# GOING VIRAL

Also by Amy Alward

*The Potion Diaries*
*The Potion Diaries: Royal Tour*

# ☙ THE ☙
# POTION DIARIES

# GOING
# VIRAL

## AMY ALWARD

SIMON & SCHUSTER | BFYR

NEW YORK   LONDON   TORONTO   SYDNEY   NEW DELHI

SIMON & SCHUSTER BFYR

An imprint of Simon & Schuster Children's Publishing Division

1230 Avenue of the Americas, New York, New York 10020

Text copyright © 2017 by Amy Alward Ltd

Published by arrangement with Simon & Schuster UK Ltd

Originally published in Great Britain in 2017 by Simon & Schuster UK Ltd

SIMON & SCHUSTER BFYR is a trademark of Simon & Schuster, Inc.

For information about special discounts for bulk purchases, please contact Simon & Schuster
Special Sales at 1-866-506-1949 or business@simonandschuster.com.

The Simon & Schuster Speakers Bureau can bring authors to your live event. For more
information or to book an event, contact the Simon & Schuster Speakers Bureau
at 1-866-248-3049 or visit our website at www.simonspeakers.com.

Also available in a SIMON & SCHUSTER BFYR hardcover edition

Cover design by nicandlou

Interior design by M. Rules

The text for this book was set in Goudy Oldstyle Std.

Manufactured in the United States of America

First SIMON & SCHUSTER BFYR paperback edition November 2018

10 9 8 7 6 5 4 3 2 1

CIP data for this title is available from the Library of Congress.

ISBN 978-1-4814-4384-5 (hc)

ISBN 978-1-4814-4385-2 (pbk)

ISBN 978-1-4814-4386-9 (eBook)

*For Elv, Rachel, Lucy, & Zareen,*
*whose magic touch brought*
*these books to life*

# GOING VIRAL

# CHAPTER ONE

# PRINCESS EVELYN

"ANY NEWS?" HE ASKED, LEANING AGAINST the doorframe, his arms folded across his chest. He was worse than Zain when it came to acting like he owned the place. But then, she supposed, he kind of did. Prince Stefan. Her new husband.

She wanted to spit out some witty retort, but when she opened her mouth she descended into one of the terrible coughing fits that left her body shaken and tissues covered in a dusting of white powder. They often brought her to her knees.

"Just as bad?" he said.

She didn't have the energy to answer. *Just as bad.* Of *course* it was just as bad. Didn't he have eyes to see?

She collapsed back down onto her bed, the voluminous duvet enveloping her body like a cocoon. She closed her eyes, unable to remember the last time she had felt this weak. She even felt like her power was waning. She knew she would feel different . . . she had given away half of her Talent to her new *husband* (dragons, she hated that word) after all. But if anything, it felt like something else was draining her. This virus, this mysterious illness she had, was becoming a serious problem. Stefan had been giving her a pill that seemed to keep the worst of it at bay—he took the same one—but he wouldn't tell her what the pills were for.

She hated being reliant on him. She hadn't left the palace since Sam's ceremony that had proclaimed her a Master Alchemist. A familiar wave of guilt washed over the princess as she thought about her friend, Samantha Kemi. Not long after the ceremony, she'd seen Sam on TV. She was being interviewed on a newscast, claiming that Stefan had been the real mastermind behind the bombing of the Laville Ball, and that the person who had taken the blame—Emilia Thoth, Evelyn's now-deceased evil aunt—had been just a pawn in Stefan's larger game.

Stefan had walked in while she'd been watching the cast and turned it off with a flick of his finger. When Evelyn tried to turn it back on again, the screen remained black.

She had meant to confront him about Sam's accusations, demand he tell her the truth! It was just that this illness was making her so weak, she could barely focus . . .

She opened her eyes as he approached her. "I was afraid of this." He reached over and put a cold hand on her forehead. She jerked away, but couldn't get far. "You were my last hope. I needed you to be strong enough to fight it. I'd always heard that you were the strongest Royal that had ever been in Nova. Now we only have one option."

"Hmm?" She knew what he was saying was important, but she kept drifting in and out of consciousness. "Fight what?" she mumbled. "Do you know why I'm ill? What are the pills for? Why haven't you told anyone?" She struggled to sit up, wondering when her limbs had turned to lead.

"Hush now, Princess. There won't be any more pills for you."

Her eyes rolled around in her head, her gaze finally landing on her arm. There was something stuck into it. A syringe. Stefan was injecting her with something. "What are you doing?" she cried. But the words came out muffled and squashed together. She wasn't even sure that they made any sense.

"Hush," he said again. "The virus is going to spread. There's no way to stop it—I see that now."

"Wait . . ." She struggled against the pull into sleep, but it dragged her down anyway, aided by Stefan's hand pressing firmly on her forehead. The last thing she saw before her eyes closed forever was Stefan's curious-looking tiger-striped eyes staring down at her, and his final words.

"Dragons help us all."

# CHAPTER TWO

# SAMANTHA

"SO ..."

"So ..."

I can't help it; I have to giggle. The laugh bubbles up out of me like soda from a can that's been shaken.

"What's so funny?" Zain asks.

"All this time building up to our first proper date, and I never expected it to be this awkward!"

To my relief, he laughs too. A strand of his black hair flops onto his forehead as he looks around the crowded restaurant, our elbows so close to the next couple I could almost share my neighbor's napkin. "I guess between my uni studies and working for ZoroAster Corp, I've forgotten how to be human," he says.

"I forgive you," I reply with a grin. "It's normally me who's the awkward one."

"True, you alchemy nerd," he teases. I throw my napkin at him, which he ducks easily. Then he leans in to whisper to me. "Are you ready to get out of here?"

"Why? Have you got a better idea?"

"I was thinking we could go see the kelpie dance?"

I grin. "I haven't done that since I was about three years old!"

"I heard they updated it recently. It could be cheesy but . . ."

"Sounds perfect," I say. Anything to get out of this place. When Anita heard that we were going out to Marco Darius Winter's signature restaurant MDW, she almost choked on her pumpkin spice latte. Even when I clarified that we would be sitting in the more casual section, not the fine dining room, she foamed with envy. "That's still one of the hottest restaurants in the city! How did you get a reservation?"

"I dunno," I'd said. "Zain got it."

"You are so lucky!"

If so, it was lost on me. I've lived in Kingstown all my life and I can count the number of times I've been to Morray Street (or "Money Street" as it's not-so-affectionately nicknamed) on one hand. It's the fancy part of town, with luxury shops and fine-dining restaurants, and the restaurant, MDW, is smack-dab in the middle. It's so fancy that they can afford Talented waiting staff, so our plates are magically whisked away the moment we're finished and our glasses are never empty.

I only hope the refills are free, but considering they're

serving special "glacier ice" in their tap water, I highly doubt it. Zain insisted on picking up the tab, so I didn't get a chance to find out.

I'm not a foodcast addict like Anita, so I just don't appreciate the artful but *tiny* dishes that are being served up, a twist on Novaen tapas. I can't help but feel out of place, sixteen-going-on-thirty, and keep thinking that I'd rather go get a burger at Hungry Joe's than drop any more money here. Besides, all anyone can talk about is Prince Stefan and Princess Evelyn. Like the couple next to us. My teeth clench as their conversation starts back up again over their dessert.

"Well, I think he's good for her—I feel so much safer now that she's married," says the woman, tapping the edge of her spoon delicately on the sugar crust of her crème brûlée. "And their honeymoon looks so beautiful. Do you think we should book a stay at the Luxe resort for our next holiday?"

The man nods. "Whatever you want, honey. And don't forget, it's a smart move politically. King Ander is no fool, and now our two countries are closer than ever."

"You're wrong," I snap, spinning in my chair so I'm facing him.

"Sam ..." Distantly I hear Zain call my name and catch the warning tone in his voice, but I can't stop.

"Stefan is dangerous," I continue. "He tricked the princess into marrying him!"

The man drops his fork and holds his hands up, like I'm attacking him over his slice of chocolate mousse cake.

"That's Prince Stefan to you, young lady," says the woman, who brandishes her spoon like it's a weapon.

The man's expression changes from wide-eyed surprise to curiosity. "Hang on, don't I know you? You're the alchemist girl who was pulled off the air during that interview on *Nova Breaking News!*"

I wince. I'm not the alchemist girl who won the Wilde Hunt and saved the princess any more. Now I'm the raving lunatic who was cut off midrant.

"I'm really sorry, sir, we were just leaving," Zain says, standing up.

The man folds his arms across his chest. "No, wait . . . I want to hear what this young lady has to say. *Why* is Prince Stefan dangerous?"

I swallow and wait for a beat. This is the news I need to get out there, and I've been preparing for just this moment—even if it's for an audience of only two. "For starters, he kidnapped me at the Laville Ball and forced me to find the recipe for an aqua vitae for him, and then when that failed, he convinced the princess to marry him and poisoned her with a contagious virus."

"I thought it was you who said that the aqua vitae was a myth," says the man. "That there was no such thing."

"There isn't, but—"

"And the princess *had* to get married or else endanger all of Nova, right?"

"Yes, but—"

"And even though the princess has some deadly virus, she's able to jet off to the beach for a fabulous honeymoon, where she's photographed looking perfectly happy and healthy?"

My face drains of color. "There are photographs?"

The man nods to his partner. She rolls her eyes at me and takes her phone from a sleek clutch purse. "Here, look." With a few taps, she pulls up a paparazzi shot of the princess on the beach, Stefan's arm draped over her tanned shoulders. Although it's a little blurry, as if taken from far away, it's obviously them.

"Come on, Sam." Zain holds out my coat for me. "We're sorry to bother you."

"But ... I don't understand," I stutter. The woman flicks through the photoset, and with every smiling photo my heart drops. I grab my coat from Zain's hands and charge out of the dining room as fast as I can—but not fast enough to avoid the woman muttering loudly about how the clientele in MDW has really gone downhill.

"You okay?" Zain asks once we're outside, slipping his hand into mine and giving it a squeeze.

"Yeah." I let out a deep sigh. "I'm sorry; I know we said we wouldn't bring it up tonight. But I couldn't help it. I couldn't listen to them talk about how great he is. Why does no one see what Stefan's really like?"

"Because he's a master manipulator with all the palace resources at his fingertips?"

"I suppose. I just wish she'd get in touch."

"I know."

He's hurting as much as me. The last time either of us saw Evelyn was at the ceremony that made me a Master Alchemist. The princess's last words were that she was "coming down with something," and then she was swept away by secret service. Since that point, I've tried everything to get in touch with her short of chaining myself to the palace gates, but I don't know how to get her attention. And since the princess won't listen, I've been trying to get the word out about Stefan in other ways: contacting everyone I've met in the media since winning the Wilde Hunt, posting on my social channels, writing letters to the palace ... but no one wants to hear it.

"Can we forget about it for the rest of the evening?" Zain tugs at my hand.

"You haven't heard anything, then?" I ask.

He winces, then covers it up with a shrug. "It's the palace. They contact you, not the other way around—even when you're long-term friends. Besides, Stefan's only just learning the ropes. Once he's settled, I'm sure Evie will be back in touch and things will go back to normal. So ... back to forgetting about it?" He stares up at me through his fringe and I feel my resolve waning.

"Okay, it's forgotten."

We walk hand-in-hand down to the waterfront, where the kelpie dance takes place. There are two big grandstands set up facing the water, and Zain pays a few crowns for a ticket inside. The atmosphere is like a fairground, with silly games and cotton-candy stands all around, and Talented business owners enchanting toys to light up in the night sky as the sun sets.

"Come on," Zain says. "I'll win you a prize."

"Really?" I say, unable to resist cringing a little. "How about I win you a prize?"

"Sorry champ, but these games are Talented only." Zain points to a sign in front of the stall.

"Well, how is that fair?" I put my hands on my hips. "Isn't that discrimination or something?" Talenteds—people like Zain, or my sister Molly—can manipulate the streams of magic in the air through an object like a wand or a pair of gloves. The most powerful Talents in Nova are the Royal family, including our incommunicado friend Princess Evelyn. They can use magic with just their hands. But I'm ordinary. And that means I can't use magic at all.

I try not to get too bummed about it. Most alchemists are ordinary, because we can work with magical ingredients without any adverse effects. The Talenteds who try mixing ingredients end up with their bodies and minds twisted—it's not normally worth the risk. There's only one Talented alchemist in the world that I know of. An icy shiver slides down my spine, despite the warmth of my jacket.

Zain nudges my shoulder, thinking I'm still insulted by the Talented-only sign. "It's just a game. Watch."

I focus back on Zain, but I know what's really given me a chill: thinking about Emilia Thoth. The Talented alchemist—and the princess's estranged aunt—who kidnapped me from the Royal Tour. *She's dead*, I remind myself. She can't hurt me, or my friends, anymore.

Zain takes out his wand and approaches the game operator, handing over the fee to play. The game is a large wheel, like a dartboard, with holes strategically cut in different locations. Each hole has a score above it. "Game's simple," the operator says. "I'll spin the board—you use your magic to shoot through the holes. The spell needs to be just a simple rubber ball—nothing fancy, please. The more holes you shoot through, the higher your score, the bigger the prize. Got it? Five holes, six attempts."

Zain nods, and the look of concentration on his face makes me giggle.

"Ready? Three, two, one . . ." The operator spins the board.

With quick flicks of his wrist, Zain sends bright red balls flying at the spinning wheel. What he certainly doesn't expect—and neither do I—is for all of them to come flying back, missing the holes completely. After the six balls are shot, his score is zero.

Zain's mouth drops open, so wide I could probably throw a ball in there. "It's rigged!" he says in mock horror.

I can't help but giggle again. "Come on, we're going to miss the show!" I say, tugging his sleeve.

"One more time."

"If you have to." I grin and catch the eye of the operator, who looks more than a little smug. Somehow I don't think Zain is going to do much better this time.

My phone buzzes and I glance down. On the screen is the subject line of an incoming email:

ATTN: SAM KEMI DOCUCAST

My first thought is, *again?*

How many times do these people need to be told? I swipe the email away, determined to deal with it another time.

A loud groan from Zain tells me he's failed. I slip my phone back into my pocket and pat him on the shoulder. "Can we go in now?"

"Yeah, okay," he says, scowling at the operator. But when he turns to me he's all smiles. I melt a little bit further into my ankle boots. We're an odd couple: He's the heir apparent to the country's largest synthetic potions manufacturer, the industry that threatens my family business. I'm a Master Alchemist of one of the oldest mixing families in Nova. Yet what we have really seems to work.

"What were you frowning at?" he asks, throwing his arm over my shoulder and pulling me close as we walk up the metal stairs of the grandstand. For the most part, the crowd is made up of families with young children, but there are a few other teenage faces around. The kelpie dance is not exactly known for being "cool," but for a *Zamantha* date it's way more our style than a stuffy restaurant. Plus, our seats are in a relatively empty part of the stands, and there are blankets for keeping warm. Nice and cosy and datelike.

"What do you mean?"

"I saw you looking down at your phone and frowning. Looked serious."

I shake my head. "No, it's nothing ... just this *really* persistent television producer person who wants to make a documentary about me. Says that the interest after the Wilde Hunt and the Royal Tour is at an all-time high and I should really 'capitalize.'" I make air quotes with my fingers and roll my eyes. "It's probably a scam. It's like the fourth or fifth email she's sent—I've already told her no."

Zain's eyes light up. "Are you serious? That sounds really cool! Show me the email?"

I laugh. "Keen much?" I pull the email up on my phone and pass it to him.

He scans it quickly. "Sam, are you kidding? This is properly real. She"—he points to the name of the sender, Daphne Golden—"is a really hot director! She did the last Yolanda film."

"Really? That was a good movie."

"See? This could be so cool. What is it they want to do? This email doesn't have any details, it's just a lot of begging," he says.

I let out a deep breath. "Well, they want to film in the store—'the average life of an alchemist' type thing, maybe follow me to school and stuff. Interview my family and friends—you too, without a doubt. She says I have a story to tell. You know, the youngest person ever to be made Master Alchemist in Nova, my experience on the Wilde Hunt and the Royal Tour ... that sort of thing."

"Sounds awesome!"

I wrinkle my nose. "Does it? I dunno. I was kind of looking forward to the fame dying down, finishing school, not ... going on TV again. It just seems like I'm asking for more attention. I'm surprised she even wants to talk to me after all the negative press that's going around."

"Look, you're a public figure in Nova now and people are going to talk to you whether you want the attention or not. Maybe it's a chance to tell your story, exactly how you want to tell it?"

"Maybe . . ."

"And I bet they're offering to pay well."

"Yeah, but . . ."

"It's something I would seriously consider. You won't have opportunities like this again. You could set all the records straight about your family, too—there are still people out there who think you guys hid an aqua vitae from the world." That was the big scandal last month—that somehow we'd developed a cure for *everything*, the most powerful potion in the world—and then either destroyed it or kept it for ourselves. So *not* true.

I stare down at the email. A documentary . . . it could be fun.

Trumpets sound all around us, and the lights dim. "I'll think about it," I whisper to Zain as the show starts, glad for the distraction. A laser display of glittering red and green beams dances across the water as a screen rises up behind. An introductory video plays, along with several adverts for ZoroAster Corp medicines. Zain and I exchange a glance, eye-rolling at the supreme cheesiness. But with my cheek against his shoulder, our hands clenched together, snuggled up underneath the warm woollen blanket, I couldn't think of a more perfect first "proper" date.

That is, until a face appears, smirking on the screen.

A smug, sharp-angled face with amber-yellow tiger eyes.

"CONGRATULATIONS TO OUR NEW PRINCE, STEFAN OF NOVA!" the caption reads. For their first stunt, the kelpies burst out of the waves in front of his serene, waving form, honoring the newest member of the Royal family with a choreographed dance of their watery hooves and frothy manes. They should take my breath away, but all I can see is red.

Beside me, Zain squeezes my hand. "Remember, just forget it . . ."

I grit my teeth for two more seconds, but when fireworks go off behind Stefan's head, I throw the blanket to the floor and stand up. "I can't watch it."

"Sam!"

"Stay if you want, but there's no way I'm honoring that creep. I don't care if no one else understands, or if they won't listen. I will never believe he's changed. I wouldn't trust Prince Stefan if my life depended on it."

# CHAPTER THREE

# SAMANTHA

THE DOOR SLAMS SHUT BEHIND ME.

Mum is sitting at the kitchen table, and she looks down at her watch in surprise. "Oh, Sam! I wasn't expecting you back until later. Your dad took Molly to swim practice . . ." She catches the expression on my face and stops talking. I stormed the whole way home from the kelpie show. Zain offered me a lift, but I needed the walk. Seeing that video brought the familiar rage bubbling back up to the surface again and now I can't disguise it. "Everything okay?" Mum asks, her calm voice cutting through the red haze in front of my eyes.

"No," I say through gritted teeth. I need to calm down. I need . . . tea.

"What is it, honey? Here, let me do that," she says, taking the kettle from my shaking hands. Mum is Talented, but her magic is weak and she doesn't tend to use it inside the house. Her object—a divining rod—sits on the dresser upstairs. "Why don't you sit down?"

I do as she says, slumping into one of our kitchen chairs. "I don't get it. How can people believe in him?"

She doesn't need to ask who I'm talking about. Every cast, every morning show, every newspaper front page features Prince Stefan at the moment. He's on a PR offensive, and that's exactly how I find it: offensive. Stefan's the one that put the princess in danger—hiring Emilia Thoth, sparking the chain of events that led to the hunting of the aqua vitae, and now marrying her only to take advantage of her immense magical power. It feels like no one has even noticed that the princess has been suspiciously absent from the public eye apart from a few blurry photographs.

My face scrunches up in disgust every time he's on air. He's impossible to escape. Everywhere, there are pictures and videos of his handsome, shining, smarmy face, his enigmatic tiger eyes, his perfectly coiffed blond hair. My voice, my lone voice, is drowned in a sea of adoration and hope.

I don't have hope. I have anger.

*Tears of seraphim mixed with roots of bodhi tree—to lift the veil of deceit from everyone's eyes so they can see the truth that's in front of them.*

Even though it would be a felony, I think about making a giant batch and putting it into the water system of Nova. At least it would be better than all this pro-Stefan juice that the world seems to have drunk.

But I'm the only one who saw him in Gergon, the only one who knows that he was behind the explosion at the Laville Ball. And the more he dominates the TV casts and the newsprint and social media, the harder it is to get anyone to believe me.

*How can anyone the princess chose to marry be that bad?*

*If what you say is true, wouldn't he have shown his true colors by now?*

Mum's voice adds to the fray: "I don't know, honey. I suppose people want to believe the best of their new Royal family."

"Even if I can find evidence against him?"

"It's your word against his. And even though we believe you—"

"What about the princess? She's been MIA from all these publicity stunts and no one thinks that's weird?"

"She's busy. Being a newlywed is never easy."

"Ugh, especially when you've married a creep like him."

"And the public want to know the new prince. None of this is that unusual, honey."

I roll my eyes. It's an argument I've now heard too many times. "What about the white powder that I saw on Evelyn's sleeve? The same symptom of the virus that

Stefan *showed* me had been spreading through his country. Does no one care about that?"

Mum's expression remains neutral, ever the diplomat, but a tiny frown line appears between her eyes. I almost want to point at it and say: "Aha! You *are* worried too!" But I don't. "You care," she says, gently. "And because you care, we care. If the princess asks for your help, you and Grandad will be ready. If she wants privacy, you just have to wait for her to get in touch. That's all you can do."

"I know," I say with a sigh. I sip my green tea and wait for my heart rate to return to normal.

"Well, maybe it's not *all* you can do."

I raise an eyebrow. "What do you mean?"

"You don't have to wait around. You have your own life. Maybe after everything you've been through this past year, you can focus on you. It's your last year at school. You have that big internship with ZoroAster Corp coming up. Maybe you and Anita should take a holiday somewhere?"

I pause, staring into my tea. "Yeah, maybe. Sorry, Mum, I guess I'm just tired. I'm going to take this upstairs, okay?"

"Are you sure you're all right?"

I shrug. "Yeah. I think I just ... miss her, you know?"

"Of course you do. The princess has been a big part of your life this year, but she is a Royal first. She'll come back in her own time."

Up in my room, I sit at my desk and open my laptop. Out of habit I log in to Connect and when it loads I see that Kirsty has posted a long message on her page. Kirsty is our store's Finder—she travels the world hunting down ingredients and restocking any dwindling supplies. She helped me out big time finding the love potion ingredients during the Wilde Hunt and in the search for my great-grandmother's diary. I like so many of her photos and posts that her latest pops up straightaway on my feed.

**CALLING ALL MY FRIENDS**

Things are not right in Nova.

The new prince comes from a place where ordinaries are treated as second-class citizens to Talenteds.

We need to listen to my friend, Samantha Kemi, when she warns us that he is dangerous!

We must be vigilant—we can't let our rights be taken away.

Stand Up For Ordinaries!

The message makes my heart swell. Kirsty is one of the few people who also knows Prince Stefan's true nature, and his connection to the aqua vitae. I haven't seen her since the Royal Tour, but I thought I spotted her in a photograph of a crowd at an Ordinary Rights Association (ORA) rally. With the spotlight on Gergon since the wedding and Prince Stefan's ascendance, she's stepped up her campaigning there for ordinaries to receive equal treatment and rights to Talenteds. She's been traveling so much that I've barely seen her.

Unlike Gergon, Nova has historically been a place where Talenteds and ordinaries have managed to live in harmony.

Princess Evelyn threatened that balance earlier this year. As the Royal princess of Nova, she needed to be married during her eighteenth year and share her Talent or else risk her power growing so out of control that it would destroy her—and the city of Kingstown too. Her initial refusal to marry—and the extreme measures she took creating the love potion to overcome it—meant that she took enormous risks with her own life and the lives of her people. The ORA called it irresponsible, reckless even. They don't think we should have a Royal family at all—that it's crazy for a few people to be in charge of so much power, even if a lot of it is for show. They think we should follow the Pays model, where the people overthrew their monarchy after a long and bloody revolution. The excess power was redistributed amongst the people once the royal bloodline had all been wiped out.

I shiver. I don't want the princess to be "wiped out."

My opinion is that the Nova model works, but only if the royal family abide by the rules. They have the power, but they are legally bound not to misuse it. We have an elected government—a mix of Talented and ordinaries—to keep things in check.

Because the reality of our world is that there are Talenteds and there are ordinaries. We need to learn to live together.

Balance is everything. Balance is peace.

Balance is harmony.

Any alchemist worth their salt knows that. You could even go as far as to say that balance is the ultimate goal of alchemy. Some people would say it was change. But alchemists change things for a reason. To find that perfect equilibrium between light and dark—whether that's elements or potions or even in ways of thinking.

So even though Kirsty has asked me a few times, I won't join the ORA. She thinks I would be a good "face" for them to use. Since all the publicity surrounding the Wilde Hunt, my social media following has shot from zero to supernova. I have a platform—even if I only use it to try to discredit Prince Stefan.

But I don't want to be anyone's puppet.

The next post almost changes my mind. It's not from any of my friends—it's one of those articles that drops into my feed based on things I've searched for before. What catches my eye is an absolutely horrible picture of me, a screenshot taken from when I had been dragged away from the *Nova Breaking News* newsroom midrant about Stefan. My hair has fallen out of its bun and my eyes are rolled back in my head. They've made me look deranged.

Which is exactly what the headline says:

*SAMANTHA KEMI: MASTER ALCHEMIST*
*OR MENACE TO SOCIETY?*

I cringe, but don't click on the article to read it. I do, however, click on the #SamanthaKemi public hashtag.

The page loads up with even more anger.

JEALOUS OR JADED? *Why Samantha Kemi just can't leave the prince and princess alone.*

QUIZ: *Can you identify these five Sam Kemi meltdown moments?*

And, worst of all, there's a bold BREAKING NEWS headline.

CAUGHT ON CAMERA: *Samantha Kemi rails against the prince at hot restaurant MDW.*

Underneath, playing automatically, is crystal-clear footage of my argument with the couple at the next table, filmed by another patron of the restaurant.

My head falls onto my desk.

Every time I try to tell people the truth about Stefan, my words get distorted. I need a way to get *my* version of events out. But to do that, I have to have control over the images that are shown, the words that are said.

A thought strikes me with a mixture of fear and excitement, and I click out of Connect and into my email. Maybe I do have an opportunity to tell my side of the story.

Daphne Golden's email sits at the very top of my in-box.

A docucast. A television show.

*But you hate the spotlight. You hate being on TV.* The voice inside my head is pretty loud this time.

Then again, it's not live TV.

With a few taps, I call Zain and wait for his face to fill my screen. "Hey, beautiful," he says with a broad smile. "What's up? Did you get home okay?"

"Yeah, no problems. I'm sorry for storming off."

"You don't have to apologize. We'll just have to research a totally Prince Stefan–free date next time."

"Definitely." I grin back at him. I'm glad he's not mad at me for cutting our date short—but I know he understands. "Look, I was thinking about what you said at the kelpie show—about the docucast?"

25

Zain's eyes light up. "You going to do it?"

"On one condition. I want you to do it with me."

Zain's face freezes, and I wonder if our connection has dropped. Then he blinks hard and says, "Wait, are you serious?"

"Why not? I'm going to intern for ZA after I graduate, so you're part of my story too. And I think it would be better if you were there. I would feel more comfortable, at least. And I know you're busy with uni but you could fit it around your lectures . . ."

"Okay." He nods, the grin returning to his face.

"Seriously?"

"Yes, okay! Let's do it!"

The grin on my face matches his. "I'll email her right now and see what she says." In another window, I open Daphne's email and scan it quickly. She does seem keen to get started right away. "Let's get going—while you're as hot as magma!" are the last words of her email.

"I'm writing back," I say to Zain. "I'm putting in the condition about you and . . . *done*." I hit send before I can change my mind.

"Let me know what she says. I'd better get back to studying."

"No problem, I'll—" My in-box pings midsentence. "Hang on a second, she's just replied. She says: "Great! You and Zain will make perfect television. We'll be there in the morning to get everything set up—make sure your

26

parents are around so we can have them sign the permis-sions—and then clear your half-term break calendar for filming.'"

I blink at the screen as it fills up with the documents Daphne pings over to me—showreels from her previous work, news articles about me that she's researched, story-boards for the filming, and a big long contract to sign.

"Sam? Are you okay?" I hear Zain now rather than see him—my screen is covered in downloading files.

I minimize everything until I'm staring at his face again. The excitement still tingles through my veins, the thrill of being so spontaneous and daring. But reality is setting in. "Um ... Zain? I'll be right back. I think I better go talk with my parents."

# CHAPTER FOUR

# SAMANTHA

I ACCIDENTALLY SPLASH HOT WATER ONTO the kitchen counter, my hands shaking out of nerves this time, not anger. The back door shuts behind my dad's cheery voice announcing that he and Molly are home, and I clench my fists to stop my fidgeting. Telling my mum and grandad about the documentary was surprisingly simple: they both thought it sounded like a good opportunity for me.

Maybe even *too* good. Mum had a lot of questions about whether this Daphne Golden was for real. After I showed her the showreels and Daphne's credentials though, she agreed that it sounded legitimate. "But honey, are you sure you want this kind of attention?"

I shrug. "Whether I wanted it or not, I've got a platform now. I guess this is a chance to use it responsibly?"

"Well, then I'm proud of you. I know I said you needed a distraction, but I didn't expect you to come up with something that quickly!"

"As long as I don't have to be on television, you can do what you like. You are a Master Alchemist," says Grandad. It's a familiar refrain from him now. But even though I'm a Master Alchemist by title, and I accept all the responsibility that comes with that, I still yearn for a hint of Grandad's approval.

He seems to know it, reserving his praise for only my most perfect mixes and tantalizing me with secrets about the store—I feel like a potion that's being drip-fed the ingredients I need, so I don't absorb too much too quickly without retaining anything. Even though I'm impatient to learn it all, it's humbling to remember how little I know, even with my fancy qualification.

Yet I still have one more hurdle to overcome. Telling Molly. Starting with the Wilde Hunt, I've been in the spotlight, stealing all my family's attention—especially Grandad's. Now, just as things were about to die down, I'm not sure how my sister will feel about cameras coming into our house to film a documentary all about ... me. "Hi, Molly, hi, Dad," I say, spinning around and plastering a smile on my face.

"Sam has big news," Mum says.

Dad's eyebrows jolt up in surprise. "Really? So does Molly. But you go first, Sam," he encourages me.

"Sure. Well ..." I draw out the syllables as both Molly and Dad look at me expectantly. "Daphne Golden, a big Tinseltown director, wants to do a documentary about me. She's going to come round with a camera crew tomorrow to start filming. But I promise it won't be too invasive—I won't let them film you if you don't want."

Dad's eyebrows rise up almost into his hairline, but I catch him exchanging a look with Mum and eventually he smiles. "Sounds . . . like an interesting experience for you."

"Thanks, Dad," I say. I brace myself for Molly's response. But, to my surprise, she smiles broadly. "That sounds so cool," she says. "Anyway, do you want to know my news now?" Her cheeks flush with excitement.

"Come on, out with it, then," says Mum with a laugh.

"My whole class got this at school today. Here." Molly pulls out an envelope, embossed with the royal seal—or the new royal seal, that is, with the twin mountain peaks of Gergon as a backdrop to the traditional unicorn and mermaid crest.

Mum opens the letter, and as she reads, her eyes widen and her mouth drops open in surprise. She reads it again, but this time out loud: "The royal family of Nova is pleased to invite Class 8A of Saint Martha's High for a formal introduction to the new prince of Nova, Stefan, and his wife, Princess Evelyn. The visit will take place on the twentieth of September. Please see the enclosed leaflet for information on how to prepare for a trip to the floating palace." There's a moment's pause as she folds the letter back into the envelope. "Molly—a visit to the palace!" Mum is so breathless she can't even finish her sentence.

"That's a big deal!" says Dad.

"Huge," I agree. I'm really happy for Molly, and I feel a weight lift from my shoulders. If the princess is receiving official visits, that means she can't be too sick.

Instinctively, I check my phone, as if Molly receiving this letter means that I should be receiving a text from the princess soon too—surely her next step would be to reach out to her friends to let them know she's okay.

But there's nothing. I text her: Hey! Molly got your invite—looks like she's coming to visit you at the palace! I miss you. Hope I can see you soon. Write back!

Molly dances around the kitchen. "I'm going to the palace!" she sings. "I'm going to the palace! Oh my god, what do you wear to the palace?" She stops dancing, her eyes wide.

I laugh. "Probably your school uniform, silly! But you're going to love it there. Even I've never really been. At least, not *officially*. They normally hold public meet-and-greets at the castle." It's a strange set-up that the Novaen royal family have, but it's kept them protected for centuries: there's the large, imposing castle at the top of Kingstown Hill, the highest point of the whole city (technically the skyscrapers that make up the industrial and business districts are outside of the city proper). But the royal family *actually* live in an invisible, floating palace somewhere above the city, totally suspended by the royal family's magic power. Its very existence is a symbol of their extreme Talent, and keeps them safe.

Kept them safe.

Until they brought danger into their midst.

"I'm nervous about meeting the prince . . ." Molly says, jumping up onto the counter next to me.

"Well, maybe I can give you a poison potion to slip into his tea?"

"*Sam*." Mum's voice is laced with her best warning tone.

The familiar wave of anger surges up inside me, but I let it wash over. At least Molly is willing to still be cautious. I give her a small smile, which she returns. I don't want to kill her buzz with my warnings about Stefan's true nature. But I can't—won't—believe he's changed in such a short period of time. If ever I get close to believing he's just a benign, good-looking, media-friendly prince, all I need to do is shut my eyes and I'm sent straight back to the dark, dripping cave underneath the crumbling Visir School—to his smarmy face as he forced me to work with the dreaded Emilia Thoth.

"Let's celebrate all the good news with ice cream!" says Mum, breaking the tension.

After stuffing our faces with mint chocolate chip goodness, I help Mum tidy up before heading upstairs. I need to talk to Molly—privately. She's been working on her Talented homework, wearing her special unicorn hair gloves—a gift from the princess—as she practices channeling her magic. She has a particular gift for healing magic and already knows she wants to go to medical school. Her help with healing Grandad after his memories were taken proved beyond doubt to me that she was going to grow up to be a great healer.

"Can I come in?" I ask, after knocking on the door-frame.

Molly sits back from her desk and peels off her gloves. "Sure ... I wasn't making much progress anyway." She frowns at the little leaf in a jar that refuses to grow.

I come in and sit on her bed. "Can I give you a message to give to Evie when you see her?"

"Sure," says Molly.

I hold out a piece of folded paper. "It's sealed with a special paste I made—she's the only one who will be able to open it."

"I understand," says Molly.

"And you will be careful around the prince, won't you?"

"Of course."

"And you'll give me a status update of everything he says and does and how the princess looks and acts?"

"You know it."

"Thanks, Molly."

"Don't be a worryworm, Sam."

*Worryworms. Known for their ability to burrow deep into the ground. Used in potions to uncover buried secrets. Very rare.*

"I'll try." But I can't help it. I won't stop worrying properly until I hear from the princess herself.

# CHAPTER FIVE

# SAMANTHA

"JUST A LITTLE TO THE LEFT. A LITTLE MORE. Now tilt your head. One more time, but to the other side. Perfect."

The camera's flash makes stars dance in my vision, but I hold my pose, feeling increasingly like a maniac with my toothy smile and wide eyes. I try to catch Zain's eye to show how over it I am, but he's being fussed over by a make-up artist who is trying to convince him to put on a stronger glamour. I think he looks perfect, but then I am a little bit biased.

I wish I had his level of comfort with glamours. My dark hair has been styled into a short bob that frames my round face; I push it back behind my ears, then in front again, then behind as the photographer snaps away. I don't know what looks best.

The photographer has been here for half an hour already, moving me around the shop floor. After getting permission from my parents, I spent half the night cleaning and straightening and wiping. Now the three stories of shelving are perfectly organized, with every glass jar and container gleaming. I replaced all the old, worn books on the shelves with the fanciest looking leatherbound tomes in our library and made sure their spines were in alphabetical order. I think it helped distract me from what I'd actually agreed to. Going on TV. Again.

"Do you have a particularly atmospheric potion we can use in a photograph?" Daphne asks me. Daphne, so far, is everything that I expected from a film producer and director: effortlessly cool, with a chic chin-brushing bob that always falls back into place no matter what she does to it—whether it's push her tortoiseshell glasses up into her hair or jab a pencil behind her ear—all thanks to a glamour. The photographer is a tall guy called Geoff with a close-shaven beard and a man-bun. These people are way too hip for me.

I wrinkle my nose. "An atmospheric potion?"

"You know, something pretty. That makes a lot of smoke and swirl." As she speaks, she gestures wildly with her arms.

*Medusa's hair—a potion that produces smoke that invades the air in the shapes of snakes.*

Except that potion is also so noxious we have to prepare it under a hood so none of the snakes escape into the atmosphere.

"I could mix a little cloud dust up?" I say. If I put a few drops in some colored water, it will rise out of a flask and settle around the opening like clouds around a mountain peak. It doesn't actually serve any specific purpose, but it's quick and fits the "pretty" bill.

"Sounds perfect," Daphne says, clapping her hands together.

I walk through the door that separates the shop from the lab, Geoff and Daphne following close behind. I haven't seen Grandad yet this morning—but I'm glad he's not here to watch me "faking" alchemy for the cameras. Still, it's fun to play around with some of the ingredients, making a bit of a show. This is my favorite part, after all: the mixing. Alchemy is the blood that runs through my veins. It's everything that I was born to do. And now that I'm a Master Alchemist—the youngest Master in Nova since my grandfather—I have equal reign over the laboratory.

Once the potion is foaming up attractively, Daphne has Geoff take a few more photos. "These will be perfect for our promo shots for the docucast marketing. It's going to be a wild ride, Sam, I hope you're ready." Finally, she taps Geoff on the shoulder and tells him to put down the camera. "I think that's it for you for today."

"Oh, great," I say, and the smile on my face is probably the first genuine one I've had all day. Things have happened so fast since I got my family's permission and

Daphne showed up with all the paperwork. "Are you doing anything else exciting?"

"We *should* have been," Geoff says. The photographer and director exchange dark looks.

"What do you mean?" I ask.

"We were supposed to do a big shoot with the princess this afternoon, but it was canceled." Geoff looks at me sideways, but I cast my eyes down. I know they expect me to have an idea about what's going on, but the truth is . . . I don't.

Daphne's eyes light up. "Maybe she's pregnant!"

"I don't think so," I say. I hate how quickly people jump to conclusions about the princess.

"Know something we don't?" Daphne quips back.

I force out what I hope is a casual-sounding laugh. "No . . . I just know Princess Evelyn, and kids aren't on the agenda just yet." When it's clear I don't have anything juicy (or even remotely interesting) to tell them, they finish packing up.

"Oh well," Daphne says with a shrug as she picks up a portable flashlight. "Everything must be okay, right? She can't be in any real danger as no Wilde Hunt has been called. I'm sure you would be the first to know if it had!"

"That's true." I smile. *Why didn't I think of that?* Evelyn can't have caught the Gergon virus, because there's been no Wilde Hunt. I hadn't realized how much the thought had been weighing on my shoulders until the anxiety lifts. But just as quickly as it lifts, a different realization sinks in. No illness means the princess really *has* just been shutting us out of her life. Zain and I exchange a look. It's worse for him than it is for me. She's been my friend only a few months. But Evie and Zain have been best friends since they were kids. "My mum says she's probably just busy being a newlywed," I say.

"She'd better release those wedding pictures one day," says Geoff with a laugh. "Whoever that photographer was will make a mint."

"So, guys, see you tomorrow, bright and early?" says Daphne. "We'll start the day off easy, just get some establishing shots of you working in the store and doing exactly as you would normally do. Then we'll go to the ZA building and shoot your angle, Zain. Sam, don't change one bit of your routine without telling us."

"Unless part of my routine is picking my nose and putting it in a potion or something, right?" I say.

She looks at me quizzically.

"Uh, I don't do that . . . it was a joke."

"Oh." She laughs, but it's only for my benefit. Since when do I make corny jokes like that, anyway? I hope being on TV doesn't turn me into some kind of blithering idiot. "And will your grandad be here tomorrow too?"

"He will . . . but he doesn't want to be in the docucast, if that's okay."

"Sure, sure, the focus is on *you*, anyway. You are the star, young lady! This is going to be so great. The two descendants of warring factions: old versus new. Natural versus technological. Synth versus potion. Tension ... tension is what drives a story! I cannot wait." Daphne claps her hands together. "Just picture it. 'Novacast presents: Sam Kemi, Mixer *Extra*ordinary.' Are you done, Geoff?"

"Ready to go," he says with a grin.

I wave them good-bye, and when I close the door, I breathe a sigh of relief. They're so high energy, so different to the normal vibe in the store. We prefer to maintain an atmosphere of calm. For a little while at least, we have to prepare for it to be frenetic.

"That was intense," says Zain. He kisses me on the cheek. "I'd better get going—I have class in an hour."

"And I've got to get to school. Thanks for doing this with me," I say.

"Are you kidding? It's going to be fun. Daphne seems nice. Enthusiastic."

"That's putting it mildly."

"Okay, see you tomorrow."

"See ya." We kiss again and I watch as he heads out of the door. My mind feels like it's been going a million miles a minute and I haven't had any time to prepare myself.

"Have they gone?" Grandad walks into the store with

armfuls of prescriptions, ready for us to open in fifteen minutes.

"They'll be back tomorrow, though," I say.

He nods. Most of our time together in the store or the lab is spent in silence, focusing on our respective mixes or interpreting each other's gestures when needed. I know that the time is coming when I won't be working in the store anymore—after graduation, I'm planning on university and then taking the Synth-Natural Research position at ZoroAster Corp. But for now, we can stick to our comfortable routine.

That's another thing the documentary will do for me, I realize. It will preserve these times, for the future. You never know how long the present is going to stay present—and after the close call with Grandad's health only a month ago, I want to hold on to every moment.

There is something I have to ask him, though. Daphne's comment about the Wilde Hunt has been turning over and over in my brain. "Grandad, is there any way for a royal family member to be seriously ill, but without a Wilde Hunt being called?"

He looks up at me from the counter, stroking his long white beard. "Theoretically, a Wilde Hunt is only called if a royal heir is in *mortal* danger and the bloodline is in trouble. Those are the two factors. So they could certainly be sick—or injure themselves—without a Wilde Hunt being called, if there was a viable heir."

"And Auden's Horn is ... wise enough to know when that is?"

"It hasn't been wrong before. But, for example, if the king fell gravely ill now, a Wilde Hunt would not be called. We would all do our best to save him, of course, but there is the princess who would succeed him." Beneath his bushy eyebrows, his eyes study mine. "Is there a reason why this has come up?"

"You know what I told you about the symptoms I saw in the princess on the day of my ceremony?"

"The coughing and the white residue on her sleeve."

I nod. "Right. The same symptoms of the virus that Prince Stefan showed me was spreading in Gergon. I saw it with my own eyes. It was so contagious it was draining all the Gergonian Talenteds of their power. But if no Wilde Hunt has been called in Nova, it can't have spread here, can it? I shouldn't be worried."

Grandad pauses, and the silence makes my insides curl.

Eventually, I can't take it any longer. "I mean, Stefan hoped that by marrying the princess, he could end the spread of the virus. Maybe that's what happened? He might have gone about it in a terrible way but ultimately he wanted to save his people." I shrug. "If his plan worked and the virus was cured ... That would be a good thing, wouldn't it?"

"I'm hearing a lot of self-doubt coming from a Master

Alchemist," says Grandad. "What does your gut say?"

"That's not what happened. Something is wrong."

"Then let me make some enquiries of my own. I'll let you know if I hear anything."

"Thanks, Grandad."

I put it to the back of my mind for now. I just have to wait for Evelyn to get in touch. If something was wrong, she would come to me.

I know she would.

*Wouldn't she?*

# CHAPTER SIX

# PRINCESS EVELYN

HER FIRST THOUGHT AS SHE SAT UP WAS that she felt better! Healthy, even. Finally, something had cured her of that awful coughing sickness that had left her so drained.

Her memory was fuzzy—the last thing she remembered was seeing Prince Stefan's face as she lay in her bedroom. She remembered thinking that as soon as Sam was done with school, she was going to make her the official alchemist to the palace—no way was she taking that ZA job. But until that time, it was still Evelyn's father's choice: and her father still chose ZA to look after the royals.

Even so, she was confused. She wasn't in her own room—it was much smaller for one thing, and she didn't recognise any of the furniture. She swung her legs out of bed, letting her toes curl into the scratchy hemp carpet on the floor. Definitely not her choice of furnishings.

She walked to the window. Outside on the street, there were people everywhere, dressed in strange, uncomfortable-looking outfits that made her think of a time centuries before. Part of her wanted to find her phone to take a picture, but that would be rude.

Then it hit her. Of *course* they were dressed in such an old-fashioned way. Hadn't she heard about this a dozen times before? They were in Gergon! And she had just married their prince. She must have come for a state visit. But why didn't she remember arriving? Or leaving Palace Great for that matter?

Startled by the realization, she scanned the room for Prince Stefan, but he wasn't there. They must have given him separate quarters, thank goodness. Someone in the street noticed her, and she waved a hand regally.

But the Gergonian stopped and shook his fist at her, shouting something in his language that did *not* sound flattering. Others began to stop, too, and the anger in the crowd grew like storm clouds gathering. She let out an "Oh!" of surprise.

That was no way to treat a princess.

Well, she wasn't going to stay cooped up in this room. She needed to find out what was going on, and she couldn't do that here.

She stepped through the door and came across the king and queen of Gergon, sitting at a long dining-room table laden with food. Also at the table was their first son, Stefan's brother, Prince Ilie. What kind of perverse interior design had bedrooms leading straight into a dining room?

"You cannot be here!" the Queen said when she saw Evelyn, her voice high and shrill. Evelyn had only met her once before, when she'd been a young girl. She'd been so confused when Prince Stefan hadn't invited his parents to their wedding. Granted, it had been organized in a heartbeat, amidst the aftermath of the attack on the Laville Ball, Samantha's abduction and the threat of her growing power. Still, they could have Transported in for the ceremony—but Stefan insisted they go ahead without them.

That should have been a clue.

Back when she'd first met the Gergonian queen, she'd been reminded of a harpy, and the impression wasn't much different now. The queen was also dressed in old-fashioned clothes, but these were much finer than the ones worn by the people on the street. On top of her piles of thick braided hair was an ornate gold crown, far too elaborate for a casual breakfast.

Evelyn let out a strangled cry as she looked down at herself. Why hadn't she checked what she was wearing before—where was her brain? Fortunately, she was decent. She frowned as she ran her hands over the heavy black woollen fabric she was wearing. She'd never seen this dress before, she was sure of it. She knew every single item of clothing in her wardrobe, and there's no way she would have chosen to wear something so dowdy and plain out of choice.

"What does this mean?" the king asked, banging the end of his fork into the table. In his high-necked cloak and with his pasty skin, he looked like a vampire—every inch the Gergon king. It turned Evelyn's stomach to see but she was practiced at controlling the expression on her face. These were her parents-in-law. (That thought, too, twinged her heart—but at least that *why* was obvious—she had not married for love, but for convenience.) She should at least try to be gracious.

The older prince, however, did not look happy. He glowered at Evelyn, his dark eyes narrowed.

"It means he's failed. She was supposed to bring us out of this mess."

"Not yet failed, my dear Ilie. We must trust in Stefan . . . that he has a plan."

Evelyn had had enough. "Excuse me, but is this how you greet your new daughter or sister-in-law in Gergon? Because it strikes me as extremely rude." She put her hands on her hips.

"Oh, do be quiet, girl," said the Queen, waving her hand dismissively. Even her voice, her accent, sounded like something from a different time. Evelyn wondered if she'd learned Novaen while only reading literature published before this century.

Prince Ilie's eyes flashed at Evelyn. "You don't know?"

"Know what?"

He laughed, but she couldn't find any joy in it. "Why, you're dreaming."

"Dreaming?" She frowned, staring at the prince, waiting for him to explain the joke. She pinched the inside of her wrist, hard, but the scene in front of her didn't change. "What do you mean, dreaming? Isn't this . . ."

"Real? No. Sorry. You've been trapped in this world same as us. All because my brother had a soft spot for that brat and my parents didn't have the courage to finish her when they should have done."

Her eyes narrowed. "Who's 'her'?"

"You'll find out soon enough." He ate a forkful of food and grimaced. "Wow, could we not have dreamed of better food?"

The queen snorted and turned her nose up. That didn't bother Evelyn. What did bother her is how comfortable they all appeared to be in this twisted dream state.

"Prince Ilie," she said through gritted teeth. It couldn't hurt to be polite. "How long have you been here?"

"Months. Maybe even a year. It's hard to tell time in here."

"What?" Evelyn felt her heart stop inside her chest. *Months?* Then she shook herself back into her senses.

"Well, if this is a dream, then I'm sorry, but I have no desire to see you in mine."

"Do whatever you wish, but if I were you, I would stay here. It's better than what's ... out there."

"I'll take my chances," she spat back.

Ilie smiled sadly. "We'll be waiting. Don't worry, Princess. We have all the time in the world."

She clenched her fists together, closed her eyes tight and, with all her might, blasted the scene away—and along with it, the nasty inhabitants.

# CHAPTER SEVEN

# SAMANTHA

"SAM, DO YOU HAVE A MOMENT?"

I look up from where I've daydreamed into a cup of coffee, my eyes unfocused. I frown for a moment, then remember where I am. In the store, a few minutes before closing. My normal routine is to take over from Mum so she can pick Molly up and take her to her after-school activities. If it's quiet, I'll use the time to catch up on homework, but often I'm too busy mixing.

"Oh, sure, Grandad." I pick up the coffee, my fingers tingling from the heat, and follow him into the library.

"Don't worry, I already asked your mother to close up," he says, answering my unasked question.

My eyebrows rise in surprise as I follow him into the back, and he slips the key to the rare books section of the library from its customary hook. He heads over to the lock, hidden behind one of the library shelves. I haven't been in the hidden library since the early hours of the Wilde Hunt.

He beckons me to follow, and, once I'm inside, he shuts the door behind us.

"Take a seat," he says, gesturing to one of the cavernous leather armchairs in the center of the room. The leather is so worn in places, it's faded from its original chestnut brown to golden yellow. Out of habit, I run my hands over the arms, the oils from my fingers working back some of the original color.

*Acacia oil—to buff marks and stains out of tough leather. Also works as a perfect base for skin-healing lotions.*

The remedy pops into my head, and I make a mental note to give the chair a rub-down later.

Grandad doesn't sit; instead, he walks over to the bookcase and reaches up on his slippered toes at something on the highest shelf.

"Let me get that for you, Grandad," I say. "At least that's one benefit to being tall." I jump out of the chair and easily stretch out to reach the shelf. My fingers brush up against a hidden catch.

"Pull that out," he says.

I do as he instructs, and the shelf expands into a hidden screen. It pulls down until it covers two shelves-worth of books, and I step back, my mouth wide open in awe.

"Ah, I'm still able to keep *some* secrets from you, I see," Grandad says with a laugh.

"This is amazing!"

"Well, you are a Master Alchemist now—so that means I will be letting you in on one more secret tonight. And it must remain a secret—we alchemists are very private, you know." He stares up at me from beneath his bushy eyebrows.

I gulp and nod. "I promise."

"Good. Now sit again."

I sink back down into the chair, grinning with anticipation. I don't know what secret Grandad is going to reveal next, but frankly the sight of a hidden Summons is cool enough for me. It reminds me never to take anything in this house—and in the shop especially—for granted. I eye up one of the paintings, wondering if it's hiding a safe of ultra-rare ingredients.

Grandad coughs loudly to get my attention back. He's standing in front of the Summons, frowning. "I never quite understand how these things work," he grumbles. I would help him, but I don't know what he's trying to do. "Ah! There we go."

He steps back to reveal three faces on the Summons and the room suddenly fills with voices. Everyone is speaking on top of everyone else. And then I realize that I recognise the face in the middle: he's looking right at me and waving.

"Oh, hi, Mr. Patel!" I say with a smile, waving back. It's my best friend Anita's dad.

"Hi, Sam," he says. "Everything okay at home?"

I nod. But before I can say any more, Grandad claps his hands together loudly. "Right! Settle down, settle down, everyone." The voices stop as Grandad steps back and slowly sits in the chair next to me. He clasps his hands under his chin, leaning his elbows on the arms of the chair. "Thank you all for taking the time today. Let me introduce my granddaughter—Master Alchemist Samantha Kemi."

A chorus of "nice to meet yous" greets me, and I am too stunned to reply with anything more articulate than a mumbled "thank you."

"Sam, welcome to your first Master Alchemist cabal!'"says Mr. Patel. I grin back at him. Mr. Patel might be the second greatest alchemist in Nova (I still gotta give the nod to my grandad), but he brought ancient techniques from Bharat and adapted them to modern Novaen society—he wrote a textbook on it that is on Zain's Synths and Potions curriculum.

A blond woman with bright pink lipstick replies in heavily accented Novaen. "It's hardly a cabal, Bikram." She turns back to me. "I am Madame Charron, *maître d'alchimie* from Laville. Just think of us as a group of old friends."

"Each of these individuals has helped me in the past with a tricky potion—or if a mix is not coming together as I would like," says Grandad. "Madame Charron, for example—"

"Eradicated a variant of fae-pox that had jumped to humans and was spreading like dragonfire," I finish for him. Of *course* I know who Madame Charron is. She's amazing.

The woman onscreen beams.

"Your grandfather is being too modest," says the final alchemist. He has a shock of short white hair, a long dark moustache, and friendly eyes that crease when he smiles, but it's his high-collared white robe, edged in blue silk, that distinguishes him. He must be from Zhonguo, where they have a uniform for their alchemists. "Ostanes has helped us far more times than we have helped him. I am the Waidan of Long-shi."

I blink in surprise. These people aren't just any Master Alchemists—they're *legends*. Long-shi is the birthplace of alchemy and one of the most powerful centers for mixing in the whole world. The Waidan is the title for their Grand Master. In taking up the role, he would have shed his real name and any ties to his family, dedicating his life to the art of mixing.

I'm surrounded by geniuses of my field.

"Well, tonight, we need your help," Grandad tells them. He turns to me, gesturing at the screen of faces. "Do you want to go over the symptoms you've described to me? I promise you what is discussed here will remain a secret. In this case, I think we want the best minds thinking about a possible diagnosis."

I bite my bottom lip, trying to remember everything that Stefan told me when I was his prisoner in Gergon. "I'm worried that Prince Stefan has brought a strange virus to Nova. The first symptom appears to be a cough, often accompanied by a white—sort of powdery—residue. Weakness in the limbs, tiredness, also reported. But the most alarming symptom is a drain of magical ability in the Talenteds that are afflicted. I've been trying to research what could be behind it, but I'm having no luck."

"That is very alarming!" says Madame Charron, echoing my thoughts exactly. "In Pays we have heard rumors along our border with Gergon that something was very wrong inside the country, but no one has been able to go in or out."

Mr. Patel rubs his chin. "I've heard of certain plagues that weaken a Talented person's ability temporarily, but not one that removes it completely. Do you know if anyone has recovered their ability after the illness has passed?"

I shake my head. "I ... I'm not able to examine the afflicted, and I don't know if anyone's recovered." This is the first time I've found myself regretting not asking Stefan *more* questions about the virus when I was in Gergon. But then, I never expected it to come into Nova.

"We should demand access to Gergon so we can get

to the bottom of this," says Mr. Patel. "Surely if we cause enough commotion they will have to let us in."

"Trust me, we have tried to contact anyone we know in Gergon. Silence. It's as if the entire country has gone dark!" replies Madame Charron.

"Then, I will do what research I can from here," says Mr. Patel.

"As will I," nods the Pays alchemist. "If this virus has been seen before, we will have record of it somewhere."

The Waidan says nothing, but he gazes off into the distance.

"Thank you, friends—and please, use the emergency call signal if you find out anything," says Grandad. "It is imperative we get to the bottom of this."

"Yes, thank you," I say. My shoulders slump. I don't know what I expected, but I hoped there would be a breakthrough.

"Until next time," says Mr. Patel.

"Au revoir," says Madame Charron.

They sign off, until it's only the Waidan left on the screen. He stares right at me, his face shifting until it is dark with anger. "Who is affected in Nova?" he demands.

"I . . . it . . . the princess," I stutter, shocked at his sudden intensity.

"Is she in quarantine?" he asks.

"I don't know. No one has heard from her."

"Then you must come to Long-shi, as soon as you can." He turns toward my grandad, and the anger on his face shifts to concern.

"You know something?" Grandad asks.

"If this is what I think it is, then it could be the start of something very serious indeed. Even deadly. But I didn't want to say in front of the others. It concerns an ancestor of yours ..."

"Tao Kemi." Grandad locks eyes with the Waidan, and a tense silence fills the air. Eventually, Grandad sighs. "Samantha will go."

"To Zhonguo?" My eyes dart between the Waidan and my grandad, confused by the sudden turn of events.

"Yes," says Grandad. "I would come with you if I thought my old bones could handle the journey."

I frown. It's true that Grandad hasn't been quite the same since recovering from the attack by Emilia Thoth that resulted in the loss of his memories. The doctors advised against any strenuous travel, but it hadn't mattered at the time—Grandad never traveled very far even before the incident.

"You don't have a choice," he continues before I can put together any sort of counter-argument. "You must go if you are going to figure out what is wrong with the princess." He turns to the Waidan. "She will come out to you as soon as she can."

"I will start the preparations," he replies solemnly.

The screen goes dark, and Grandad hurries to put it away.

"What do you think the Waidan knows?" I ask. "What does Tao Kemi have to do with this?" Tao Kemi was the last of our family to be named Waidan of Long-shi, before his brother immigrated to Nova. He disappeared at a young age, along with his diaries, so not much is known about him.

"That is what you are going to have to find out."

I gulp. *Dragons, I'm going to Zhonguo ...* A country half a world away from Nova, beyond Pays and Runustan and Bharat—it will be the furthest place I've ever traveled. It's a place I've always longed to visit— and I had secretly hoped that Grandad would take me one day. I force myself to take a deep breath. At least we'll be able to stay in touch throughout the journey. Maybe I can convince someone else to come with me instead ...

"It will take a day or so to get everything in order— you'll need a visa and a Wilds pass. Thursday morning should do it, and in light of the circumstances, you should Transport there. Much faster."

Thursday. Only two days away. My brain suddenly wakes up with the realization of what I'm about to do. "What about school?"

"You'll miss a week, no more."

"And what about the documentary? They shot the

promos today and they wanted to start shooting tomorrow . . ."

"They'll live. They can film it when we get back."

"But—"

"Samantha Kemi, you are a Master Alchemist now and if your hunch is true, then the princess could be in grave danger. This documentary is about *you*—it can fit around your schedule. Now, let me go prepare." He swings open the bookcase leading to the main library, and I'm left alone with the rare books and my thoughts.

Then I can't help but smile. Even though this has all happened so quickly, the sooner I get to Zhonguo and find out what's going on, the sooner I can work on a potion to cure it.

I pull my phone out of my pocket and scroll through the messages I've sent to Evelyn, all getting increasingly more desperate. **Just one word from you, Evie. Just let me know you're okay.**

Still, I'm not giving up.

**I'm going away for a few days,** I write to her. **Stay safe for just a little while longer.**

One week. The trip is only a week.

And when I'm back, I hope I'll know exactly what is wrong with the princess.

# CHAPTER EIGHT

# PRINCESS EVELYN

TO HER RELIEF, WHEN SHE OPENED HER EYES, everyone was gone, replaced by a serene space in tones of white and blue.

If she hadn't been convinced before, she was now.

A dream, then.

She relaxed. Well, a dream was okay. That meant that soon she would wake up and all would be different.

As always in her dreams, her mind turned to her friend and bodyguard, Katrina. But no longer were those gentle thoughts of wonder, or excited sparks of desire. Now she felt supreme guilt. Especially at the memory of their last conversation—the day after the wedding.

"You're . . . you're married?"

Evelyn could see the look of devastation on Katrina's face as clear as if she was standing in front of her. Then she realized she *was* looking at her—an almost-perfect vision conjured up by the dream world. The same tall, strong body—honed by her bodyguard training—clad in the sleek navy suit that was her uniform. Her bright copper hair was in wild waves around her shoulders, free from its regulation braid. The only thing that threatened the illusion was that she kept flickering in and out of existence like those old-time ordinary television shows.

Then she saw a vision of herself standing opposite Katrina. She still hated the sight of herself—it reminded her of the time she had accidentally taken that love potion. She'd spent a couple of weeks head over heels in love with her own reflection—and now she couldn't stand to look in mirrors.

"I didn't have a choice," vision-Evelyn explained. "You saw me, Trina! I was out of control! I had to marry someone or else my power was going to destroy me. The prince is as good a choice as any, and he wanted to marry me now."

"I wanted to marry you too."

"Don't make this harder than it already is. Marrying you was not an option. It was never an option. You're *ordinary*."

The hurt on Katrina's face stung as much as a slap. The real Evelyn squeezed her eyes shut, and when she opened them again, the vision of their final conversation was gone.

As though in reaction to the turn in her thoughts, the scene around her changed to sickening gray-green storm clouds, heavy with the likelihood of rain. She bit her lip hard, to stop the downpour of emotion that threatened to come.

She had to be strong! That's what Katrina liked about her, anyway. Katrina loved Evelyn as someone in control, decisive. A future queen.

Well, a queen had to make hard decisions. That was just the way of it. And marrying Prince Stefan meant safety for Nova, happiness for her parents, a new alliance with a former enemy nation.

All those things were so incredibly, overwhelmingly positive that she couldn't possibly be blamed for making the decision to marry Prince Stefan. Then why these suffocating, infuriating feelings of guilt?

The clouds drew around her like a shroud. She beat at them with her arms, flailing wildly, but it was no use. She sank down, let her head fall into her hands and allowed the clouds in.

She knew why. It was the way she had gone about it. There had been nothing queenly about her actions—she had acted the coward. She'd let herself be swept away by the Novaen Secret Service after the explosion at the Laville Ball, hidden away as her power grew more overwhelming every day. When the prince had come to her, it had seemed like the only way out. What a mess. If only she'd waited for Samantha before agreeing to marry Stefan. Samantha had figured out a way that Evelyn could have stored her extra power—like a magical battery.

But instead, she'd gone ahead with the wedding and the next thing she knew, the weakness had taken over. She hadn't even checked in to see how Katrina was doing.

This was ridiculous. She was a princess. She needed to wake up, to grow up, find Katrina and apologize. No more weakness. No more bed rest. No more sleeping.

She stood up and with one sweep of her arm pushed the clouds of guilt away.

"Now I must wake up!" she said aloud, as if the force of her request would be obeyed by her subconscious mind.

"Wake up!" she cried again.

But nothing happened.

The first creeping vines of doubt began to edge their way into her mind. Images of her worst fears flashed before her eyes, threatening to take up permanent residence. Katrina, turning away from her in disgust. Samantha's store burning to the ground, a blazing inferno. Her citizens terrorized by an unknown enemy.

Her hands gripped at her hair and she closed her eyes. "No," she said. She would not let nightmares in.

"You can join us inside again. It's safe here."

When she opened her eyes again, she saw Prince Ilie holding open an iron gate that was attached to an enormous stone wall, like the ones that used to surround medieval fortresses. Through the gap in the gate she could see a bustling town, full of quaint stone buildings and people dressed in traditional Gergonian clothes.

"Safe from what?" she asked, taking a step toward the gate.

"From the nightmare-bringers." He opened it a little wider and stretched out a gloved hand to meet hers.

It did look inviting inside the walled town. And even though it would mean interacting with the Gergon royals again, she wouldn't be alone. She would have company inside the strange dream world, while she tried to figure out how to wake up.

A flash of movement caught her eye, a trail of white smoke. She craned her neck back, and what she spotted made her heart stop.

Oneiros. *Dream-wraiths.*

She'd only ever heard of them in books. Creatures that lived solely in dreams—that could take a happy thought and turn it into a nightmare.

"Come, quickly!" the prince said. "They'll reach you soon. The walls keep us safe."

But Evelyn didn't come. The oneiros were circling on top of the walled village, almost as if they were guarding it. The sight sent shivers down her spine. She wasn't going to go anywhere near this walled-in place where so many of the creatures congregated.

"No," she said.

"Suit yourself." Prince Ilie saw her look of determination and slammed the gate shut in her face.

She didn't mind.

She was Princess Evelyn. She was a Novaen royal. And she was going to handle this dream world on her own.

Let the oneiros come.

# CHAPTER NINE

# SAMANTHA

"HANG ON, EXPLAIN TO ME AGAIN WHY I need to take notes for you in class for the next week?" asks Anita, sitting on the steps outside the door to our high school. She's rebraiding her dark hair, so long it falls almost to her waist. "Yesterday you told me you were starring in your own documentary, and now you're off to Zhonguo?"

I cringe. "I know. But something came up yesterday."

"A secret alchemist mission."

"Yeah . . ."

"That has to do with the mystery virus and Prince Stefan."

"Exactly."

"But you can't tell me any more."

"Not yet . . ."

"It's a Master Alchemist thing, huh? What even *is* your life? Does Zain know about your trip yet?"

"I'm meeting up with him later to tell him. I didn't want to explain it over text."

Anita nods. "Good plan. If you need anything, you know Arjun and I are just a call away."

"I know. Thanks, Ani."

The bell rings behind us, so we gather up our book bags and swing them over our shoulders. Then my phone buzzes. "I better get this," I say to Anita, registering the central Novaen area code on the call. My heart leaps. It might be the princess on a new number. "I'll catch you up." Anita nods and waves, so I answer the call. "Hello?"

"Sam? This is Daphne. Listen, I got your email and—though it's a little crazy—I love your idea. It's brilliant. Are you sure you've never had aspirations to work in TV? No? Never mind. Listen, it took a lot of wrangling from me—lord KNOWS things are tight at the studio—but we've got the permission and it's full speed ahead! We're only bringing along a skeleton crew so we can travel light—I can do almost everything with magic these days but some of the technology is finicky, so I'm bringing along an ordinary camerawoman. She's great and she can do some of the techy stuff too. Magic's no substitute for computer skills—I never bothered learning that stuff! Anyway, she comes highly recommended so it's all going to go off without a hitch—"

Daphne's talking so fast, I can't slip a single word into the conversation—until now. "Wait . . . what idea?"

"Your idea! To film you going back to your roots in Zhonguo, discovering your past. The network's going crazy for it, I tell you. It's genius."

It takes me a couple of seconds to process her words.

"You mean ... you're not going to postpone the filming?"

"Postpone? Are you nuts? We're not going to have an opportunity like this again! You leave on Thursday, right?"

"Yeah."

"I'll see you with the film crew then. Ciao, babe."

She hangs up, and I'm left staring at the phone in disbelief. But then I think, *what's the harm?* I set myself a reminder in my phone to ask Grandad to get the Waidan's permission for the film crew to accompany us. If he says it's okay, then I don't see why they can't come along.

The rest of the school day passes ever-so-slowly, my eyes flicking up to the clock every thirty seconds. There's so much I need to do to prepare that I'm itching to head back home. I've got a list going on my phone and it's filling up with things like:

– Pack potion-making kit ... what supplies??

– Look up videos on how to say basic phrases in Zhonguo (I don't want to appear like a total ignorant Novaen)

– Dig out hiking boots

– Download Zhonguo guidebook or find one in library

I'm still adding things to the list when the final bell rings and I'm out the door in a flash. My mind feels like it's racing a million miles a minute. It's spinning so much that when I get to the park I almost miss the moment a pile of fallen leaves lifts up and drifts through the air, morphing into shapes: a bird with flapping wings, a galloping horse, and, finally, a heart. I just watch, transfixed by the shifting confetti of red and gold, and clap wildly when the leaves drop. I see the mastermind—Zain—standing with his wand outstretched like a conductor's baton, orchestrating the dance of the leaves.

Talenteds. They're always showing off. But even as an ordinary—someone without the ability to use magic—I can appreciate the gesture. Plus, I've learned that there's magic in being ordinary too. In not having to rely on any outside power, and in our ability to interact with the magical creatures and plants of the world without danger. Being ordinary enables me to be an alchemist, and I wouldn't change that for all the Talented power in the world.

"Hi," Zain says as he sees me. The way he looks at me sends a blush rising in my cheeks, but before I can say anything back, he kisses me hard on the lips, and all thought temporarily disappears from my brain.

"Hi," I say, a quivery mess when we break apart. Zain's kisses do that to me. His fingers lace through mine and we walk down the leaf-topped path. The air is crisp, but I don't feel a chill. Next to Zain, I feel nothing but warmth.

"So, what was it that you wanted to talk to me about? Still feeling okay about the documentary?"

"Yeah, it's not that. Listen, I got a lead yesterday on the virus."

"A lead? What sort of lead?"

"The kind I *have* to investigate ... I spoke to the Waidan of Long-shi."

Zain whistles low. "How did you manage that?"

"Grandad."

Zain chuckles. "Makes sense."

"Anyway, so I described Evie's symptoms to him and he might have an idea of what's causing it. But I have to go there myself to find out. To Zhonguo."

To Zain's credit, he takes this announcement totally within his stride, barely missing a beat. I guess he's come to expect that life with me at the moment is *never* normal for long. "Long-shi ... isn't that where they found that buried village a few months ago?"

I frown. "What?"

"Don't you ever watch the newscasts? It was a really cool story about archaeologists uncovering an ancient alchemical monastery that had been buried by a lava flow."

"I *think* that rings a bell. So, can you come with me? Can you get out of uni for a week?"

He blinks. "Are you serious?"

"Deadly. I could really use your help out there."

He pauses, and the ghost of a smile creeps onto his face. "I can try. Maybe I can swing it so I don't have to go back at all."

I squeeze his arm. "Really not enjoying it, huh?"

He shrugs. "I know Synths and Potions is supposed to be my 'perfect' major, what I'm most passionate about. It's what I've been working toward my whole life! But to be honest, I think I hate it. It's my dad's job, not mine."

"What you would do instead?" I ask.

He pulls away from me and shoves his hands deep in his jacket pockets. "No clue."

A cool breeze wraps its way around my body, making me shiver. I touch the sleeve of his jacket. "You don't have to have it all figured out."

"Easy for you to say, Master Alchemist. You're making your own path and I'm following my father every step of the way."

"Hey!" I freeze, indignant. If anyone knows how hard I worked to get that title, Zain does.

Zain scuffs his foot along the ground. "Sorry, I didn't mean it. Look, Daphne wanted this documentary to be about you. I'm just supporting cast. I think you should go to Long-shi on your own."

"What? No . . . Don't be stubborn—"

"I'm not being stubborn," he interrupts (in my opinion, stubbornly).

"But I need you."

"No, you don't. Look, I'll talk to you later, okay? I have a paper to write." He spins on his heels and walks toward the park exit.

By contrast, my feet are rooted to the floor. I feel like if I move, I'll fall over: His total 180 in attitude has sent my world spinning on its axis.

I look down at my watch. Anita should be out of school now. I dig my phone out of my pocket, dial her number, and wait anxiously for her to pick up.

"Anita?"

"Yeah?"

"I think Zain and I have had our first fight."

# CHAPTER TEN

# SAMANTHA

I FOLD A T-SHIRT NEATLY AND PUT IT IN THE small rolling suitcase I'm taking to Zhonguo. Anita lies on my bed—she's supposed to be helping me, but she's too distracted trying to process my conversation with Zain.

Finally, she sits up and stares me in the face. "He's threatened. He's threatened and now he's scared and he's hurt."

"Threatened? By what?"

"By you, stupid."

I scoff.

"No, think about it. You've got so much figured out already—you know your life plan and passion and you're damn good at it. You're on a mission that might save the princess *again*—with a film crew who want to make it into this incredible story—and he doesn't know what's happening in his life. You've told me he's confused about his major, thinking about dropping out of uni, his best friend has gone totally incommunicado, and now his super kick-ass girlfriend is reminding him just how super kick-ass she is. He's just lashing out. He will be back, I promise you."

I stop packing for a moment and sit down cross-legged on my bedroom floor. "Dragons, why is it all so complicated?"

"Probably because people aren't potions, Sam. Just because you have all the right ingredients doesn't mean they're going to mix properly."

"Hmm, I suppose so."

Anita laughs. She can tell that's not what I want to hear. "You guys will figure it out. It's your first fight. After all, you have the best *chemistry*."

I groan at the pun and throw a pair of rolled-up socks at her head.

"But enough about Zain," Anita continues. "And I know you can't tell me anything more about the trip. Tell me more about the documentary! That's so exciting that they want to continue to do the show even though you'll be traveling."

"I know! It surprised me."

"Not me. People are desperate for a distraction. Did you read the piece in the *Novaen Mail* about how the princess has cheated the country out of a national holiday by not having a big, televised wedding? And they're claiming that not showing us the wedding dress is a violation of our human rights!"

"Well, that's just nuts."

"I know. But the media are desperate to fill the giant hole that is Princess Evelyn's disappearing act. Enter, stage left, Samantha Kemi—alchemist extraordinaire, savior of the princess, beloved of the people . . ."

"Okay, you can stop that now!" I fiddle with the zip on my suitcase, trying to get everything to fit inside. "But what if I'm no good at it? They want to film it 'reality' style, as if I don't even know the cameras are there— well, apart from the 'one-on-one' interviews. Reality television means you have to be natural. What if I'm a total flake? You remember what happened on my last television interview, and this is going to be much more intense."

"You don't have any more deep, dark family secrets to reveal, do you?"

"I don't think so."

"Then you'll be fine. The worst thing that will happen will be if you hate the film crew. You're going to be spending a couple of weeks in each other's pockets, in Zhonguo and here. It could be annoying."

I bite my lip. "I hadn't thought about that."

"You'll be fine. Despite your grouchy ways, you're pretty easy to get along with."

"Can't you come with me?"

"What? No. Besides, someone needs to take your notes, remember?"

This is what I love about Anita. I don't even have to ask her—she just knows exactly what to say (and do).

"Thanks," I reply. "By the way, how's it going with Jacob?" I ask slyly. Jacob is in our joint geography class, and he asked Anita out not long after she came back from helping me at Lake Karst. I'm sure he's had a crush on her for much longer than that, but took a while to pluck up the courage.

"All right," she says, blushing a shade of peach. I put down the pair of jeans I'm folding. If she's shy, that means it's getting serious.

"You've been on a few dates now . . ."

"It's almost our one month anniversary," she says with a small smile. "I have no idea what to get him though."

"Are you supposed to get him something?"

"Did you get something for Zain?"

"Well, we technically hadn't been on a first date yet, so what day would we even use for an anniversary?"

"What about the mountain top?"

"Hmm, if that was the case then our first month anniversary would've been on a plane to Runustan trying to track down my great-grandmother's potion diary . . . so I wouldn't have been in the best place to think about a gift."

Anita frowns. "Oh yeah, I forgot about that—and

how quickly you guys have moved. Do you still feel good about it all?"

I stop and think for a second.

*Rosehip and grace of a woodland elf—for reflection on your feelings, to establish and diagnose emotional problems, to find the necessary remedy.*

"I think so," I say, honestly. "When I'm with him, I feel like I can do anything. He gives me that confidence, and I never feel like I have to hide who I am."

"That's good," Anita grins.

"Plus he's really hot," I say, waggling my eyebrows.

Anita laughs and throws a pair of socks at my head. But all I can think is one thing:

I really hope he comes with me to Zhonguo. I check my phone out of habit, but there are no messages from him.

"Sam? Anita?" Mum's voice drifts up the stairs.

"Yeah?" I shout back.

"We're about to have dinner. Does Anita want to stay?"

I raise my eyebrows at her.

The idea ticks over in her brain. "I saw your dad was preparing dumplings, and they're the best . . ." But finally, she shakes her head, even as I see the hesitation in her eyes. "I'd better get back—Mum wants help clearing out the attic before bed. She's on one of her 'sprees.'"

"But I thought your mum was a massive hoarder?"

"Exactly. This is the consequence: biannual mega clearouts!"

"Okay, good luck."

"Save me a *jiaozi?*"

"No guarantees!" I say with a laugh.

We squeeze each other in a long hug, but Anita lingers longer than me. "Don't worry, it'll be okay. He'll come around and everything will be back to normal."

"Thanks. I really hope you're right."

There's a tiny crack in the wall I've built, and it threatens to spill over into tears. I bite my lip, hard, to hold them back. But Anita sees the truth. She hugs me again, and all I can think is, *thank the dragons for good friends.*

## CHAPTER ELEVEN

# PRINCESS EVELYN

THE PRICKLING ON HER SKIN STARTED AT her wrist.

It moved gradually up her arm, every hair slowly standing up on end. She didn't dare look at what was causing it. Then she forced herself to open one eye.

On her arm was a tarantula, as large as her hand and black as a stain, and it was crawling up toward her face. She wanted to scream but her throat constricted, no sound came out but a choke. She tried to move but her muscles wouldn't obey. All she could do was watch, helpless as it approached her collarbone, as it drew back into a strike position, two of its legs rearing back, fangs outstretched ...

She was in a maze of mirrors. Everywhere she looked, she saw her own face staring back at her. *Don't you love me?* the mirrors said. *Don't you love me?*

She tried to find a way out. She started slowly,

methodically, at first. Her fingers reached out to feel what was glass and what was a potential pathway through the maze, her eyes cast down to avoid looking at her reflection. But with every turn she took, there were more and more mirrors, mirrors on the floor and on the ceiling, mirrors in front and behind, her face reflected back and back and back, a million Evelyns staring at her, their faces mimicking her blind terror, mocking her. She sank to the ground and tried to close her eyes but it was as if matchsticks held them open and she had no choice but to look at herself for eternity . . .

Kingstown was burning, and she was powerless to stop it. She could only look down at the flames from her invisible palace, watching as her people fled their homes in terror, crying out for lost loved ones.

The Z from the top of ZA toppled to the ground, its steel girders melting in the heat.

Kemi's Potion Shop, lost in the inferno.

Royal Lane, almost indistinguishable through thick clouds of black smoke.

Her city, slowly being destroyed.

It was too much for her to bear.

*It's safe here from nightmare-bringers.* That's what the prince had said about the walled city. Maybe she should go there. Anything to get away from what her mind was showing her. She looked up and there she was, outside the gates. All she needed to do was step through and the vision of the burning Kingstown would disappear.

A flash of copper caught her eye. "Katrina?" Evelyn spoke her name out loud, spinning around away from the gate, her heart spiked with hope—and happiness. The vision of the burning city faltered in front of her eyes. "Katrina, are you there?"

She thought of one of the first times she realized she had a crush on Katrina. Not long after the Wilde Hunt was over, when she had sworn off love for good. But wasn't that always the way? The moment she stopped looking for it, love came by and swept her off her feet ... Katrina had been helping her set up an alternative, secure social media profile so she could keep up with her friends (like Zain and Sam) without attracting media attention. She remembered sitting at the desk as Katrina leaned over her to point at the screen, the end of her braid brushing Evelyn's shoulder. She caught the lightly floral scent of her shampoo, and she found herself shifting position, ever so slightly, so that their fingers touched. She could've sworn in that moment, a real current of electricity passed between them, connecting them. The memory made Evelyn smile.

And it made the vision of the burning city disappear— and in its place were the oneiros, their white wispy hands circling, trying to conjure up another, even more awful vision.

Evelyn clenched her fists. She didn't need to enter

Prince Ilie's walled city to protect herself.

She could do it on her own.

All she needed to do was remember who she was, and who she loved.

# CHAPTER TWELVE

# SAMANTHA

THE NEXT MORNING, I'M UP EARLY. THE house is a whirlwind of preparations. Daphne asks me not to pack up my potions supplies until the TV crew arrive, which makes me nervous. I like being prepared—and I hate waiting around in case I forget something. Everything else I need is packed up in my suitcase and already sitting by the front door, ready to go.

There's still no sign of Zain in my texts or messages. He really has decided not to come.

"Sam! They're here!" Mum's voice drifts up the stairs. I swallow, hard. Now that this is finally happening, dread settles in my stomach like dregs in the bottom of a teacup. I wish I could read my doubt and find out if it's valid or blown out of proportion. But thoughts aren't leaves, and there's no way for me to know.

I give myself a shake and head downstairs. I only make it halfway down the staircase before I see the "crew," and it stops me dead. There are two people staring up at me: one is Daphne, the director. But the other gives me pause. It's . . . for a moment, her name escapes me, but I know I recognise her gorgeous, copper-bright hair. She's the palace bodyguard, the one that I thought Princess Evelyn was falling for—before she went and got married. Katrina! That's her name.

As I come to a halt on the stairs, her eyes lift to meet mine. They seem to shoot me a warning, as if she doesn't want me to show Daphne that I recognise her. Then she lifts a big camera to her shoulder—one of the type they use to film documentaries—and before I know it, Daphne conjures the microphone so it floats near my head, and a little red light appears on the side of the camera: recording.

I stare, my feet frozen to the stairs. After a few awkward seconds, Daphne jerks her head to the side, where my family is standing in a line waiting for me. I realize she wants to film me saying good-bye. I rush down the stairs and dole out big hugs, starting with my mum and dad, and then Molly. Grandad's opted out of the filming, so I'll say good-bye to him privately.

"Cut! Perfect!" says Daphne, staring at a little floating monitor in front of her. "Although for the future, Sam, don't look at the camera so much when we're rolling—we want you to act as naturally as possible. The only time you'll look dead into camera will be for the one-on-ones. We might have to reshoot that entrance. Can you go back upstairs?"

I shake my head, heat rising in my cheeks. *I can't do this*, I think. My heart beats wildly in my chest and my throat begins to close. The door to the kitchen looms in the hallway behind my parents and with a few quick steps I lunge my way past them and through.

My vision is a blur. I grip the edges of the counter and close my eyes, trying to focus on my breathing. "Acting naturally" doesn't feel natural at all. Having those cameras pointed at me, the red lights blinking, the microphones floating just out of shot . . . *Pull yourself together, Sam*, I tell myself.

Two loud knocks sound on the door. I open it up to Mum. "Everything okay in here?"

"Yeah, fine," I say with a small smile.

She puts her arm around my shoulders and pulls me tight. "We've set Daphne up in the store and she's got the camerawoman filming some background shots, so they're occupied for now."

"Thanks, Mum," I say, glad I can have a moment to myself.

"Where's Zain?" she asks, rubbing her hand on my back.

I shrug. "I don't know. We had a fight yesterday and I thought I would have heard from him by now. I don't know if he's coming and . . . I don't know if I can do this without him."

Mum scoffs. "Sam, if there's anything you should have learned over the past few months, it's that you can do anything you set your mind to. Zain is a lovely boy but you don't need him by your side."

"But the cameras ... the documentary ... it's so not me." I bury my face in my hands. "I thought I wanted to do this to have control of my own story for a change, rather than wait for the media to write stuff about me. Zain was going to help me navigate all that."

With light pressure from her hands, Mum spins me around so that I face her. She takes my hands down from my eyes and lifts up my chin. "You can do both," she says. "And if you don't want to do the documentary anymore because you'd rather not be on television, that's one thing. But if what's stopping you is Zain not being here? I won't allow that."

Mum's forceful words, so much in contrast to her normally sweet demeanor, bring a reluctant smile to my face. In fact, I do want this. The Novaen people have been told enough lies. I might have the chance to show them some truth. And Mum's right. I don't need Zain to do that. "Okay."

"So you're going back out there?"

"Yes."

"Good girl," she says, pulling me in tight for a hug.

I take a deep breath and step back into the fray.

Daphne spots me immediately. "There you are! We've just finished up our establishing shots, so we're almost good to go! Oh, wait—I forgot to introduce you to the new member of our team. This superwoman over here is Katrina Pickard."

Katrina lowers the camera from her shoulder and extends her hand out to mine. "Nice to meet you. But, call me Trina. Everyone does." She doesn't give any sign that we've met before.

"And you," I say cautiously, following her lead.

"I call her superwoman because she's going to be doing the duties of ten people. It was very hard to find anyone who has the right visas and paperwork and availability for a job like this. We got lucky!"

"I'm . . . uh, glad you could join us," I say.

Trina smiles. "No problem. Now I'm going to put a mic on you. These are really easy, wireless microphones that will stick onto any piece of clothing. If we just put it on top of your collar . . . There, perfect." The microphone is tiny, and fits on the collar-button of my plaid shirt. "How about we get some shots of you packing away your potion-mixing stuff?"

"Okay," I say. Katrina heaves the camera back onto her shoulder.

Daphne pipes up. "And narrate your actions as if you're showing people at home around your store— imagine you're giving them the big guided tour. We want people to discover alchemy for themselves, through your eyes. Are you ready?"

"Don't people normally script this stuff? What if I say the wrong thing?" My face must betray my panic, because Daphne rushes to reassure me.

"We can edit any mumbles out. Remember, this is something you've lived and breathed your whole life. All that's changing is that the camera is here."

"Oh, and the millions of people that might watch," I mumble. Then I remind myself: *That's what you want.* I take a deep breath. "Okay, well. This is Kemi's Potion Shop, which has been in our family for over three centuries. There's a lot of history here." I stare up at the wall of ingredients—the Kemi pride and joy. The jars, bottles, and vials containing the ingredients are fully stocked and neatly labeled, but if you didn't know what you were looking at, it would seem chaotic. Jumbled. That's how Grandad and I demonstrate our skill without having to lift a finger. It's impressive. I know because my heart expands with pride whenever I look at it.

"I won't be taking many ingredients with me," I continue, "because they will have almost everything in Zhonguo. But I will be bringing a few special Novaen gifts for the Long-shi alchemists that they might not have: a merpearl and a kelpie bridle.

"I'll also be taking a lot of books," I say, stopping in front of the mini-library we have in the store. The main library is behind, but I also keep the shelf out here stocked with my current "TBR" pile. "I can't seem to travel anywhere without them—even though Zain has tried to convince me to switch to an e-reader." I take down three thick paperbacks: a guide to the flora and fauna of Zhonguo, a travelogue of a Finder's journey through the country and finally, a book of Zhonguo fairytales.

"Cut! Much better," Daphne says. Trina reaches up and turns off the camera. "I think we've got something to work with here." Daphne gives me an encouraging smile, which I awkwardly return. At least someone is optimistic about my abilities.

Mum comes over and envelops me in a hug. "Be safe, honey. And even though you're there for a serious job, try to enjoy yourself."

"Your mum's right," says Dad. "This is your first trip back to the Kemi homeland. I wish we were taking you there ourselves, so we could show you some of where our family came from."

"Me too," I say. My heart twinges, and I know if I stay any longer I'll get emotional. I try to step away from the hug, but Mum's arms remain tightly wrapped around me. "Uh . . . Mum?"

"Come on, Katie," says my dad, gently.

"Oh, I know I can't keep you wrapped up in cotton wool forever." She gives me one last squeeze and then finally lets go. "Now, Molly, on the other hand . . ."

"Hey!" says Molly indignantly, from behind Mum's back.

"Hey yourself," Mum says with a laugh. "You've got at least four more years of overprotective Mum, okay?"

"Fine," says Molly, rolling her eyes.

"Let's go." Trina grabs my suitcase from the floor and takes it outside to the car. I finish my second round of hugs. The first ones were played out for the camera and didn't feel quite real.

"Let me know how it goes with the princess," I say to Molly.

"I will."

My final stop is Grandad. "Keep me informed every step of the way. The Waidan won't have asked you to come all that distance without good reason. And lastly, remember: You are not only a Master Alchemist, but a Kemi. If there is any threat to Nova that can be fixed with a potion, you will figure it out. It's the Kemi way."

"Don't worry, Grandad," I say. "I won't let you down."

# CHAPTER THIRTEEN

# PRINCESS EVELYN

GOOD THOUGHTS KEPT THE ONEIROS AT bay—that much she'd figured out—so Katrina's face was never far from her mind.

But she still had questions, and only one person she could ask. She marched straight up to the gates of the town and pounded on the metal bars. "Come out!" she cried. "Prince Ilie, show yourself."

She'd had enough of waiting around. If she wasn't going to wake up, she needed to figure out what was going on. And to do that, she had to talk to the people that had been here the longest. The Gergon royal family.

"Have you not heard the legend of the sleeping princess?"

His voice startled her, but she quickly composed her face to get rid of any shock. The rules were different in this dream world, and she didn't want him to know that he had taken her by surprise. Prince Ilie—Stefan's older brother—appeared without warning on the other side of the bars, stiffly formal in a long black suit.

"I've heard of it," she replied. "A princess who slept for a hundred years. My kingdom won't allow that. There are people working to wake me, I know it."

"Who said I was talking about your kingdom?" He cast his eyes down, but she didn't trust him for a second.

"So you are all asleep too. In Gergon." Evelyn blinked, attempting to process what she was hearing.

"Yes."

"But *why?* I don't understand."

The prince sighed dramatically. "It is easier if I show you," he said. He took out a large key from his pocket and turned it in the lock of the gates.

"I won't come inside." Evelyn took several steps backward.

"There is no need. I will step out—but only for a moment. I will not be able to stay away from the walled town for long. The nightmares are too terrible." He glanced up at where the oneiros were circling, and shuddered. He locked the gate behind him. "Hold out your hand like this," he said, laying his palm out flat.

Evelyn hesitated. But what choice did she have? She wanted to know what was happening, why she had been put into this dream state, and here was someone who appeared to know. Slowly, finger by finger, she opened her hand until her palm was face up to the sky.

"You are not only royal, but the heir to the throne—and like me, you have the ability to control magic through your skin." The prince reached out and ran his finger lightly across her palm. As he did so, beams of light shot from her fingertips, rivers of light infused with bright sparks that glittered and shone as they danced in the rays. Tears sprung up into Evelyn's eyes. For the first time in her life she was *seeing* magic. Her magic. The streams that she had under her control. That gave her power.

Or so she thought. The strands of light began to twist, turning her hand, closing her fingers together until the strands all traveled in the same direction.

The prince looked sad. "I thought so. It is the same for me." He opened his palm and the same magic burst to life. But though magic spread from his fingertips, his strands were weaker, thinner—only single specks of glitter compared to Evelyn's rivers, and further up they twisted and braided together until they joined Evelyn's.

"Where is it going?" asked Evelyn, her eyes following the streams of magic as they flew up and over the city walls, leading deeper within, where they joined innumerable tributaries of magic flowing up from every inhabitant of the dream world. The river then flowed to one place—a tall, dark stone tower right in the very center of the city.

"Who lives in that tower?" Evelyn asked.

"She does. She's taking all of it. All the magic she can ..."

The resignation in the prince's voice only caused Evelyn's resolve to strengthen. "How do we stop her? Can we storm the building and take our magic back?"

Prince Ilie shook his head. "I'm afraid we have an even more urgent problem than that."

"Which is?" Evelyn demanded.

The stone tower shook, threatening to topple over at any moment.

"We think she's about to wake up. And when she does—she will have the power to drain the whole world."

# CHAPTER FOURTEEN

# SAMANTHA

"START ROLLING THE CAMERAS," DAPHNE says as we approach the check-in desk at the terminal.

I frown. I can't see how checking in for a Transport will be of any interest to viewers at home. But then I see why. Standing with his elbow propped up on the counter, his hair glamoured so each black strand is iridescent in the bright lights of the Transport terminal, is Zain.

It's thrown me so totally off guard that it gives him a moment to leap forward and lift me into a twirl. He grabs my hands and kisses me on the lips before I can react. "I did it, Sam," he says, a charming grin on his face.

"Did . . . did what?" I stutter. My eyes flicker between him and the camera.

"I got the time off! I'm coming with you to Zhonguo."

Emotions war within me. I'm so confused by this

total 180 from Zain. But the cameras are on, Zain's squeezing my fingers and staring up at me with his startling blue eyes, and I find myself smiling back. "That's great!" I say, trying to inject the same enthusiasm into my voice.

"Cut!" says Daphne. "What an entrance. Oh, I knew you two would be television gold."

I barely register what she's saying.

I step back from the embrace as fast as I can, my eyes flickering back to Trina to make sure the cameras are off. As soon as I can see they are, I say: "What the hell, Zain?"

"Sam—I'm sorry. I overreacted yesterday."

"And the best way to spring that on me was on camera? You couldn't text? Phone? Email? DM? Anything?"

"My fault!" says Daphne, throwing her hands up in the air between us. "I had called Zain to confirm his details and he told me about your little disagreement. I knew you two would work things out so I thought we could capture the tension for the documentary! You know, you can't manufacture this kind of dramatic storytelling . . ."

I blink in disbelief at Daphne, and then at Zain. At least he has the decency to look bashful. "I'm sorry I blindsided you. Daphne wouldn't let me get in touch. She said it would ruin the 'authenticity of the moment.' Will you forgive me?" he says.

I feel myself soften. This is our first fight. You're supposed to be able to get over your first fight, aren't you? "Yes."

"So we're okay?" He lifts my fingers to his lips and kisses them gently.

"We're okay."

"Good."

I allow myself to smile. Now that the shock of seeing him has worn off, I'm relieved I won't be going to Zhonguo on my own. "Well, I'm glad you decided to come. I didn't really want to do this without you, you know."

"I know."

Daphne steps in and I cringe as I realize she's been listening the whole time. "Oh, lovely! Just lovely . . . all back to happy families, yes? Come on, let's get checked in for the Transport then."

We have an hour to wait in the terminal until our Transport is called, so we settle in the comfortable waiting lounge. Except for Katrina and me, almost everyone in here is Talented. They're the only ones who can afford such an expensive mode of travel. Huge Summons screens line the far wall, with strong Talenteds guiding passengers along streams of magic from one destination to another. A journey that might take several hours by plane can be accomplished in only a few minutes by Transport. Flights might be slower, but they're also cheaper—and they come with the added bonus of not having to witness the entire journey from midair.

I wait for a moment when Daphne takes Trina aside to do some shot planning, and I drag Zain over to a nearby coffee counter. I need a hit of caffeine before the Transport, but I also need to speak to him in private.

I drop my voice to a whisper. "Hey, did you recognise that camerawoman?"

Zain frowns and looks back over his shoulder. "You mean the woman with the red hair? Um, I don't think so. Should I?"

"Don't just stare at her! That's *Katrina*. Formerly of Princess Evelyn's private guard service."

Zain's eyes open wide with surprise. "Seriously? Wow. What do you think she's doing here?"

"I don't know. But I'm going to find out. It can't be a coincidence." On the tip of my tongue is to explain to Zain the chemistry I saw between them . . . but that's Evelyn's business. It's not my place to say.

"Hang on, they're coming back over here. Order your coffee."

"I'll take a caramel macchiato, please," I tell the barista.

"There you guys are! Oh, another caffeine addict I see—just like me! I'll take a triple shot no foam latte." Daphne says that last bit to Zain, and grabs me by the shoulders. "Now you, our little *star*, let's set up in the corner of the lounge—make sure you get shots of people Transporting via Summons in the background, Trina, okay? I'm thinking adventure, I'm thinking excitement, I'm thinking *transporting* people out of their everyday lives and into Sam's world." Daphne moves me until I'm sitting down on a small ledge with a huge window behind me.

"What do you want me to say?" I ask, shuffling my feet. The cold glass presses up against my back but the air from the lounge is too warm. My tummy rumbles. I want my macchiato. My whole body is uncomfortable and—not for the first time—I wonder what the hell I'm doing.

"Just talk about where we're going. This is going to be a one-on-one video, totally unscripted, a chance for you to open up a bit. Let us in. Tell us what's going on in the mind of Sam Kemi." She punctuates every word of her final sentence with a finger jab at my forehead. I wonder if she's going to leave a mark. "I've left some questions on a notepad down there, so feel free to look at those if you need some inspiration. And Sam?"

"Yeah?"

"Don't hold back. If it goes too long, we'll edit it down. The more you speak from the heart, the better you're going to come across."

"Um, can Trina stay with me?"

Daphne looks surprised. "Sure. Why?"

"I just think it will be easier to talk to a person, rather than to a camera lens."

"Okay, but remember you *will* have to stare into the camera. We want it to be confession-booth style. Can you deal with that?"

I swallow, but I nod.

"Great. Okay, this works out! Trina can hold up the prompts while you talk. I'll set up a spell around you that will block sound coming in and out so that we don't get interference on camera." She pulls out her object—a wand like Zain's—and with a few flicks of her wrist, manipulates the magical energy in the air around us to raise a sound barrier. My first thought is how *loud* the Transport terminal really is, now that all the background noise is gone. My ears ring in the silence.

Trina slips a pair of thick round headphones over her ears all the same and turns on the camera, so the red light blinks in front of me again, a winking distraction.

I swallow hard, taking a few deep breaths to compose myself. I glance over Trina's shoulder and see Daphne has joined Zain in the coffee queue, wildly gesticulating with her arms as she talks. This is my chance. "I know you," I say, staring past the camera and straight at Katrina instead.

"What do you mean?" she asks, but I don't buy her ignorance. Her face turns stoney, she's bracing herself for my curiosity. And, most tellingly of all, she turns off the camera—but continues to point it at me as if we're doing our assigned confessional.

"Why are you here?" I blurt out. I had wanted to ask more lead-up questions, but out of the corner of my eye I can see Daphne looking over at us. "I remember you. From the palace. You and the princess . . ." I don't even know how to finish that statement, but the flash of red color that appears on Trina's cheeks is proof enough that my assumptions were correct. "Why aren't you at the palace? Is she okay?"

"I was fired from the palace," Trina says through gritted teeth.

"What? Why?"

"Stefan. But that's not all. Before they fired me, I also saw that the princess was sick—she can't stop coughing, she's weak; she can't stand up to him."

"I knew it," I say. "No one else would believe me— not outside my family and friends. Especially not when those honeymoon photos came out."

"Those were fake. Doctored. I know, because I used to run all the computer systems inside the palace and I saw a memo going around that the prince was looking for an 'experienced Talented photo editor.' Then a few hours later—boom—those photos showed up. Didn't you notice how fuzzy they were? And they didn't even show the princess without giant sunglasses and a huge hat."

I think back to the photos I saw in the restaurant. They hadn't seemed right to me then, but everyone else had been so *sure*. I'm glad for the confirmation I'm not imagining things, but I'm equally terrified for the princess. What's really going on at Palace Great?

"And what are *you* doing, going to Zhonguo?" Trina asks me. "Up until yesterday you were doing this documentary in Nova. What's with the change of mind? It's to do with the princess's sickness, isn't it? You've found something out, haven't you?" She stares at me with her piercing green eyes and I feel stripped bare under that look. I'm taken back to the moment at the Laville Ball where I saw her help Princess Evelyn after she lost control of her overwhelming power.

It's impressive. Anyone who can hold their own in a face-off with the princess earns my respect.

But not necessarily my trust. "How do you know what I was doing? Have you been spying on me?" I move to stand up—I don't know what's going on, but suddenly I no longer feel comfortable.

A look of panic flares up in Trina's eyes and she flaps her hands at me to sit down. "Okay, you don't have to tell me anything," she concedes. "I know because of what I just said—I ran the computer systems in the palace. I've been following your movements, because you're not only her friend—you're her alchemist. And you've been vocal about your feelings about Stefan. I knew you wouldn't be leaving the country unless you had a lead that could help her. So if your plan involves helping the princess somehow ... please. Let me be there with you."

I hesitate, still not 100 percent convinced.

"Look." She pulls down the edge of her collar, and around her neck is a delicate silver chain with a ring hanging from it. A ring I recognise. It belonged to Princess Evelyn. "Evie gave this to me. All I want to do is help you help her."

Staring up into the woman's pleading green eyes, I know there's no way I can refuse her. I need all the help I can get. "Okay," I say, quietly.

"Good. Now let's get some confessional shots down or else Daphne is going to get suspicious."

I nod and take a deep breath. "So, um, we're in Kingstown International Transport Terminal about to head to, uh, um, Long-shi village in Zhonguo. I am, er, really excited about the trip ..."

Trina puts up her hand to stop me, but I've already stopped myself. My shoulders drop and I lean forward onto my knees, a loud groan escaping my lips. "Wow, this is harder than I thought," I say, aiming for a sheepish grin but probably ending up with an unconvincing grimace.

"Don't worry about it," says Trina. "Shake it off and try again. Oh, here's your first question." She holds up a white sign that reads: *How do you feel about Transporting?*

I feel myself relax as I read the question: this is something I can answer easily. "I'd never done much Transporting until this year—it's way too expensive for me."

Trina holds up her hand to stop me again. "That was great, loads more natural, but make sure you're looking at the camera when you say it, not at me."

"Oh right, I forgot about that." I grip the edge of the seat with my fingers, annoyed that I've messed up *again*. I return my gaze right to the center of the camera lens, trying not to focus on my upside-down reflection in the smooth black glass. "I hadn't really Transported that much until this year—it was always way too expensive for me—but because of the Wilde Hunt, I've had to get used to it quickly!"

Trina smiles at me and nods encouragingly. Then she picks up the next card. *What are you hoping to find in Long-shi?*

I pause for a moment. This is something I've been thinking a lot about, and I'm not sure that I have a definite answer. Then I realize that this is supposed to be confessional. I decide to go ahead and be honest. "I don't know what I'm going to find in Long-shi. I'm going with a completely open mind. Something my grandad taught me is that alchemists always look to the past to find answers. Take, for example, the buried monastery they just discovered—it's one of the greatest archaeological finds of the past century. This is where alchemy was *born*; this is where my ancestors come from. There might be answers there to questions we don't even know to ask. That's what appeals to me. And if I return to my roots, test myself, and dig down deep into my past, I might find out what else I'm really capable of."

"It sounds a bit like you're treating yourself like a potion ingredient."

I laugh. "I suppose it does! And in a way, that's exactly what I'm doing. I'm examining myself. I want to find out what my properties are, so I can find out exactly where I belong. Just like an ingredient in a mix."

*And do you have your diary with you?*

"My potion diary? But of course." I pat the tan leather satchel at my feet—my present to myself after escaping from Stefan. "It's always by my side. And—I know this is nerdy—but part of me can't wait to put my potion diary on the same shelf as those of some of the most revered alchemists of all time—and not just those related to the Kemi family! I was doing some reading and I found out there's an ancient library in Long-shi that has potion diaries going back a thousand years! Just to be near that sort of history ..." I can't help myself; I shiver with delight.

Trina gives me a nod and smiles at me. "That's great, thanks Sam. I think we got what we need." She turns around and gives a thumbs-up to Daphne.

Daphne drops the sound barrier. "How did it go?"

"Sam did great," says Trina.

"Oh, good, because our Transport is ready. Only a few more minutes to go and we'll be in Zhonguo! This is all so exciting," says Daphne.

But I'm not listening any more. Instead, I'm staring at Katrina, who is packing up the camera equipment. The princess never would have let her go—so it must have been all Prince Stefan's idea.

I wonder what's really going on inside the palace walls.

# CHAPTER FIFTEEN

# SAMANTHA

"HEY, ARE YOU OKAY?" ZAIN ASKS AS WE jump into one of the cars Daphne rented to take us to Long-shi. Daphne and Trina are in the second car, along with the massive amounts of camera and computer equipment they've brought along with them. I was sure that couldn't all be for the documentary, but Daphne laughed when I commented on it. She called it "traveling light" in her industry.

Anyway, I'm glad Zain and I get a few hours of privacy—even if it is while driving.

We still have a long journey ahead of us. Long-shi is miles away, and cannot be accessed via Transport panel—they're just not set up for that. It's also surrounded by the Wilds, where magic becomes less predictable. Wilds are natural reserves spread all around the world, where magical creatures and plants can survive without interference from Talenteds. In towns and cities, streams of magic are tightly bound and controlled, like strands of hair woven into a braid, so it can be used predictably. In the Wilds, it's a different story. I've seen Zain's dad's object—his ring—explode in front of his eyes when he attempted to use magic in the Wild Hallah mountain range. It's dangerous, so I'm glad we're not Transporting there.

I know exactly why Zain's asking if I'm okay. I can't seem to shift this permanent frown that has etched itself onto my forehead. I have this feeling deep in the pit of my stomach that I normally only get when a potion isn't cooperating. It usually means I'm missing something.

If only I knew what it was.

*Tincture of nightshade—to see into black holes of knowledge. Web of a Persian spider—to help the brain make connections.*

I try to shake it off. Soon I'll be meeting the Waidan and I'll be able to get some answers. "Yeah, just anxious to get to Long-shi," I say.

"Me too. I know you'll be in talks with the Waidan that I can't be a part of . . ." His arms tense and I brace myself for another argument. But instead, he lets out a long breath and his muscles relax. "Because I'm not a Master Alchemist. But I'm excited to go up and visit the archaeological dig. The history side really interests me—I can't believe we'll be one of the first people to see it." His eyes light up as he talks, and it brings a smile to my face. "I know we're going to have the film crew with us, but I'm going to bring my own camera too. Want to see?"

I nod, and he digs around in his backpack. A moment later, he pulls out a small, nondescript black camera with a bulbous lens. "It's one of these new FollowMe things. If you look here, the top folds out into its own propeller. I can send it to places we can't see—like getting awesome aerial shots or down into the dig site or something. Maybe they'll let me do my own videos on the side to promote the docucast."

"That would be amazing!" I say. "You should mention that to Daphne."

"So that's all?" Zain asks, as he packs away the FollowMe. "Just anxious to get there?"

"I guess I'm also nervous about being on camera all the time."

He smiles. "You don't have to worry about that. You're a natural! Even that weird thing you do with your nose looks cute on TV."

"What weird thing?!"

"You know, where you scrunch up one side . . ."

I cover my nose with the palm of my hand. "I do that?"

He nudges me gently. "Yeah, but like I said, it's cute. I promise."

"Okay," I say, not fully convinced. I've never cared much about how I look—I'm normally covered in dust from the shop and once even went to school with fluff from giant swan feathers in my hair. I'd grown up assuming I'd never be able to afford the fancy glamours that I saw Talented kids using, and I'd embraced that. We can't create our own glamours—we can only buy them, often at outrageous prices. At least I can just throw my hair into a ponytail and be done with it. My thick brown hair is so straight it barely needs any kind of styling to look at least a little bit polished. I know that's lucky, even if I sometimes wish for the soft, natural blond curls that Princess Evelyn has—or bold, fiery copper hair like Trina. The grass is always greener.

Still, I agreed to do this documentary so I could tell my own story, in my own words. But now it's only just dawning on me that thousands of people might tune in to watch.

In close up.

In full HD.

I close my eyes and let the nerves wash over me. It's not like this is my first time on TV. I was filmed all through the Wilde Hunt and that was okay. This will be okay too.

I look up at Zain. He doesn't have to worry. He's comfortable using glamours—in fact, I've only ever seen him without them once: when we were stranded on the mountainside in a tent, worried about whether we were going to survive the night. He's one of those people that looks naturally camera-ready all the time.

I put it to the back of my mind for now, and stare out of the window as we pull away from the terminal. I'm eager to get my first glimpse of the country the Kemis once called home.

We've not Transported into the capital city of Zhonguo, but one of the smaller cities closer to the Bharat border called Zhen. It's almost unbelievable that this isn't the biggest city in Zhonguo, though. All I can see for miles around are skyscrapers: gleaming steel towers that put Kingstown's business district to shame. I don't think there's anywhere like this near Nova. The streams of magic are bundled up so tight, I can almost feel them slicing through my body as we drive.

If there really is a virus that can affect Talenteds . . . It would be chaos in a city like this.

Once we leave the city limits, we enter rolling countryside. This isn't the Wilds. These are cultivated fields: rice paddies and tea plantations—neatly constructed and controlled, still touched by humanity. There's an almost clinical beauty to the broad sweeps of lines that run up and down the hills. It's almost hypnotic to look at.

I gently nod off while leaning against the window, and am only jolted awake when we hit a large bump in the road. When I look outside, I see that the landscape has changed again, the sky tinting to a dusky violet as the sun sets. "Wow, I've never seen a sky that color before."

"I think it's because of that," Zain says, pointing at the windscreen.

My jaw drops.

It's impossible to miss. Directly in front of us is an enormous volcano, rising up out of the landscape like a triangular fist punching through the countryside. It looks almost alien on the horizon, surrounded by nothing but flat land.

The mighty Yanhuo volcano.

*The volcano of Yanhuo. Where alchemists first discovered fires hot enough to transmutate a solid ingredient into liquid, so it could be integrated into a potion. Now, what was the name of that ingredient again?*

"The dust and particles thrown up by the volcano can make the sunsets look even more dramatic," says Zain.

I'm barely listening as I drum my fingers against my temple. "I can't think of this potions ingredient that was first created after being melted in lava from the Yanhuo volcano . . ."

"Look it up—my tablet is in my bag." Zain gestures to his backpack at my feet and reluctantly I take out the tablet. With a few taps, I have the answer.

I slap myself on the forehead so hard, Zain jumps up in his seat. I wave off his concern. "Of course! I can't believe I forgot that. *Phoenix* feathers." Phoenix feathers are one of the world's rarest ingredients. It would be my dream to use them in a potion, but they're not only difficult to acquire, they're also volatile and highly combustible.

"Hey, you can't remember *everything*. That's why we have the internet."

"You can't always access the internet, but I can always access my brain," I shoot back, sticking my tongue out at him. My memory is what I rely on the most when it comes to all things potions. It's one of my best features. When I get home, I vow to amp up my studying.

"Not long now," says Zain, his wand enchanted to act as our GPS. It sits on the dashboard, swivelling in the direction we should drive and every so often letting us know how much time we have left.

We continue driving closer and closer to the bottom of the volcano, its presence getting more and more menacing by the mile. My stomach turns with unease. I can't imagine what it must be like to live permanently at the base of such a monumental landmark: its sheer size a reminder of nature's power. It suddenly puts everything I know about Talenteds and ordinaries into perspective. I might have my potions and Zain might have his magic, but we are still nothing compared to nature's own immense power.

"I think I bookmarked a video on Yanhuo," says Zain. "It should be on the front page of my tablet." I pull up the page he's talking about, and the voice of one of the most popular naturecast presenters in Nova, Sir Malcolm Renfrew, fills the car.

"While the Yanhuo volcano is labeled as 'active,' the last known eruption was a thousand years ago, and so it is considered dormant. The eruption was devastating, burying nearby settlements beneath ash or swamping them with lava. While some settlements were rebuilt, it wasn't until a local hiker fell through a lava tube and came across an old, cracked pestle and mortar, like the ones used by traditional alchemists—totally out of place on the mountainside—that historians and archaeologists realized the true extent of what had been hidden beneath the lava. Since that initial discovery, an entire village has been unearthed, which experts now believe to be the ancient alchemical monastery of Long-shi. Excavations are still ongoing.

"According to historical documents of that time, the Talented villagers living near the monastery blamed the ordinary alchemists for the eruption, claiming that in their search for new elixirs, they'd disturbed and angered the gods. The few surviving alchemists were rounded up for execution. But when a sickness descended as a result of the residual ash cloud, it ended up being the surviving alchemists who helped the villagers get well and start to rebuild their lives. So they were pardoned and allowed to continue their work. The site is now one of the most preeminent centers of alchemy, with the mixers and villagers living in harmony, and the volcano has remained quiet ever since. Though for some thrill-seekers who brave the volcano's rocky slopes, lava can still be seen boiling deep in the heart of the top-most caldera." The video changes to an aerial shot of the volcano, a desolate landscape of grays, browns, and rust. But I don't need to watch it on a video—I can look at it right outside our window.

"We're here," says Zain, snapping my attention back to the road. We lean forward in our seats as we pass underneath the ornate gateway to the town of Long-shi, an arch richly painted in bright red with gold accents. I spy a carving of a snake winding its way around one of the columns—the symbol of alchemists everywhere.

I feel tears springing up in my eyes despite myself. The birthplace of alchemy. In a funny way, it feels like I've come home.

# CHAPTER SIXTEEN

# SAMANTHA

I STRETCH MY ARMS WIDE WHEN WE GET out of the car, my spine popping as I twist from one side to the other. We've driven into a gated compound at the edge of the town of Long-shi and have arrived in a neatly manicured courtyard surrounded by three low buildings, Daphne and Trina pulling in behind us. Rising over the top of one of the living quarters is the dominating sight of the Yanhuo volcano. Now that we are closer, I can see its snow-capped peak more clearly. I even think I see smoke lifting from the very top, but it could just be clouds gathering.

"Stop that, or you're going to get even taller," grumbles Zain.

I laugh. "I don't think that's possible." I'm already approaching six feet—plenty tall enough for me. Only in the past few months have I learned to embrace my height, not hide from it. Slouching is not a good look for anyone.

It might just be my imagination, but already I feel the wonder of this place seeping into my bones. A place that feels like home. The town of Long-shi is modern and clean, but every so often there are little touches that remind me we are really in Zhonguo. The rooftops, for example, are peaked at each corner, and along their gable edges small, intricately carved figurines of animals dance in single file: tigers following lions, with dragons and unicorns and Garudas, too. The main street that runs through the center of town is dominated at either end by bright red gates, the ornate decorations edged in gold leaf.

The compound is the home of the Waidan, with one building his living quarters and the other two dedicated to alchemy: a lab and a store.

"Wow, this place is so ... relaxing," says Zain, taking in a deep breath.

"I know. It's beautiful," I say. The courtyard has a rock garden in one corner, with a bubbling stream tumbling between the rocks and into a pool below. Large, bright orange carp drift lazily around the pool, occasionally rising to snatch food off the surface.

"Ah, hello, Samantha! You're here!" says a voice from behind me.

I spin around. Even if I hadn't met the Waidan before on the Summons screen, he would be easily recognizable. He is dressed in the traditional long white robes with sky-blue ribbon trim that I've seen in ancient portraits of Zhonguo alchemists.

"Hello, Waidan," I say slowly, faltering over every syllable. I feel like I'm butchering the basic Zhonguoan phrases I learned from the internet. I bow my head like Grandad taught me. "I'm very pleased to meet you in person."

The Waidan smiles and nods his head back to me. "It is nice to meet you too," he replies in Novaen.

My cheeks redden with embarrassment—I'm sure he knows my Zhonguoan doesn't stretch much further. "Waidan, please meet my boyfriend, Zain Aster. And here is the documentary team my grandad told you about: meet Daphne Golden, the director, and Katrina Porter, our camerawoman."

"You are welcome to my humble home and laboratory." His eyes linger on the wand holstered underneath Zain's arm, and on Daphne's wand, which she is currently using to keep a large microphone hoisted above our heads. "We have much to discuss, but first, come and meet my team," he continues. Three people enter the courtyard from the laboratory building. "This is Mei, Dai, and James. They are all apprentices here at Jing Potion Laboratories."

"Nice to meet you," I say with a smile, and this time it's handshakes all around.

"You too," says Mei. She grins at me. "We've heard a

lot about you—of course. Would you like a tour of our facilities?"

"Um, I would love that but …" I look over at the Waidan expectantly. I'm anxious to hear what he has to say about the virus. Everything else can wait.

"Do the tour first," says the Waidan. "I will meet you at the end. I have a few things I need to prepare."

I nod. "Then a tour would be great," I say to Mei.

"Fantastic. First of all, are you having any trouble understanding me?"

I frown. "No, not at all. You speak Novaen like you were born there."

Mei turns to Dai and they give each other a high five. James, however, folds his arms across his chest and huffs. "Don't mind him," says Mei. "He just lost a bet. We've been working on a translator potion for months and you are our test subjects. But it looks like we've hammered it!"

"I think you mean nailed it," says Zain.

"Ah! See, not quite perfect yet," James pipes in. Mei rolls her eyes and flicks her sheet of long black hair over her shoulder. I'm a bit in love with her already.

"It's amazing," I say. "What are the ingredients, if you don't mind me asking?"

"Not at all," she says, as we enter the lab building. "The main ingredient of course is Babel fish scales—we have some in the pond outside—but it was getting them to work with the brain to produce accurate translations for a specific language that was the challenge."

*Babel fish—legend had it that if you caught and ate a Babel fish, you would go mad and speak in tongues for hours. Turns out those "tongues" were languages, and the scales can now be used in potions for translation.*

"Oh wow, I've heard of Babel fish scales being used in potions to help someone read or listen in another language, but not speak. That's absolutely amazing if you've cracked it: It could be worth a fortune!"

Mei looks from me to Zain, then back again. "We have many more tests to do first," she says, ducking the statement.

"Of course," I say. I probably wouldn't give too much away if I were in the presence of the heir to a massive synth corporation either. Zain might not be in the business now, but his father is keeping a seat warm for him at the boardroom table.

The lab is a lot more modern than I was expecting, with tablets on the front of every workstation and sophisticated ventilation systems running through the ceiling, but there are traditional elements too: brushed wooden countertops and large clay mixing pots over open fires. It's nice to see that they still use natural materials, as we do in our lab in Kingstown, but our set-up still feels a lot more ... medieval than theirs. There are also huge stainless steel barrels full of rosewater-and-moon-milk potion base and their ingredients are stored in a hermetically-sealed refrigerated store room. I almost faint with envy when I see their electronic database listing their ingredient stock, including warning symbols that are automatically pinged to their Finders when they're getting low. The Jing labs are a blend of technology with tradition and a model for my future dream lab.

Trina's camera captures all my gasps and excitement, and I'm glad. If the docucast can also show Nova that alchemy has its place in the modern age, then that's no bad thing.

"I think you've been wanting to see this?" Mei says, standing in the doorway to the next room.

I eagerly follow in her footsteps, and almost fall to my knees when I get inside. We've entered the library.

It's only a single-story room, but the shelving space goes on for what seems like miles: a maze of glass-enclosed bookcases organized by century. There must be hundreds of potion diaries in here.

"As well as being the Waidan's apprentice, I'm also the official potion diaries librarian here at the Jing labs," says Dai, with a smile. "The earliest journal in here is from a thousand years ago. You will especially appreciate that one. It is written by the last Kemi to have taken the title 'Waidan.'"

My entire body quivers with excitement. A thousand-year-old Kemi diary. And who knows what other treasures are hidden inside that library. I wonder what it must be like to have so many diaries in one place, you need a librarian to sort through them all. With his gelled, spiky blue hair and tattoos peeking out from the top of his white coat, Dai doesn't look much like a typical librarian. He does have round glasses though, which I suppose is one point in the librarian column. "If you come here, I'll show you—because it will be of most definite interest to you."

I follow him through the maze of glass shelves, Zain hot on my heels. "How do you preserve the diaries?" Zain asks. "Do you have to wear special gloves?"

"Actually, using your fingers is better for the diaries than using gloves."

"Really?" Zain sounds sceptical. "But don't the oils from your fingers risk destroying the paper over time?"

"It hasn't happened yet. In fact, if you use gloves, you're less likely to be aware of how firmly you're gripping the paper and you're more likely to tear it—which causes more damage in the long run."

"Oh, I get it," says Zain. "And what about temperature fluctuations? It feels pretty cool in here."

I look over at Zain in surprise. I hadn't known he had such an interest in book preservation. He winks at me.

"We keep the temperature in the room as controlled as we can, along with the humidity. But these are meant to be working diaries—no one wants the knowledge that's in here to be locked away. That's why we welcome visits from international alchemists such as Sam Kemi here. Especially those with such a pedigree as yours," he says to me with a slight bow of his head.

A blush rises in my cheeks. "You must have diaries from some of the other ancient families here too."

"Of course. But the Kemi diary we have is the oldest."

"What happened to the older diaries?" Zain asks. "There's been a monastery here for two millennia, so there should be older ones ... maybe that haven't been discovered yet?"

"Almost everything that had been kept at the original Jing monastery on the volcano was destroyed in the eruption. We are still doing excavation work to this day, but it's slow-going. Paper and fire, well ... they don't exactly mix."

Zain is persistent. "Then how did Tao Kemi's diary survive? Wasn't he the Waidan at the time of the eruption?"

"The diary was kept inside a sealed stone chamber that the lava didn't penetrate. In fact, we believe it had already been buried at the time of the eruption."

"Why would that be?" I ask.

But Dai continues walking without answering my question. Zain and I exchange a look as we follow him through the maze.

We stop in front of a glass case that is much more heavily guarded than the others. I can spot thin, wavering red lines indicating motion sensors, and there are cameras pointed in our direction too. I would bet the rest of my Wilde Hunt earnings that there are magical forms of protection that I can't see.

Zain asks the question on my lips. "What's with the heavy security here?"

Dai's face darkens. "A few months ago, when the discovery was first announced, we had a flurry of activity in the village—publicity for the dig, but also lots of Finders and alchemists—some with good intentions, only interested in the history, and some no better than treasure hunters, trying to see what they could pillage to sell on the black market. On the day we found the diary, someone tried to steal it. They didn't succeed—but they did manage to vandalize it. They stole one of the pages."

"You're kidding!" I gasp. I can't believe anyone would do that to an ancient book.

"I'm afraid not. That's why you can see it through the glass, but no closer."

I try to conceal the disappointment on my face. I would love to be able to touch the diary—almost like reaching back in time and bringing history back to life.

"He was the last Kemi Waidan of the Jing monastery," says Dai.

I nod. It's one of the reasons that my ancestors moved to Nova. Our family wanted to establish our own brand of alchemy, not be forced to give up our name.

I dig my potion diary out of my satchel, gripping its buttery soft leather cover. I place it on the shelf, right next to the case where Tao Kemi's is kept. Then I take a step back as a swell of pride washes over me. This is a moment I didn't know I had been waiting for. A connection to a past I knew too little about. Now I feel parched—my thirst for knowledge only partially quenched. There is so much reading to do in the world. I want to absorb it all.

A tear rolls down my cheek as I feel the weight of all those diaries. And mine, so small and thin beside them. It doesn't yet deserve to be there. I need to earn my place on that shelf. I take my diary back and put it back in my bag, where it belongs.

"Cut!" says Daphne. "That was fantastic, Sam. A real emotional moment and a perfect closer to episode one. More of those please!"

# CHAPTER SEVENTEEN

# SAMANTHA

"MISS KEMI?" THE WAIDAN'S VOICE ECHOES across the library. "I'm ready for you now."

I nod. Just as I turn to leave, Zain grabs my hand. "Will you tell me what happens?"

"I'll fill you in as much as I can. I promise." I can feel Trina's eyes following my every move, and I nod to her as well.

He hesitates, keeping his grip on my hand. But then he lets me go. "I trust you," he says.

"Sorry, but this can't be part of the docucast," I say to Daphne. I take the microphone off my collar and pass it over to Trina. In a way, I wish we could film what's going to happen next. This is part of my story—but for now, it will have to be a secret part. I don't want any unnecessary rumors circulating about the princess before I really know what's going on.

Daphne frowns but I don't give her room to protest.

She seems to think better of it and waves her arms back toward the laboratory. "Let's get some more shots of Zain in action," she says, back to directing already.

Meanwhile, I make my way to the Waidan, with Mei following close behind. We pass by a greenhouse stocked with ingredients, and I make a mental note to head back there later to see what they are growing. We seem to be in a more administrative part of the building, with doors leading to small offices. We stop outside a room marked WAIDAN.

No sooner am I through the door than Mei grabs my arms behind my back and pins me down on the floor before I can muster up any sort of resistance. I turn my head to the side just in time to avoid bashing my chin against the floor, and I end up with my cheek against the rough carpet instead.

"Are you working for him?" the Waidan demands. All I can see are the embroidered toes of his traditional silk slippers.

I try to get up but Mei's knee digs into my back. "What do you mean?" I ask through gasping breaths, wincing against the pain.

"Tell us—are you working for Prince Stefan?"

"Prince Stefan? No! I hate him. I just want to know if my friend . . . if the princess is in trouble."

"Are you here to steal secrets from the Jing monastery?"

"No!"

"Would you take a truth potion to swear it?"

"Of course!"

There are several heartbeats of silence before I seem to pass their test. The pressure on my spine releases and my arms are no longer being pulled from their sockets. "Let her go," says the Waidan, finally. "I believe her." Mei lets my hands drop to the floor.

I creak to my feet, my blood boiling. Heat rises in my cheeks—especially the one that was scraped on the floor. I press my palm against it. "Is this how you treat fellow alchemists? My grandad would be outraged!"

"I apologize, but I could not chance that you would try to escape," says the Waidan, his eyes dark. He leans back against his desk, suddenly looking as old—if not older—than my grandad. His face is lined with worry and even his robe seems to hang limply around his thin frame. "And it was a *fellow alchemist* who started this trouble in the first place."

I blink back tears from the shock and pain. "What do you mean?"

It's Mei who answers. "It was an alchemist who stole the page out of Tao Kemi's diary that Dai was telling you about. We managed to stop them before they could take the whole thing, but . . ."

"They got what they needed," finished the Waidan.

"Yes. We suspected the thief was in the employ of

Prince Stefan of Gergon based on their style of dress. That is why we had to make sure you were not working for him. He is, after all, now a member of the Novaen royal family," continues Mei.

"I can promise you I only want to find out what is wrong with the princess—and if the spread in Gergon is an indication of how contagious it is, then all of Nova could be in danger. What page was stolen?" I ask.

"That's the problem," says the Waidan. "We don't know exactly. We've only been able to read the pages following, which list some of the side effects of a virus— and it's the same symptoms that you've described: coughing, weakness, and a drain of power in the Talenteds. We believe they must have stolen the recipe that unleashed this virus. I've been monitoring the news and online chatter to see if there was any sign that an illness with similar symptoms had taken hold. We sent messages to Gergon but weren't able to find out if they had been affected. When you called about the princess's symptoms, I feared the worst ... that maybe it has spread to Nova."

"What could the virus be?" I ask, but my voice rises barely above a whisper.

"Now that you're here, you might be able to help answer that question," says the Waidan.

I rub the joint where my arm meets my shoulder. It's still sore. "That's if I want to," I grumble.

"But you must—for your princess," says Mei.

"Yes, I know!" I snap back. "I'm just not feeling too helpful right now."

The Waidan ignores my outburst and sits down behind his desk, lacing his fingers underneath his chin. "Tao Kemi was a very secretive man—we know that from other primary source material we have found at the site. But from our investigations, we have reason to believe he left the story of the illness behind, in the same chamber as we found the diary. Tomorrow, we will take you there."

I shake my head. "No."

"But—"

I lift my eyes to meet the Waidan's, not letting him finish his sentence. "No, I won't wait until tomorrow. I'm here. I want to go now."

He stares back at me with equal intensity, and I don't back down. Unease slithers in my stomach and I feel like I'm being disrespectful, but if Princess Evelyn is infected with a deadly virus then I can't wait another second. After what feels like an eternity, he nods. "Mei, get the car."

# CHAPTER EIGHTEEN

# SAMANTHA

"WAIT!"

I halt, one leg already halfway into the backseat. Trina is flying out of the door of the laboratory toward me. She skids to a stop by the car and puts her hand on the door, preventing me from closing it.

"If you're going somewhere, let me come with you. If it's to do with the princess, I want to help. Please."

Her eyes are wild with determination, but I don't give my answer a second thought. "Of course, come on." I slide across the seat. Having a former palace bodyguard along can't be a bad thing—my bruised cheek is a reminder of that. And I can trust Trina. Anyone who cares so deeply about Princess Evelyn won't betray her.

Mei is in the driver's seat and she looks back at us. "No Talenteds allowed. Magic behaves strangely in the Wilds and we can't take the risk—"

"She's not Talented. She's coming with us."

"Let her come," says the Waidan from next to Mei. Trina pulls the back door shut and with a screech of tires we drive off.

"Where are Daphne and Zain?" I ask Trina. I feel a twinge of guilt at leaving Zain behind, but Daphne will complicate things. I can't trust her.

"They were filming some one-on-ones. I saw you heading to the car and sprinted to catch up with you. I'm not here for the documentary. I'm here to help you. And wow—it looks like you need it." She reaches up and touches the sore spot on my cheek. Trina rounds on the Waidan. "What did you do?"

I put my hand on Trina's arm. "It's okay. I'm not hurt."

"This woman is not part of the documentary team, is she?" asks the Waidan.

"She is but also . . . not." I struggle to explain.

"I was part of Princess Evelyn's ordinary security team," says Trina, her chin jutting forward.

"Ordinary security?" I ask. I've never heard it described that way.

"Her computer systems. The princess has all the magic power she could ever want, so she doesn't exactly need bodyguards for physical protection. But from technological intrusion, hack-prevention of her devices, that sort of thing, she still needs help. That's how we met in the first place. She wanted assistance setting up a private Connect page so that she could be in touch with her friends ... like you and Zain."

"I always wondered how she pulled that off," I say. I'm touched that Evie would do all that for me. I shouldn't have doubted that our friendship was real.

"Gradually it was our connection that grew. I knew that the princess and I, our ... we ... were a long shot. But I never trusted that slimy prince. You seemed to be the only person in all of Nova that was speaking any sense about him." She leans in close, so that she's talking only to me. "They fired me before I could really get a sense of anything happening in the palace. I don't know if the princess is the only one affected, or if what she has has spread to the rest of the royal family. There's no way for me to check. But I was keeping tabs on your television appearances, your social media, and what people were saying about you. When I got all these pings through from my notifications in some of the government databases that showed you applying for emergency Wilds passes in Zhonguo, I knew it had to be to do with the princess. You wouldn't leave Nova unless it was for a cure. That's why I had to find a way to come along with you."

My eyes open wide. "That's kind of terrifying that you can find out so much from the internet."

"I'm not being modest when I say I'm the best. Luckily I'd learned some film-making skills at college, so I knew I could fake the basics, and with my tech background I can edit video with the best of them. Plus I could hack my CV to make it look *really* good to Daphne Golden."

I nod. "This is the most number of words I've heard you string together since I met you!"

She leans back in the seat, finally relaxing her shoulders. "I guess I'm more the quiet type."

She's right. Her loosening up from her normally rigid stance makes me smile—and then I feel a pang in my heart as I realize it's because I miss my friend and Finder, Kirsty. Trina is an iron bar, whereas Kirsty is a whip. One sturdy, the other flexible. Knowing me, I *should* prefer the sturdy one. But I need Kirsty's flexibility to make my brain work. That's why we make such a good partnership. That's also maybe why Evelyn needs someone like Trina. Trina offers her stability, normality, and a sense of comfort in her world that is manic, unique, and oddly sheltered.

"That's probably why she liked you." I say the thought out loud. "She was always surrounded by so much noise. I saw how you were together, in that Laville Palace room. You kept her calm. You were like ... her oasis."

Trina smiles sadly. "Thank you for saying that, Sam."

I pull my potion diary out of my bag. I need to be scientific about this. Put my Master Alchemist skills to the test. I open to the pages where I've been jotting down everything I know under the heading *The Virus*. "So, tell me what you saw inside the palace. How did the princess act? How did Stefan act toward her?"

Trina frowns, then closes her eyes as if she is trying to remember. "I wasn't allowed to see much, but the prince was on the charm-offensive before the wedding day. It was after that that things changed. Once they were married, it's like he walked around with a dark cloud over his head. And the most strange thing was that he started giving Evelyn some kind of pill each evening."

"Ah!" I flip back a few pages, where I'd written about the pill Emilia Thoth had created for Prince Stefan. "That would keep her from being contagious for a time, so she could interact with people."

"That makes sense. But I got notice that the prince had terminated my contract with the palace. Well, I say 'got notice,' but I showed up for work one day and I wasn't allowed to Transport up. The coward's way of saying 'you're fired.'"

"Huh." I clench my fingers into fists. I have a few pages of notes but I'm no closer to figuring out what the virus is—or how dangerous it is. I hope there are answers in this village.

Trina grabs my hand. "You are doing more for her than anyone else in Nova. And that's why my place is by your side."

Tears threaten to spring up in my eyes, but I hold them back. I need to be serious. Focused.

The car climbs higher on a winding road up the volcano's base, through some sparse forest, the trees struggling to grow on the hard volcanic ground. We pass through a Wilds border, although it's not manned—the only people who come up to the village, after all, are the Waidan and his approved excavation crew. It's the only road, so he swipes our passes and a barrier lifts, allowing us to pass through.

"We're very close now," says the Waidan.

My first thought is that "monastery" is a bit of a misnomer. The place is huge. We enter through a stone gate into what appears to be a circular village—every wall we encounter is curved. As we drive further into the monastery, I get the sense that it is made up of a series of concentric circles, almost like a maze. The low stone buildings are a pale shade of yellow, their walls stretching up toward the open sky. "The buildings would have once had roofs," says Mei, "but they were made of wood and would have disintegrated in the lava flow." She parks up in front of one of the buildings, which has a sign taped across it that warns of cavities hidden beneath the floor. It's written in both Zhonguoan characters and Novaen lettering, which is why it catches my eye.

"This way," the Waidan says. "I've given the excavation crew a couple of days off, so we have the place to ourselves while we try to solve this mystery."

Outside, I shield my eyes with my arm, before digging

out my sunglasses. We've made it about a quarter of the way up the side of the volcano, and the sun is fiercely bright, especially where it reflects off the light stone.

There's a searing heat on my ankle. I scream and jump back, almost knocking into Trina. "What is that?" I cry. In front of me is a lizard—but the lizard is consumed by fire. Its scales are black and red like magma, and it is engulfed in orange-yellow flames.

The Waidan is around to our side of the car in a flash, brandishing a hemp bag. He takes a handful of powder from the bag and tosses it at the lizard. It lands with a sizzle, and the lizard cools off instantly, turning all-black. It scurries away into a nearby crack in the ground and my breathing levels return to normal.

"Lava lizard," says the Waidan. "It's one of a number of rare creatures we discovered here that were either on the endangered list or—in some cases—presumed extinct."

"Are you kidding me, that was a lava lizard?"

*Lava lizard—creature said to be born of fire itself. A small portion of its tail can keep a fire burning for days or weeks on end.*

"And that was a baby one," Mei adds.

I want to kick myself. Lava lizards are such cool creatures—almost like mascots for alchemists—I didn't think I'd behave like such a baby on seeing one for the first time.

"Oh, don't fret too much—you were wise to be wary

of it. It might be small but its fire burns the same as any other and is fiendishly hard to put out. Watch your step," says Mei.

"I will."

"We have a lot of unusual creatures here—like those lava lizards. Some of the ancient Finders' logs mention being able to collect phoenix feathers from the summit. So it's quite possible that a phoenix once lived in the volcano's caldera—although there hasn't been a sighting in my time."

"Seriously?" I stop and look up at the summit of the volcano, where a steady stream of smoke puffs into the sky. Seeing a phoenix would blow my mind: they're by far my favorite magical creature. It makes the volcano seem even more mysterious and intriguing.

"She's more active again," Mei says to the Waidan, referencing the volcano.

"We'll check the seismic monitors when we get back."

"Are you able to predict if the volcano is going to erupt?" Katrina asks, unable to hide the alarm from her voice.

Mei nods. "We have sensors buried deep into the ground and we monitor seismic activity in a wide radius around Yanhuo. But a volcano is never fully predictable."

I shiver despite the heat, and stare up one more time at the ominous smoke. Then I put it to the back of my mind. We're currently walking on the best evidence of a volcano's incredible destructive power. If we were in any imminent danger, the Waidan and his team wouldn't let us come here.

We walk past more ruins, which Mei explains were once the living quarters of the alchemist-monks, tiny cells just large enough for a bed and sink. Part of me wants to stop and examine and ask questions, but it can wait for another time. The Waidan leads us through a maze of narrow side streets, until we reach a doorway framed on either side by two misshapen lumps of stone. "These would have represented a dragon and a phoenix," says the Waidan. If I squint, I can just about see what he means—I can make out the curved, sinewy body of a dragon and the long, pointed beak of a phoenix. They would have been impressive statues in their time. A similar sign to the one I saw out front is posted across this doorway: BEWARE OF HIDDEN CAVITIES BENEATH THE FLOOR.

Once we pass through the doorway, I notice that this room has a large window that perfectly frames the summit of the volcano. "Wow, that's some view," I say.

"This is Tao Kemi's former residence," says Mei. "He was the last Waidan to live here. If you look through this window, you can see a part of the monastery that hasn't been excavated yet. Those would have been the living quarters of the Waidan's servants."

I peer through the window and all I can see is a great

swathe of hardened lava. "You mean ... there were houses underneath that once?" I ask her.

"Indeed. When we found this house, we knew it was special, which is why we began our excavations immediately. Look over here, and tread carefully. There is a cavern underneath this floor, and though we have made every effort to make the floor safe, there is a risk that it may collapse."

Picking my way gently around the outside of the living room, I follow Mei and the Waidan into the former bedroom of Tao Kemi—there's a raised stone platform that would have acted as a bed. A warm breeze wraps its way around my ankles—there's a huge hole in the floor of the bedroom and the warm air is rising up from underneath it.

"We ... have to go down there?" I ask.

"There is a small room underneath the floor of this bedroom—it's where we found Tao Kemi's diary. There is only room for two of us." He looks pointedly at Katrina and Mei.

"We'll stay here and guard the entrance," Mei says.

Katrina frowns. "Are there any other exits I should know about?"

Mei shakes her head. "This is the only one."

"Got it. Sam—I'll be right here if you need anything."

I nod back. It does make me feel more relaxed knowing that Katrina is watching out for me.

The Waidan turns to me. "Tell me, Samantha Kemi, have you ever thought why *this place* is the birthplace of alchemy? Zhonguo is a big country. But for some reason this area drew the interest of the men and women who would become the very first mixers."

I pause for a moment, thinking about all the reasons *I* would be interested in a place like this. It's far from the most hospitable land . . . but maybe that would form part of the appeal. "The fire," I blurt out, before I can think about it much harder.

The Waidan appraises me with one eyebrow raised. "Well done. Why the fire?"

"Alchemists are interested in balance—but to create balance you sometimes have to force change. Forcing change requires a lot of energy—intense heat or cold, most of the time. I imagine you can't get fires hotter than the ones in a volcano. It provides access to the center of the planet. The heat of the planet itself . . . if there's anywhere that could 'fuel' alchemy, this would be it."

The Waidan nods. "This earth has many unique properties. But the most unique aspect of this volcano lies far beneath our feet. In the flow of lava that disappears into the center of the earth. The alchemists of old believed that the lava could transport magic all around the world, that it, in fact, was a physical embodiment of the streams of magic in the air."

"Wow. But it's just molten rocks and crystals and gas, right?" I say with a laugh.

The Waidan doesn't answer, but fixes me with a stern look. "Some of the world's greatest potions were created here. Long before the Visir School or even Kemi's Potion Shop," he says. "Some of the recipes have been lost to the sands of time. But others survived . . . even underneath the weight of one of the worst natural disasters in history. Even though a thousand years have passed."

"You mean to say . . . you discovered a *potion* here?"

"This is what we cannot yet show to the world because we do not understand it. And yet you are a descendant of the man who created it, and also a Master Alchemist yourself. It won't respond to me or my team, but maybe you will have more luck."

The floor rocks beneath me. It's not just the effect of the Waidan's words—it's the volcano rumbling.

But rather than look alarmed, the Waidan closes his eyes. "The volcano knows something. She has been dormant for hundreds of years but now is more active than ever. This way."

I follow him down into the chamber beneath Tao Kemi's old sleeping quarters. It's almost pitch-dark until he lights a sconce on the wall with a match. "Once we realized this chamber was here, we didn't have to excavate," he says. "It was still perfectly intact when we discovered it."

I can hardly believe my eyes. The room itself is sparsely decorated, with just a couple of iron hooks on the wall for additional sconces, but right in the center is what looks like a shallow pool of water. A pond, a millennium old, still shimmering and crystal clear as if it had been filled only yesterday.

"What is it?" I ask, almost breathless with awe. My eyes are wide open, drinking in the entire scene. I kneel down by the pond's edge, my hand reaching out to touch it. I draw back at just the last moment. It goes against my alchemist instincts to dive straight into an unknown liquid. Yet something about the pond calls to me.

My hand rests on one of the stone tiles at the edge of the pool, which is decorated with Zhonguoan characters. My fingers trace the shape of the carvings, and I wish I knew what they said.

"It reads 'Kemi,'" says the Waidan, answering my unasked question. "We initially thought it was carved to identify the builder of this chamber, but now we think it could mean something more. Go ahead and touch the water. We have tested it thoroughly and as far as we can see, it is safe."

I nod and take a deep breath, reaching down to the pond's surface. My fingertip breaks the shimmering surface, and I gasp at the cold. Stranger still, rather than ripple out away from me the water gathers toward my fingertip. The liquid lifts as I pull away until it's standing before my eyes, a waterfall in reverse. I'm simultaneously entranced and terrified.

"My god ..." says the Waidan. He drops to his knees beside me, his white robes pooling around him. "I've heard of such a thing, but never thought I would witness it. Liquid magic. Your touch must have awoken it. He must have charmed it to respond to Kemi blood."

My eyes widen. If this is really magic ... then everything I've been taught is wrong. It's not invisible—it can be made tangible. What I thought were limits to possibility were only limits to my imagination.

I snatch my hand away, but the water remains standing, like a screen. It reflects the image of the volcano behind me. No—wait—it can't be reflecting the image—we're under the ground. It's *showing* us something.

"That is Yanhuo! What is this magic?" asks the Waidan, his eyes darting across the watery screen. The image shifts to focus in on a sprawling complex of curved-wall buildings with gilded copper roofs, designed in a series of concentric circles on the side the volcano. "I've never seen anything like this ... And that must be the Jing monastery! But as it once was."

So not wooden roofs at all, but copper.

As the image zooms in closer, we see monks wandering the narrow laneways between the buildings, all dressed the same way as the Waidan is today—with the long white robes edged in blue silk. The scene shifts to the

144

house we are in now, closing in on one of the rooms the archaeologists thought was a bedroom. But it turned out it was more like a laboratory—and the raised platform wasn't a bed at all. It's a table. There's a man in the room, back bent over a mixing bowl, his thin black moustache so long it drips off the edge of his chin like a line of ink.

"Is that ... Tao Kemi?"

"It must be," says the Waidan, but his mouth snaps shut as Zhonguoan characters appear on the top edge of the watery screen. The Waidan rushes to translate as the characters fade in and out. "I am about to finish the greatest potion I will ever make. The culmination of years of single-minded effort. Everything is abandoned. All is focused on the mixing."

I bite my lip. I have so many questions, but I can also sense the tension in the Waidan's voice. Could the words be referring to the *aqua vitae* again? It was the potion that ruined my great-grandmother's career—and almost ruined mine. I wonder if it's the Kemi family curse to search for it.

The scene shifts and is replaced by the image of a woman, her pale round face glowing as brightly as the moon as she lifts her dark eyes toward us and smiles. "This is the woman I love," translates the Waidan. "Her name is Xi Shi. A woman so beautiful she could topple entire nations—with a wit to match. For her, I will move

145

every star in the heavens until they align according to her wishes.

"But she has only one wish. She is an ordinary woman and her dream is to manipulate the element of magic, as the rest of her family are able to do.

"It is an impossible task."

The woman's face dissolves in the water, replaced once again by the scene of Tao at his station, mixing. Failing. Throwing his hands up in exasperation. I see the passage of time fly by in the window outside his room, and Yanhuo begins to smoke.

Beside me, the Waidan shivers as he reads the next sentence. "But I succeeded."

The writing disappears, and instead we watch Tao as he descends into the village. He meets with the beautiful Xi Shi, who at first seems angry with him. She shakes her head, walks away. But then Tao pulls out a small wooden box. He kneels at Xi Shi's feet and opens the box to reveal a delicate blown-glass vial, the glass the same pale pink of a fresh cherry blossom. She takes it from the box with her long, elegant fingers, releases the stopper, and drinks the potion. In the next moment, she whips a slim twig of wood—a wand—from her sleeve and points it at a flower growing in a bed a few feet away. With a swish of her object, she plucks the flower and it drifts through the air toward her. Once the flower is grasped within her fingers, she throws her arms around Tao Kemi.

"No . . ." My eyes are tricking me. This must be a story. A legend. It cannot be showing something true. The potion Tao was creating was not an *aqua vitae*, then.

If anything, it was something more unimaginable than a potion that could cure all illness.

It was a potion to give an ordinary person magic.

"It can't be." The Waidan's voice quavers with as much disbelief as mine. Characters flicker up on the screen again and the Waidan shakes himself to read them. "I succeeded. But at a price."

The scene shifts to show Xi Shi and Tao standing over the bed of an old woman. The woman leans forward and coughs violently, leaving a tell-tale white residue on her hands and sheets. Then she falls back on the bed and the light steadily leaves her eyes. Xi Shi presses her face into Tao's shoulder, sobbing. "A sickness descended on the village. A terrible disease that spread like dragonfire. At the monastery, we were helpless. There was no cure."

There are scenes of great sadness playing out on the watery screen in front of me, families being torn apart with grief. But then the next phase comes. I can see it building in front of me like clouds gathering for a storm. Anger. Everyone wanted someone to blame.

"It soon became clear that this illness had a particular target. The Talented. Every Talented that met Xi Shi found their power drained away from them, and then they passed on the sickness to every Talented they met.

147

And so it went that the magic drain spread around the village. The Talented blamed me. They weren't wrong. For with every Talented who weakened, Xi Shi grew stronger. I had upset the natural balance."

The action returns to the monastery, to the very chamber that we are in. Xi Shi and Tao are sitting almost in the place that I am now, kneeling at the edge of the pond. "We fled to the monastery. Xi Shi begged me to reverse the potion. This was power she did not ask for. She wanted only to make flowers bloom and lights appear in the sky. She wanted only to be the same as the rest of her family."

There's a pause as Tao Kemi appears to collect his thoughts.

"As for a cure? I may have a recipe, but I have no hope of acquiring the necessary ingredients in time and no writing implement to set the recipe down in my diary. All I can do is speak these words in hope that a future Kemi will hear this in their time of need. The key ingredient is phoenix flame. Enough flame would restore Xi Shi to her original state and return the magic she has taken. But getting enough is almost impossible, so there are other ingredients that can help amplify the properties of even a small amount of flame."

As soon as the Waidan translates those words for me, I drag my bag toward me, shaking it so my diary falls out. I grab a pen, biting the cap off between my teeth, scrambling to write down each ingredient as he speaks.

"Nature prepares to take her revenge. We sit here now, leaving this story written in magic, a warning to be heard by my descendants. Do not upset the balance—for you will bring destruction down on your own heads.

"Tonight, Xi Shi and I will say farewell to the mortal world."

Abruptly, the water screen tumbles back into the pool, coming to rest again as flat as a mirror. It feels like there had been more to the story, but that Tao had been cut off.

"Yanhuo must have erupted . . ." the Waidan finishes. "Burying Tao and Xi Shi and the secret of what they did."

My throat closes up as I think of the two of them trapped in the monastery as fire and lava and ash descended on them from the volcano. Xi Shi may have been the source of the drain of magic from the Talented villagers, but the cost of stopping her was terrible. Part of me wishes Tao had destroyed his diary, and the recipe for the potion to make an ordinary person Talented with it. But another part of me—the proud alchemist inside—knows that Tao Kemi never would have made that choice. Despite the consequences, the potion was the culmination of years of hard work and determination that he would have found impossible to throw away. The only saving grace now? I stare down at my scrawls on the page of my diary. The recipe for a cure to a potion I had no idea could exist.

My brain races to process what I've just seen, turning over the pieces of the puzzle. As the conclusion dawns on me, a chill settles in my bones, shaking me to the core. A sense of wrongness. Of something impossible being true.

The Waidan stares at me. "You understand what this means?"

I force myself to nod, although my mind feels separated from my body, floating above reality. "It means the Gergon virus isn't a virus at all. It's a person."

# CHAPTER NINETEEN

# SAMANTHA

"I'VE GOT TO GET BACK TO NOVA." I JUMP to my feet. *What am I doing sitting around here?* I've got to warn the palace that someone is draining all the Talented power. My mind races as I try to think how I can get into Palace Great and demand an audience. *Will they even listen to you? Will Prince Stefan let you in?* But it doesn't matter—if I go with Zain, with Daphne—the palace will have to listen to us.

"Wait!" says the Waidan. "Stop. Think."

"There's no time for that!"

But the Waidan fixes me with a fierce gaze. "Samantha Kemi, you are a Master Alchemist. You do not rush to conclusions. You think things through. You examine every possibility. Then you find the solution. If it is true that a person—an ordinary person now made Talented— is the source of the Talented drain in Gergon, who could it be?"

The Waidan is right. I need to breathe and think about this. I force myself to delve deep into my memories of my time in Gergon. The prince did have the symptoms—so he couldn't be the source. Besides, he's been Talented his whole life—I remember at least that much from the history books. It has to be someone ordinary.

Every thought is whizzing through my brain at a million miles an hour. I think I can even hear them as they pass by, buzzing in my ear. Buzzing.

That noise isn't my thoughts after all. I scan the room frantically, checking in every corner. Finally I spot it, hovering in the doorway, darting away from the room. A FollowMe cam.

"Zain?" I cry out, chasing after the drone-camera. It spins away from me, and I'm slowed by the fact that I have to climb the steep ladder up from out of the basement. "Trina!" I shout, hoping she's stayed close by. "Get the camera!"

I catch a glimpse of her flaming red hair as she races to catch it. I'm up the ladder as quickly as I can manage, my feet pounding the stone floor. "Careful!" shouts the Waidan from behind me. Just as he says it, I stumble as one of my feet drops through the floor. Then, I'm yanked backwards, pulled away from the hole that's quickly opening up by a pair of strong hands. Trina.

We slam back against one of the walls, safe. "Thanks,"

I manage to squeeze out between gasps of breath, my heart pounding in my chest.

"Come on," she says, dragging me to my feet and leading me back outside, and through the maze of streets. We can see the drone still—just—disappearing around the corners ahead of us.

We burst through into the outer ring of the monastery, where the streets widen out. Standing there, holding the drone, is Zain—and behind him, Daphne.

I'm about to shout at him for sending the FollowMe into the monastery without permission, but the look on his face stops me short. He walks toward me, his arms open, his eyes glassy with held-back tears. Zain doesn't cry easily. Panic grips my throat. "Sam . . ."

I stop moving toward him. I'm not sure I want to hear what he has to say. "You have to come back to the town. Something's happened at the palace."

"Castle Nova?"

Zain shakes his head. "No, not the castle, the floating palace."

"But that's impossible—" The floating palace is impenetrable. There has never been a successful attack on the royals' hidden residence. Then it hits me. "Oh god, but Molly is there!" I look down at my watch and mentally try to calculate the time difference. They're several hours behind us. "She should have been back already."

I don't know how it's possible, but Zain's face turns even whiter. "She was there at the time. We're not sure exactly what's happened yet . . ."

"And the princess?" Trina asks from behind me.

Zain's silence is the worst answer he could give.

I jump in the front seat of the car next to Zain, and Daphne and Trina get in behind. Mei and the Waidan get back in the 4×4 we took up here initially.

"Sorry for the FollowMe," Zain says. "When the news came through we couldn't find you anywhere in the compound—you didn't let me know you were going."

"I was in a hurry," I say, defensively.

"We assumed you'd come up here, so we drove up as fast as we could. But this place is huge. I only used the FollowMe to help us search for you faster than we could."

"It's okay," I say. "Please. Let's just get back as soon as possible." I can tell Zain wants to ask me more about what I've learned, but I don't feel like sharing yet. I wrap my arms around my body, hugging myself. The winding journey down the volcano feels like it's taking twice as long as it did on the way up.

Once we arrive, I follow Zain as he races through the residential part of the compound to a large communal space where a television screen is set up. Dai and James are there, leaning forward on their knees. Their eyes are glued to the screen, where a breaking newscast is unfolding live. I burst in, almost colliding with the back of the sofa.

"... We are told that the palace is going to be making a statement any second now, but Phillip, what do you think this means for the future of Nova? And who do you think could be responsible?"

"What's happened?" I ask Dai as the newscasters drone on.

"It's all speculation at this point, but it doesn't sound good. They're just waiting for the official word ..."

I let out a long groan. Then I turn to Zain. "I should call Mum and Dad—"

"I tried already. Your grandad told me they'd gone to Castle Nova to get answers, so they'll call you as soon as they know anything. Oh, look—the headlines are on again."

I whip my attention from Zain back to the screen.

The newscaster says: "Once again, folks, we have breaking news: a group of school children have been involved in an incident inside the floating palace of Nova. We don't yet know the condition of the students, but we are being told that they are all alive and in safe hands—Hang on one second, we're going to go live to the palace now, where Prince Stefan is ready to make an announcement to the crowd."

"Prince Stefan?" I whisper to no one in particular, but my unease is growing by the moment. I'm surprised—and scared—that it's not the king and queen, who would normally make this sort of announcement.

The screen shows an empty podium outside of Castle Nova, the new crest of Nova emblazoned on the wall behind. Otherwise it is a somber affair: There are no elaborate flower arrangements or oversized flags in the background. After a brief moment of dead air, the prince suddenly appears on the screen, passing through the wall behind the podium with the crest on it. It's a casual display of his new power—the power that he received from Evelyn on their wedding day. Seeing him makes me dig my nails into the back of the leather sofa. He's dressed in a military uniform: a sharply tailored navy blue suit with golden buttons polished to a mirror shine. A thin band of gold nestles in his thick blond hair: the prince is *really* trying to remind the Novaen public that he's royal today. If he's worried or nervous, he's doing a good job of hiding it. There's strength in his tiger-striped eyes. Determination.

"Citizens of Nova," he begins, his voice clear and—god I hate him—powerful. "Today, I have some terrible news for our nation. This morning, a dangerous and highly contagious virus was unleashed on palace grounds. This attack took place during a royal visit with local schoolchildren that my wife, Princess Evelyn, was hosting. The group of Talented young students who were in attendance were also affected. While we have managed to contain the worst symptoms of the virus for now, we are keeping the affected people—including the princess—in quarantine until we can find a suitable cure.

"Your king and queen have also been taken into quarantine while we race to control the spread of this awful contagion." A slight drop of his eyes is the only show of respect he gives the royal family, before he returns his intense gaze to the cameras.

"This was obviously a targeted, coordinated attack on the princess and her Talented visitors. While the palace doctors, in partnership with ZoroAster Corp, are doing all they can to help those that have been affected, you can rest assured that we are also looking for justice. I, personally, will not rest until those responsible for this heinous attack are either behind bars or banned from Nova for good."

He disappears off the screen in another flash of power, and the television presenters take over, repeating and dissecting the prince's every word. Within a few moments they've drafted in experts to weigh in on what the "virus" could be.

There's still nothing from my parents.

"Are you okay?" Zain asks.

"I can't wait any longer. I don't care what Grandad said; I need to call them. Is there somewhere I can go?" I ask the Waidan. He points me down the hallway to his office, where I can use video chat on my laptop. Zain tries to follow, but I shake my head. Thankfully, he seems to understand and leaves me alone in the small room.

It takes a few tries before it connects. Mum looks distraught, her face a mess of dried tear tracks and deep lines. "Sam, thank goodness."

"I'll come back straightaway," I say, almost over the top of her words. "I'm sure that I can get a Transport—"

"No," says a voice from offscreen. Mum moves the computer so that it shows Dad inside the screen. He looks just as distraught as Mum, rubbing his eyebrows with his thumbs. There's more gray in his hair than there's ever been—between the Wilde Hunt and the Royal Tour and now this, this year has been stressful for him, to say the least.

"What do you mean?" I ask.

"You need to stay where you are. It's too dangerous for you to come back here."

"Too dangerous?" Panic rises in my voice.

"There's all sorts of talk that the prince is going to put sanctions on ordinaries—and there's even news coming in about ordinaries being attacked by Talenteds on the street. You're safer there."

I swallow hard and clench my fists under the office table, where my dad can't see. "I just saw the prince's broadcast."

Dad nods, looking glum. "We were watching too in case he released any new information."

"And what about Molly? Is she okay?"

"We don't know," says Mum, her voice trembling. "All the palace will tell us is that she has been quarantined as they're worried about the virus spreading. They have assured us that they have the best doctors and the ZA synthmakers on it."

"Did they give you any information at all about her symptoms?"

"They're barely telling us anything!" Dad throws his hands up in the air.

Surprisingly, Mum is the one with the cooler demeanor. She frowns in concentration. "They sounded similar to what you thought the princess had before, at your ceremony. A cough—the white powder . . ."

I bite my lip. If that's the case, then it looks more and more likely that the drain has spread from Gergon to Nova. *But who could be the source?*

As I'm lost in thought, I see my mum and dad being ushered off the screen and Grandad moves into their place.

"Tell me what you've found out in Long-shi," he says.

I struggle to bring my mind back to what I saw inside the Jing monastery and the story locked away in that pool of liquefied magic. But once I start telling Grandad, it gushes out of me—everything, from how Tao Kemi created the potion to make an ordinary person Talented, all the way through to how a cure now lies within my potion diary, with phoenix flame the main ingredient. It fits all the symptoms. Grandad's expression barely changes as I tell the story, though I can tell from the occasional twitch of his eyebrows that he's listening intently.

"That's why I *have* to come back to Nova, Grandad," I say. "I need to confirm we're dealing with the same potion—so I don't make the wrong cure." It's the only option. I'm not going to risk being wrong—not when it's my sister's life on the line.

"Tell me again about the pool," says Grandad. "Describe it to me."

I frown, but do as he says, describing every detail of the pool that I can remember. I can't see the relevance it has to me getting back to Nova.

"Amazing. I wish I was there to see it myself," he says. I don't often hear my grandad sound so filled with wonder. Then, his demeanor changes again—from awe-filled to determined. "Can you get back to the pool?"

"I . . . I think so."

"Go, immediately."

"But why? I don't understand."

"There might be another way to get you into the palace. I just need to pray Tabitha answers."

The screen goes dark.

I have to trust him.

# CHAPTER TWENTY

# PRINCESS EVELYN

THE STORYBOOK LESSONS CAME FLOOD-
ing back to her.

Tales of princesses fallen into enchanted sleeps,
sometimes for hundreds of years. Sometimes for eternity.
Just lying there, waiting for their prince to come. It was
something she'd always wondered about when she heard
the stories. What did those sleeping princesses dream
about? Did they live decades in their dreams, only to
wake up from suspended animation to expect to live life
again?

Maybe that was immortality. Living hundreds of real-
ities that never really happened.

Waiting ... but who was she waiting for? To her
knowledge, no one even knew she was asleep. Surely the
prince would keep the fact that he injected her a secret.
She should have never let him in her room in the first
place.

No, there was going to be no Prince Charming in her story.

*There might be a Princess Charming, she thought. Or at least . . . a bodyguard?*

*You blew that,* she reminded herself.

No, no one was coming to save her. So, the only solution was that she was going to have to save herself.

First, she had to understand the rules. She took a deep breath and opened the palm of her hand. This time it was easier to summon the vision of magic on her own, and she gasped as the beams of light spread once again from her fingers in different directions. Still, she could sense pressure on her magic, drawing it toward the tower inside the walled town. Here, far from the town, she could still resist.

But the Gergons, inside their walled city, could not. The oneiros wanted to terrify her with their nightmares, driving her into the "safety" of the city. Her good thoughts were still powerful enough to ward them off—for now.

But every moment that passed, she felt a little weaker. A single strand of her magic traveled in the direction of the tower. No matter how hard she tried, she could not change its flow. She needed to find out who was drawing the magic.

The second question she had was: How long had she been here?

How many days had passed since the prince had sent her to sleep? This question plagued Evelyn, as Prince Ilie seemed to imply he had been in this state for months. Was there even time here? Maybe it was simply an illusion.

"Hello?" a voice cried out, interrupting the princess's thoughts.

In a flash, the princess dismantled the walls of her dream bedroom, so that she was in a completely white space. And what she saw there was no longer a dream but a nightmare. She immediately searched for oneiros, but there were none to be seen. In front of her was a group of young girls who didn't have the same wavy quality of the people she usually dreamed up. They were new arrivals to the dream world. And since they weren't dressed in old-fashioned clothes, that meant new arrivals from *Nova*.

One of the girls stepped to the front, and Evie realized she recognised her.

"Molly?" The name came out of her mouth before she could stop it.

"Princess!" Molly's word came out as barely a whisper, but the fear on Molly's face vanished, replaced by a relieved smile. "Guys, it's okay! The princess is here. Everything must be all right. We'll be going home soon."

She was talking to the whole group of kids—students, by the looks of their neat school uniforms—all about the same age.

Evie put on her best smile, to keep this dream-Molly calm. "What's going on?"

The other children gathered round behind Molly, who took the lead—not so different from her older sister after all. The others were staring up at the princess in wide-eyed awe that seemed to border on terror. Molly took a moment to answer, her brows knitting together in concentration.

"It's all a bit fuzzy. We were invited to the palace to meet you and Prince Stefan. It was like ... an official royal visit."

"So have I been ... awake?" Evelyn felt idiotic asking the question, but the reality was, she didn't know.

"Um, well, nobody's seen you ... you haven't been on a cast for ages."

At Molly's words, Evelyn felt the blood turn to ice in her veins. "Nobody's seen me? In how long?"

Molly blinked. "Since your wedding. There were some pictures of you on honeymoon but no one's actually seen you in person."

"On honeymoon?" Evelyn frowned. "But I haven't left the palace at all. I've been too unwell to travel."

"That's what Sam was afraid of. So it's true ..."

"The prince must have faked the pictures." Evelyn slumped back, and the dream caught her in a chair of her own making. Then she stood up again, and just as quickly the chair disappeared. "So what does it mean that you're here? Are you even real?" In a very un-princess-like manner, she strode toward Molly and poked her hard in the arm.

Molly winced and jumped back. "Hey! Of course we're real."

Now the other students around her started to panic. The noise within the dream rose, static filling Evelyn's ears, their voices crying out for their parents, for help, for anything.

Evelyn knew she had to take control of the situation, or else she would never be able to get to the bottom of this. There was also the question of the oneiros. She didn't want them anywhere near Molly and these children. These children were her subjects. She wasn't going to let them be taken into the Gergon village.

She would build them their own place here. And she would keep them safe.

"Tell me what you remember," she said, putting her arm gently around Molly's shoulders. "Tell me what you can remember about today." She employed her most princess-y tone, and she felt Molly's shoulders relax.

Molly closed her eyes. "I woke up this morning, and immediately panicked about what to wear. Then Mum came in and said that actually we'd been instructed to wear our school uniforms just like Sam predicted—at first, I didn't want to, but then I realized that made perfect sense. And plus, it took the pressure off in a major way from deciding what to wear. We were meeting at school, so Mum took me in early. That's when I saw all these guys."

"And everyone who you came to the palace with is here? There's no one missing?"

Molly craned her neck to look around. "Yup, everyone's here. Except our teachers."

Evelyn frowned, then motioned for Molly to continue.

"The palace had provided special coaches for us to travel in. It was pretty exciting because no one had ever been to the floating palace before. Not even any of the teachers. And everyone was so excited to meet you. I overheard Mr. Rosetta saying that this was just proof of the new era that Prince Stefan was ushering in. One where Talenteds would get the position in society that we deserve, or something. But then, he would say that, seeing as he's our main Talented Arts teacher."

"I see," said Evelyn. "So you assumed I was at the palace." That was one thing she had needed to confirm. It was unusual that members of the public had been invited up to the floating palace, but not unprecedented. In fact, it was something she had wanted to reinstate once she was Queen.

"Oh yes, the letter said that we were going to meet both you and the prince. When we reached the castle, we were let out of the coach and then one by one we were taken up to the palace via Transport screen. That was so exciting. The palace is so beautiful. I can remember seeing all these candles floating in the hallway and these huge marble steps leading up to the different floors. We met the prince in the entranceway, took some pictures with him, and were given a guided tour of the palace. Then it was finished. We were going to be sent home. And—" Her breath caught in her throat, and tears sprung up in the girl's eyes. She covered her face with her hands. "It's all my fault."

Princess Evelyn placed her arms around her. "What do you mean?"

"I started to worry because we hadn't seen you—and the invitation specifically said that we would. Besides, Sam had given me a letter that I was supposed to give to you—and only you. I didn't want to let her down. We were left alone for a moment in the palace entranceway as we waited for the Transport home so I thought I'd try to find you. I ran back down the hallway and opened this pair of brown doors and—"

"What did you see?" Evie's eyes opened wide.

Molly swallowed. "It was a huge great ballroom. But it was so strange, because against the far wall there was a massive four-poster bed. You were lying on it, underneath the covers. No one was around, so I walked over to it and I ... I tried to wake you. You were fast asleep. Then I touched your hand as I placed the letter beside you and it was almost like I got an electric shock.

"When I got back to the group, the prince was there. I asked him what was wrong with you? Why you were asleep? I thought he was going to be so mad at me, but he didn't look angry. He looked . . . panicked.

"And then I coughed so hard, I doubled over. My friend Bethany grabbed my hand . . ." Molly looked around until her eyes stopped on the face of one of her classmates—a young girl, her dark skin covered in a sheen of sweat.

"What happened, Bethany?" Evelyn asked.

"Well, I took Molly's hand and the next thing I knew, I was coughing too. It was a really bad cough," Bethany said.

"Like we were hacking up our lungs," added Molly.

"And then it spread," Bethany continued.

Evelyn could picture it in her mind: the children standing in a line and the cough jumping from person to person like an infestation of fleas.

"I was at the end of the line," said Molly. "And I could see the prince. He called out to some of the servants and they came over to us and gave us each a glass of juice to ease our coughs. Of course we all drank. Then Bethany fainted. I don't remember anything else until waking up here."

"The prince—what did he look like? What was his expression?"

Molly frowned. "He looked pretty scared—his face turned this really weird shade of gray."

Evelyn's heart dropped. The story confirmed what she had been worried about. That whatever virus she had was contagious.

Molly looked up at her, her eyes wide with fear.

*Get a grip, Evelyn.* She couldn't cause these children who had come to visit her to descend into panic. Whoever they were—whether this was real or a dream—she had a duty, and that duty was to protect her subjects. "Right." She clapped her hands together. "The fact is, you all came here to meet me, and now—here is your opportunity. How about we all think really hard about what the palace looked like, and maybe we can recreate it here."

The young teens looked terrified, but they nodded, glad to have a task. Molly was one of the first to close her eyes and almost immediately, up popped the floating candles that illuminated the hallways of Palace Great.

"Perfect!" Evelyn cried out. "What else do you guys remember?"

Suddenly there was a rich red carpet at their feet, decorated in geometric gold patterns. Up popped the marble walls, not a single bright, clean white slate out of place. A window appeared above them, flooding their feet with natural light. Evelyn began to feel more and more at home. She beamed at the group of teens.

"Now, what do you see in terms of people? Who is around?"

Immediately, a selection of bodyguards popped up—although their features were fuzzy—as if the children couldn't quite conjure up their faces, only significant details. Evelyn recognised the particularly square head of one of her bodyguards, and the tall cane that was the new Palace Secretary's object. Prince Stefan also appeared, surrounded by a pool of light. His features were the clearest—but then his face had been all over the casts and the newspapers, so he was more familiar to the kids—yet his form had the shimmery quality of those she had dreamed up, not those living in the dream with her.

She couldn't figure it out. It was a puzzle that made her brain throb.

Something else was strange. "Was this really all the people that you saw?"

Molly and the others looked at the collection of shimmering people, then nodded slowly. "Our teacher stayed behind in the other room."

"You didn't see anyone who looked like this?" She thought of Renel—easily recognizable by his strong beak nose—and a shimmering version of him instantly appeared.

There was no hint of recognition on anyone's face.

That didn't make any sense. For an official royal visit, Renel should absolutely have been there.

"And what about this person?" She swallowed, pausing for a moment before conjuring an image of Katrina in her head. Katrina's bright red hair and lithe form appeared standing next to her, and Evelyn was momentarily captivated by the sight of her piercing green eyes.

"Oh, I know her!" said Molly.

Evelyn was so relieved she thought her heart would burst. "You saw her at the palace? How did she look—was she well?"

Molly shook her head. "No, not at the palace. I saw her at home. I remember her amazing red hair . . . I've always wanted hair like that."

"At home? You mean . . . she came into Kemi's Potion Shop?" Evelyn frowned. She couldn't think why Katrina would need to visit an alchemist, but there were probably plenty of things she didn't know about her.

"No, not at the shop. She came to the house to help film Sam's docucast. She was the camerawoman."

Evelyn's face fell. "Oh, it must have been someone else then. This woman is not a camerawoman. She's one of my bodyguards."

Now it was Molly's turn to frown. "It definitely was her. I even noticed because she had a star-shaped freckle on her nose. But then she couldn't have been one of your guards, as she was ordinary. She definitely wasn't carrying any kind of magical object."

"I have ordinary guards too," Evelyn said, with a distant smile. Combined with the star-shaped freckle and the red hair . . . maybe it *was* Katrina. But why would she be with Samantha and not with her? Unless … a cold feeling like ice water dripped down the back of Evelyn's neck. Unless while she was stuck in this dream world, Stefan was slowly getting rid of everyone at the palace who really meant something to her.

She had to get all of them out of this dream world.

Fast.

# CHAPTER TWENTY-ONE

# SAMANTHA

"IS MOLLY OKAY?" ZAIN IS THE FIRST TO ASK as I close the door of the office.

"They don't know," I say, shaking my head. "She's being held in quarantine at the palace and they won't let my parents in to see her. I'm so worried. They said that synthmakers from ZA are working on the cure—do you think you can find out what's happening?"

"Sure, of course." Zain digs his phone out of his pocket.

"I have to speak to the Waidan," I tell him.

"Guys, you might want to come back in here," says Trina, appearing at the door of the living room before Zain has a chance to dial. "The prince is coming back to the mic."

Zain and I exchange a look and then hurry back to the television screen, where the prince is returning into view. He clears his throat, places his hands on either side of the podium and takes a beat, before staring straight down the barrel of the camera lens. I gulp down a breath. I have to admit: he's impressive. I'm reminded of when I first met him, at the Laville Ball. He had shown up as my unexpected escort and charmed me with his tiger eyes.

I had even *kissed* him.

Okay—so that had been to slip a poison leaf into his mouth, but still. I knew his true nature. He was a man desperate to preserve his power but equally desperate to save face. His—and his family's—pride came first, no matter what the consequences were for anyone else.

Pride and power. A dangerous combination.

Prince Stefan's voice grabs my attention and pulls it back toward him, like a twisted tug-of-war. "Good people of Nova. This is the second time that I have had to address you today, and I wish the news was better. But it is still news, and I promised you that I would share what was happening. The palace security team have been working around the clock to find the source of the disease—and we have an answer." He takes a deep breath, his eyes closing for a moment. It makes the instant when he opens them again even more impactful.

"Oh, he's good," says Trina from beside me. I can't help but agree.

"We believe this was an orchestrated attack by the ORA. We are examining evidence found at the scene now and will update the public as soon as we know more.

"This is a very serious matter. We are sending out urgent messages to every Talented person in Nova who might be at risk of contracting the virus, and advising them of specific steps to take. We urge you not to ignore these messages, and to follow the directions within. We are also warning the ORA—and, indeed, all the ordinary people of Nova—we will find out who is responsible. And nobody is to leave Nova until we do."

My jaw drops as the cast ends. "What in the name of kelpies is he doing? He's delusional! Surely no one believes that the ORA are behind this—and what does he mean by *nobody is to leave Nova?*"

"I have no idea," says Trina. "Something like that would be hard to implement . . ."

At the same time, Daphne and Zain's phones begin to buzz. My head whips around to look at Zain, and I stare over his shoulder as he opens the message.

ATTENTION: TALENTED CITIZEN OF NOVA. IF YOU ARE OUT OF THE COUNTRY, PLEASE TRANSPORT BACK TO NOVA IMMEDIATELY. ANY PLANNED TRAVEL OUTSIDE OF NOVA WILL BE SUSPENDED. IF YOU FOLLOW THESE DIRECTIONS, WE CAN KEEP YOU SAFE FROM THE SPREAD OF THE ORA VIRUS—THE ROYAL PALACE OF NOVA

I cover my mouth with my hand. "He's calling it 'the ORA virus' . . . but why? Zain, you can't go back. You'll be putting your Talent at risk."

He frowns so deep, his eyebrows almost knit together. But he shakes his head. "No, of course not—" His phone buzzes in his hand again. "I have to take this," he says. I can hear the tension in his voice and the muffled concern of his father on the line. "I'm here, I'm okay," I hear him say, as he disappears off into the next room.

Daphne's face is as white as a sheet. It's clear she's just received the same text message. When she's finished reading it, she starts gathering her things—packing away her laptop and her camera equipment.

"But Daphne, you can't go—what about the documentary?" asks Trina.

"I . . . some other time," she replies, for once short on words. "I want to stay, Sam, I really do. But the palace instructions are really clear."

"Hang on a second," I say. Zain walks into the room, his face unreadable. I can't think about what that means right now. "Zain, you used the FollowMe to find me in the monastery, right?"

"Um, yeah . . ." He stares at me, not sure where I'm going with this train of thought.

"How much did you film? If you caught what I saw on camera . . . then I can show you both what I've seen and you can judge for yourselves whether you should return to Nova. Will you at least wait until you've seen it until you decide?"

Daphne hesitates, then nods. "Okay, I'll watch the footage."

"Good." I hope I can convince her to stay.

Trina rushes over with a laptop. We take the memory stick out of the FollowMe and plug it into the laptop. The latest file is at the top. We double-click on it and I can't tell whether to be relieved or disappointed: it only shows the last few sentences of my conversation with the Waidan, and none of the story told by the liquid magic.

*"You understand what this means?"* says the Waidan on the screen.

*"It means the Gergon virus isn't a virus at all. It's a person."*

I stare at Daphne and Zain's faces as they're watching it. I can see emotions warring within Daphne, but eventually she shakes her head. "Do you know who this mysterious person is?" she asks.

"No," I admit. "But I have a recipe for a cure—stay here and film me make it!" I feel her slipping away even as I keep trying to bring her onside.

"I'm sorry, Sam. But you *might* have a recipe for a cure and you don't know who's really behind this. I can't disobey the palace." In a few seconds, she has her phone out again. "Hi, set me up a Transport link out of Long-shi?"

I catch her say, before she turns away, her hand covering the mouthpiece. "Come on, pack up the cameras—we're leaving tonight," she says to Trina.

But Trina puts her hands on her hips and shakes her head. "I'm staying here. With Samantha."

Daphne stares at her for a second, then shrugs. "Suit yourself. I'm out of here."

I turn to Trina, my eyes wide. Then she looks pointedly over my shoulder. I spin around and see Zain has returned, holding his phone limply in his right hand. I pray that Zain is going to make a different decision to Daphne.

"My parents called," he says, his voice sounding far away.

"Oh yeah, I heard your dad on the line. What did they say? Do they know what's wrong with Molly and the others?"

"I need to go home," he says.

I take a step back. "What? Even after seeing the footage?"

"I'm sorry, Sam."

"But the answers are *here*. I know it."

He gives himself a shake. "Look, if I go back, I can be your eyes and ears in Nova. And I can help the ZA team on the ground." He joins Daphne in her frantic packing, throwing his belongings into his backpack. "Dad says that the prince isn't joking about shutting down the borders. There's already rumors that Transport links are being blocked all around the country—they're going to restrict plane travel next. No one's going to be allowed in or out of Nova. Don't you want me on the ground, keeping an eye on Molly and the princess from the inside? And once you have your cure, you'll need someone to get you access to the palace."

"You would risk your power being drained?" I ask, my eyes wide with surprise.

"Sam, if you're the one working on the cure, I know I won't have anything to worry about." He stares at me, straight in my eyes. "I know you can do this." He pulls me toward him and kisses me fiercely. Even though my heart is filled with fear for him, my head knows it *would* be best to have him in Nova, where he can report back. He picks up his backpack. "I'd better go."

I can just about bring myself to nod.

"Stay safe," he says.

As soon as he's gone from the room, I find the Waidan and grab him by his sleeve. Even though I know it's a terrible breach of etiquette, all notion of politeness has gone out the window. "Please—I need your help. Grandad said I need to get back to the magic pool inside the monastery."

The Waidan nods and fishes a set of keys out of the pocket of his robes. "You take the car. I will stay behind here and research how to find phoenix flame. We don't have any here, you know."

"You would do that?" I ask.

"Of course. We would have done more to help Gergon if we could, and now we must help Nova before this drain becomes a global problem we cannot stop. My entire team is at your service."

"Thank you," I say, blinking tears from my eyes. But before I can take a single step, Katrina leaps forward and grabs the keys out of the Waidan's hands.

"I'll drive," she says.

I nod. I'm going to need all the help I can get.

# CHAPTER TWENTY-TWO

# PRINCESS EVELYN

SHE DECIDED SHE HAD TO BE HONEST with them.

"I can't tell you exactly why you're here," she told the shining, expectant faces of the school children. "Because the truth is, I don't know myself."

The disappointment on their faces cut her to the bone.

It wasn't the answer that they wanted. But she didn't know how to tell them the truth: that she had no idea why they had all been put to sleep. All she knew was that she had to keep the children from succumbing to whoever it was that wanted their magic and controlled the oneiros.

"Everyone, listen up," she said, clapping her hands together. "I want you to close your eyes for a moment, take out your objects and picture the stream of magic that runs through your body. I know normally you can't see it—but here you can."

Molly closed her eyes first, then Bethany, and the rest of the class followed suit. A split second later, a stream of magic shot from Molly's gloved hands and into the sky. Her eyes snapped open. "Wow," she breathed out, the awe in her voice making all the other children open their eyes too.

It was an amazing sight. Streams of magic flew out from every one of the children's objects—wands, gloves, and rings—flowing in different directions. But one strand from each joined the river of magic that led to that mysterious tower inside the walled city.

Whoever it was, was draining these children too.

She prayed that somewhere out there, in the real world, someone was getting to work figuring out how to stop the drain.

"Thank you, guys." She closed her fist, and the children's magic faded from sight. But even though they couldn't see it, she bet they could feel it, just as she could. A low thrumming through her veins. Their magic—and it was slowly being stolen away.

An idea flickered in the back of Evelyn's mind. She turned her ice-blue eyes on Molly. "What was your sister doing while you were going to the palace?" she asked.

"She left yesterday to go to Zhonguo."

Evelyn felt her already pale face drain of whatever color was left. "Samantha left Nova? Did she know about my illness?"

Molly shrugged. "There had been rumors, and you know Sam—she's like a dog with a bone if she thinks something is up. Well, that's what I assume," Molly added hastily. "She doesn't share that much with me. Zain's with her too. And some people filming a documentary about her."

"I wish there was some way to get a message to her," Evelyn said. She felt annoyed, and then she felt annoyed that she was annoyed. Sam was out of the country. Did she know that someone was stealing her magic? All their magic?

"I'm sure she'll be on her way back," Molly said, as if reading Evelyn's mind. "I mean, everyone will be wondering what has happened to us."

"That's true," she mused.

"My mum and dad will be Freaking. Out," said Bethany.

"I miss my mum," said another classmate. The thought jumped through the class and Evelyn realized she needed to distract them or else they might become hysterical with worry. There was no time for hysteria. They needed to work together.

"Come on now, guys," Evelyn said. "We can fight this. Who wants to join my princess fight squad?"

Molly's hand shot up, along with the rest of the class.

"He's saying it's an ORA virus," said a voice that the princess recognised. She looked up to see Renel standing in the dream world in front of her. He wasn't the only one to appear. She recognised several of Renel's assistants, palace cooking staff, a few members of the janitorial team, and Molly's teachers.

"Oh no," she said. "Not you as well."

"I'm afraid so," said Renel. "It's spreading throughout the palace. Stefan can barely control it. He is being very open now that the only way to stop the virus from getting worse is to quarantine our minds and our magic in sleep. ZA have been developing an advanced sleeping potion based on the formula Prince Stefan had in his possession, but there wasn't enough to go around."

Evelyn swallowed hard. "Is that what he's calling it? A virus?"

Renel frowned. "What do you mean?"

But there were too many people around to explain.

"Molly, Bethany, can you come here a moment?" She took the two girls aside. "You see all these new people? We need to work together to keep ourselves safe. Have you heard of the oneiros?"

"Nightmare-bringers ..." Bethany replied, terror clinging to her words.

"We are all living in a dream, which means we could also be living in a nightmare. But we can stop them. You see this palace hallway, that you've already designed around us? If you tell everyone here to keep on imagining the palace, filling it with all the good thoughts we can remember, we can create a safe place for us all. Can you do that?"

Molly's jaw set, determination in her eyes. "Yes, Princess."

The two girls rushed off to inform the others about how to fortify the dream-palace. It was only then that Evelyn was able to get a moment alone with Renel.

"It's not a virus," she said.

"What do you mean?"

"It's a *person*. Someone is purposefully draining us of Talent. Keeping us in this sleep state ... this dream world ... slows the process. It means we can't be drained of our magic completely."

"How do you know this?"

"I met the other Prince of Gergon here, when I first arrived."

"Ah." Renel stroked his beard.

"He showed me what was going on. There's a tower in the center of a walled town the dream-Gergons are living in. Whoever is in that tower is taking the magic. As long as we stay outside the walled city, we can slow the drain—but the oneiros are powerful and terrifying— they will push us toward the city unless we can be strong against them."

"Why don't the Gergons leave?" Renel asked. "We could bring them here?"

She shook her head. "They've given up. They're too

afraid of the nightmares. It's easier to stay in the city."

Renel frowns. "Well, in Nova the spread is contained to the palace for the moment, but all it will take is one affected person to leave and it will spread throughout the country."

"How dare the Prince blame the ORA, when he knows full well the drain originated in Gergon!" said the princess.

Renel nodded. "Ordinaries and Talenteds pitted against each other. I haven't heard of anything more disgusting." This, coming from Renel—who might have been the world's biggest Talented snob—meant Stefan had seriously crossed a line.

Evelyn bit her lower lip and stared at the dream-palace slowly being fortified around them. It was something, but it wouldn't be enough. The longer they waited, the harder it would be to block out the nightmares brought by the oneiros. She locked eyes with Renel and clenched her hands into fists. "We can't sit around here and wait for someone in the outside world to help us. We have to find out who is in that tower. And then we have to figure out how to stop them."

# CHAPTER TWENTY-THREE

# SAMANTHA

KATRINA TAKES THE ROAD MUCH FASTER than the Waidan did, and I'm thrown against the car door as she whips up the mountain roads. I brace my hands against the ceiling, gritting my teeth as we skid dangerously close to the edge and a steep drop.

I have a million questions careening through my brain, but there are people who know more than me, and I have to trust them. Grandad is *definitely* one of them. I call him from the car as Trina drives, and he rapidly gives me instructions for what to do when I reach the magic pool again. I have to repeat some of the instructions back to him, and Trina shoots me a worried glance. I can't think about it now. His plan sounds crazy but it has to work.

I shake the doubt out of my head, along with my worries about Molly and my fervent wish that Zain was with me. I need to focus. If I can get inside the palace to see Molly and the princess, I can verify for myself that it is the same problem that affected the villagers in Long-shi a thousand years ago.

And then I can ask the prince if he knows who the source is in Gergon.

We pass through the ancient archway and Katrina stops the car. It takes me a moment to get my bearings, but I remember that we walked past the ancient theater on the way through. Once I locate it, I hurry through the twisting pathways, pausing only to make sure I pass the landmarks that I remember: the living quarters, the weighing station, and the stables.

We reach the ancient house of Tao Kemi. Stepping inside, the same feeling of unsettling dread creeps around my shoulders. I feel magic thrumming through these walls and it's disturbing precisely because there *shouldn't* be so much magic here. He broke the natural order of the world for his beloved, and then paid the consequences with his life.

I shake off the dread and dash through the living quarters—avoiding the new holes in the floor—to the hidden basement. The pool looks innocuous, its dark, serene waters holding secrets beyond measure.

"What is this place?" Trina asks.

"It's a pool of liquid magic," I say. "When I touched it, it unlocked a story that Tao Kemi had preserved here."

"Wow. I wonder what other secrets this place must hold."

"One of them Grandad told me about on the phone in the car. He said I could use this place as a kind of Transport into the palace."

Trina's eyes bulge out of their sockets. "What?"

"I know. It sounds kind of insane."

I stare at the pond with new eyes. I've heard of other forms of Transport screens, early trials that were notable for *lots* of errors. It would be the equivalent of traveling in one of the first cars ever made: cool, but insanely dangerous. Especially without someone on the other side to pull us through. Not dangerous. Impossible. That word seemed to be coming up a lot lately. "Grandad explained it like this: the volcano connects all the streams of magic around the world, so it works like a modern Transport screen ... except *a lot* more dangerous. It hasn't been attempted in at least a thousand years, so who knows if this is going to work."

"Wow. Do you think the Waidan knows?" Trina asks.

"Probably. But I was the one who was able to activate Tao's hidden message, when no one else could." I stare at the "Kemi" tile on the floor and feel determination settle in my bones. "Now I've got to see if its magic will work for me again." I give my phone to Katrina, take off my shoes and socks, and slide tentatively to the edge of the pool.

"Wait—you can't really be traveling to the palace using this pool of magic, can you?"

"Not my body, but my mind can, apparently. If there is someone on the other end to receive me."

"And who will that be? Prince Stefan won't want you in the palace—he thinks the ordinaries are behind this."

I shake my head. "Too many questions, Trina. At this point, I just have to trust in Grandad. Just ... watch me, okay? If I start to sink, or anything looks strange, then pull me out."

Trina flexes her arms. "I'm trained to react in these situations. I won't let you down, Sam."

"I guess there's nothing else for it ..." I gulp, and, after a deep breath, I take the plunge, slowly lowering my whole body inside the magical water. It pools around me, encasing me in its strange warmth. It tingles against the bare skin of my feet and ankles. I lift my palm up through the surface, and liquid slips through my fingers, slightly more viscous than normal water, dripping slowly back into the pool.

Automatically I tilt my head back, so I'm lying in the water. I'm not convinced that it will support me, but when I raise my legs I end up supported, floating like a rubber duck on the surface.

Now all I have to do is repeat the last of Grandad's instructions. I close my eyes and speak the words: "Tabitha. Tabitha of Nova, I call you. Answer me."

*Tabitha?* I know that I know that name. *But from where?* I do as Grandad said and continue to repeat the words.

Suddenly the liquid that's been surrounding me turns to solid. I'm locked in the water. My body instantly switches into panic mode; I want to flail my arms and legs but I can't move them. I can't turn my head. I open my eyes, darting them right to left. The water looks normal. But all I know is that I can't move.

"Try to relax," says Trina, sounding much further away than the edge of the pool.

*Relax? She wants me to relax?! It's not possible. It's—*

The view in front of my eyes changes. No longer can I see the dusty ceiling and stone walls. The world blurs and shifts in front of my eyes, and when it settles again, it looks as if I'm standing inside the palace. It's a room I've been in before: a small suite next to the princess's room.

"Are you there?" says a gruff female voice that seems to reverberate in my skull.

"Wait, who is this?" I'm so confused. Am I really here, inside the palace, or am I still floating in the pool?

"Oh good, you are there. Here, hopefully this will help explain things."

My vision spins around the room, stopping in front of a mirror. "Oh my god," I say, but the mouth in the mirror doesn't move. That's because I'm looking through the eyes of the Queen Mother. *That's who Tabitha is. But of course—only Grandad would be so audacious as to refer to her by her first name.*

The wrinkled but determined face in the mirror grimaces. "'Oh my god, *your* Highness,' is much more appropriate."

I choke back a groan at how rude I've been, but the Queen Mother doesn't seem to have any time for apologies. She turns away from the mirror. "We have to move—if the prince finds us then we are in big trouble."

"How bad is it?" I ask.

"I'm worried. Very worried."

The dread that's been eating at me takes another bite out of my nerves. The last time the Queen Mother was worried, it was when ZA were about to administer the *wrong* cure to the princess during the Wilde Hunt.

"What do you need to see?" she asks me.

"The princess—and Molly. I need to find out how they are so I can figure out a cure."

The Queen Mother nods, then passes through the wall of the room, into a long hallway. "You, girl, were the only one who saw through the prince's act. I don't believe the ORA is behind this—the changes started when my granddaughter married him. Look at the havoc he has brought to Nova." Bitterness laces her words. "I hope you can stop him. The Kemis have never let us down."

"Your Highness, if you don't mind me asking, how

have you managed to avoid the spread of the virus?"

"I haven't been in such fine form myself," she says, as she stifles a cough. "So I have kept to my quarters these past few days. I do not want to end up like the rest. But when Ostanes got in touch—I knew I had to help."

"Do you feel like your magic is weakening?" I ask.

The Queen Mother's voice raises a pitch in alarm. "How did you know that? I thought it was just the fact that I was getting older."

It's sounding more and more likely that this is the same potion that Tao Kemi created.

The Queen Mother comes to an abrupt halt outside a pair of ornate double doors. "They're in here," she says. "They've had to use rooms with doors, as one of the symptoms of the virus is a drain in Talent." Princess Evelyn once told me that many of the rooms used by the royal family had no doors—because their magic was so strong, they didn't need them. They could walk straight through the walls.

There's a sound like a door slamming shut behind us. Without wasting another moment, we enter the room.

"Oh no," I say. Even the Queen Mother seems shocked—through her eyes, I see her hand flying to her mouth.

We've entered a huge room that looks like it might have once functioned as a ballroom—three enormous chandeliers hang in a line down the center of the room, and richly patterned damask wallpaper covers the walls. Now it's a makeshift hospital. There are at least thirty beds, each with a child in it, wrapped in sheets up to their necks. They all have their eyes closed and are still—deathly still. There's no moaning, no writhing in pain, no whimpers.

The Queen Mother's eyes scan the children lying in the beds until I catch sight of long dark hair in thick braids—Molly. I try to run toward her, then remember I'm stuck inside the Queen Mother. "There! Can you go to my sister, please?"

The Queen Mother nods, then pads over to the bed. She leans down over my sleeping sister, pulling back the tightly tucked-in covers.

She puts her hand on her forehead. "She feels very warm," says the Queen Mother. "But otherwise, it looks like she's simply asleep."

"This is no normal sleep," I say. Molly's breathing is far too even—and though on the surface her expression is serene, I can almost see her battling beneath it, in the tiny flexing of the muscles on her face. *I will save you, Molly*, I think as I look at her through the Queen Mother's eyes.

The Queen Mother moves away from the bed. She covers her mouth as she coughs violently, and when she pulls away her sleeve I can see specks of white powder on the rich fabric. "I won't be able to sustain you here much longer. And besides," her voice drops to a whisper, "the prince will be looking for me. He wants to put me in this dream state too."

There's a loud shout from the far end of the room and Prince Stefan bursts through. Behind him, through the wide double doors, comes his contingent of guards, their wands drawn and ready.

"There she is!" shouts Stefan, staring down the Queen Mother with laserlike intensity. "You must let me put you into enchanted sleep," he continues in a more normal tone. "It's the only way to keep you safe."

"Over my dead body," the Queen Mother snarls.

"Make sure she doesn't leave," the prince says to his guards. I feel a shove—the Queen Mother trying to send me back.

I cry out into her mind before she has a chance to get rid of me completely. "Wait, tell the prince something for me!"

The Queen Mother moves until she's standing in front of the prince. With her hands she raises a barrier of magic that sends the guards' spells bouncing harmlessly off. "Prince Stefan, I have a message for you. It's from someone who can help stop the spread of the virus."

"Save it. There is no one who can stop it."

The Queen Mother repeats the words I say to her. "Prince Stefan, I know it's not a virus that's causing this.

I know some*one* is draining the Talenteds of their power. Someone who once was ordinary. Tell me who it is and I can reverse it. I can save them—and save everyone who has been affected."

The prince stills—every muscle in his body so tense I wonder if he's been hit with a paralysis spell. Then his eyes flash and he raises his tiger eyes. And even though I know he's staring at the Queen Mother, it feels like he's looking right at me. "Who is speaking through you?" he asks. "There is no one! It is a virus from the ORA! Guards—we have an infiltrator. Take the Queen Mother into custody."

"You might have been able to hide what was happening in Gergon, Stefan," I say through the Queen Mother's mouth. "But you won't be able to hide it in Nova. Let me help you."

"No!" says the Prince.

"My magic is weakening," says the Queen Mother to me. "I must send you back." She shoves me one more time, and as she does my last sight is of her magical barrier tumbling to the ground. She is hit with the guards' spells and crumples to the ground.

I burst into my body, the water suddenly an icy shock I'm not expecting, all warmth gone. I gasp for air, gulping down a breath so large it kills the scream inside my throat. Trina yanks my arm, and with one mighty pull, drags me onto the tiled edge.

I splutter on my knees, coughing up the liquid—which tastes foul. Nothing that pretty should taste that bad.

"What did you see? Do you know what's wrong with the princess?" Trina asks, desperation clinging to her every word.

*Honey and lemongrass tea—a potion to help soothe fits of coughing. (That's an easy one. What we have to do is going to be much, much, harder.)*

"Yes. She's been put in an enchanted sleep. It's definitely the same root cause as what happened here a millennium ago. I have to call Grandad back."

Trina passes me the phone.

Thankfully he picks up almost immediately, and his face appears on the screen. "Grandad—it worked!" I say. "I was able to see *inside* the palace."

"Fantastic. What did you learn?"

"It's the same symptoms that Tao Kemi described. And Stefan is putting the affected people to sleep. Do you have any idea why?"

"You said that in the story Tao Kemi told you, the Talented person died once their Talent had drained away completely. The sleep might slow the drain of Talent from the affected. That must be how he's keeping everyone in Gergon alive, too."

I shake my head, my mind spinning. This is so much bigger than anything I've had to deal with before. "Stefan wouldn't tell me who the source was. Maybe he doesn't know? But there must be someone—like Xi Shi in the story—who is causing all this."

"You can't worry about that now. You have to make the cure."

"Yes. I wonder if the Waidan has made any progress finding phoenix flame ..." I shiver, and it's then that I realize I'm still dripping wet.

"I saw a towel in the back of the car," says Trina. "I'll go get it, okay? I'll just be a moment."

I nod. I shift on my bum so that I'm sitting propped up against the wall, the phone in my hand. "Grandad, there's something else. The Queen Mother ... right at the end, she was hit by several paralyzing spells. Her magic failed her at the last moment. I don't know if she—" I can't finish the sentence. When I close my eyes, I see her smouldering gown. I see the look on Stefan's face, his whole expression lit with anger.

Grandad lets out a sigh that says he understands. I pray that she managed to survive. But she was already ill, and with her defenses down ...

Suddenly everything has just gotten more real. Twice this year already, real lives have been at stake. But we've always managed to get there in time.

Maybe not now.

"Grandad, did ... something ever go on between you and the Queen Mother?"

As his brows knit together, I can almost see the

whirring of my grandad's mind as he calculates how much of the story to tell me. It's the silence that confirms it for me more than anything else. "It ... it was a long time ago," he says, eventually.

"What happened?"

"It's the same old story," he says, a rueful smile on his face. "We were too young. Too arrogant. And we thought we could break the taboo. But a Talented with royal blood couldn't marry an ordinary. That's just one barrier that we couldn't overcome, a forest of opinions and prejudices we weren't brave enough to blast a trail through. Maybe one day someone can accomplish what Tabitha and I couldn't."

"But first, we need to save the Talenteds."

"Exactly. Now, where can you get some fresh phoenix flames, and fast?"

## CHAPTER TWENTY-FOUR

# PRINCESS EVELYN

WHERE WAS THE DINING ROOM IN THIS place? She felt so hungry. All she wanted to do was sit down, have a nice meal, and relax. But her stomach growled and she felt hollow with emptiness. She thought she heard signs of people eating and talking, the cheerful clink of cutlery against plates ... but every time she turned a corner, there was nothing but the empty tables, not even a spare crumb for her to nibble. *There's plenty of food inside the walled city*, she thought. *I should just go ...*

"Be gone!" Molly screamed, her gloved hands splayed open, sending the oneiros that had been surrounding Evelyn flying away. "Get that one! And that one!" Each of the children used their objects against the oneiros, Bethany pointing her wand, another using a ring, and with their combined power they managed to send them away in a swirl of trailing white cloud.

"What happened?" Evelyn shook herself and the gnawing hunger instantly went away.

Molly stopped, her face flushed with exertion, breathing hard. "The oneiros were all over you."

"Thank you for stopping them," she said, shaken that she had almost been taken in. She thought they'd have a bit more time, but the oneiros were just too strong.

"Um, there's something else."

"What is it?" The look on Molly's face was enough to give Evelyn shivers. "Molly?"

"Well, we think there's a reason why there are more oneiros than ever." The girl rocked back on her heels. "The king and queen are here."

"They are? Where? I must speak with them—"

"They couldn't handle the nightmares that the oneiros brought, so they took refuge in the walled city—it is the only place they could get relief. Then our teachers and all of the people you knew from the palace followed— including that beak-nosed guy. All the adults went. Our class wasn't able to think enough good thoughts to drive the nightmares away. With every new person that comes, there seem to be more oneiros."

"My parents went to the walled city? That's bad. That's very bad." That meant there was only Prince Stefan left in the palace. She paused. "What about the Queen Mother?"

Molly shook her head. "I haven't seen her." Her face was pale.

That was one thin ray of hope, at least. Evelyn's grandmother was strong. Maybe she could accomplish what everyone else had failed to do, and resist?

There was a darker alternative reason to why her grandmother might not be here. But Evelyn refused to let her thoughts turn in that direction. She put them to the back of her mind and returned her attention to Molly. "So who is left?"

"It's just you, me, and the rest of my class."

Evelyn blinked, taking in the scene. Her and twenty thirteen-year-olds against the oneiros—and whoever was in that tower. She would worry about Prince Stefan once she'd figured out how to wake up.

She forced a smile. "Well done, you guys. The nightmares would have been too much for me if it wasn't for you." She pulled Molly into a big hug.

"Oh my god, oh my god," said Molly.

"What?"

"I've just been hugged by a princess!" she squealed. Evelyn couldn't help but laugh. Then Molly turned serious. "We're all ready to help you. Whatever you need."

Evelyn nodded. "We need to get into the walled city on our own terms to find out who lives in that tower. And then we're going to bring them down."

Bethany looked confused. "But there's no way in—except through the iron gate."

"We won't go that way," said Evelyn. "We don't want

to be stuck there." She didn't know how much control the person in the tower had over the inhabitants of the city, but she didn't want to test it. "How did you fight off the oneiros that were around me?"

"The only way we could think of was to use our good thoughts and throw them at the oneiros as if they were spells. Our magic doesn't seem to work the same way here, but if I point my wand at the oneiros and think about something good, like taking the first bite of a chocolate mooncake, it seems to work," said Bethany.

Molly nodded. "Same with me—except I use my gloves and think about the time I rode a unicorn."

"That's perfect." Evelyn clapped her hands together. "Okay, we had better move fast, before even more people arrive in the dream world. And besides, I have an idea. Do you trust me?"

Collectively they nodded, and Evelyn's heart threatened to burst with pride at her young citizens.

The school group ended up being a safe way to travel—with their numbers, it was easier to form a protective barrier of good thoughts to ward off the oneiros. It wasn't long before they'd left the palace of their own making and were traveling through the blank white space of the dream-world toward the walled city. It loomed before them, a dazzling white-brick fortress. It looked as if it had doubled in size since the last time Evelyn had seen it. And there were the imposing iron gates.

"Everyone, gather around and look at me. We're going to have to use our imaginations for this one. Because I don't want to go through the iron gates. I want to go over the wall."

The children stared up at her in awe, and Evelyn took a deep breath. "Remember. If you can dream it here, it can be." Then she closed her eyes. And when she opened them again, she was sitting atop an enormous golden dragon, its wings flapping beneath her feet, her knees digging into its back.

"Right," said Molly. She closed her eyes until she was riding on the back of a winged unicorn.

Evelyn smiled. "That's it! You've got it!" One by one, the others followed suit, until Evelyn and Molly were surrounded by children on winged animals—from a fierce gryphon to other dragons. One girl was even riding in a miniature airplane, goggles on her face and a scarf sweeping out behind her.

"Let's go," said Evelyn. She urged her dragon up into the sky with pressure from her legs, and soon she was flying up, up, and over the walls of the city. The oneiros came at them, their sightless white eyes hungry to bring them down to the ground below, but the group surrounded themselves with the very best thoughts they could muster—and the oneiros were repelled.

"To the tower!" Evelyn yelled, and as one unit they aimed for a small round window near the top of the tower, in the very center of the city. "Come out and show yourself," Evelyn demanded as the dragon beat its wings to keep her in place.

"All right, no need to shout," said a high-pitched voice from inside the tower.

Evelyn frowned. It didn't sound like the voice of a powerful magician. It was the voice of a little girl. She swallowed as the darkness of the window shifted, as if someone was approaching. She braced herself, in case the voice was a deception.

And then, the person stepped into the light.

Standing in the window in front of them was a young woman about Evelyn's age, wearing what could only be described as a nightdress from a previous century. She had messy dark hair and eyes that were round and glassy, with bright green irises. Something about those eyes was more cat than human. Her features were sharp—too sharp, like she had razorblades under her skin rather than bone.

She was familiar in a way that Evelyn couldn't pinpoint.

"Who are you?" Evelyn demanded, trying to keep her voice commanding and strong.

"I'm Raluca," answered the girl. "And soon I'm going to be your Queen."

# CHAPTER TWENTY-FIVE

# SAMANTHA

BACK IN THE COMPOUND, TRINA AND I SIT around the table. Mum, Dad, and Grandad join us on my laptop. In front of me is my potion diary, where I'm examining the recipe that Tao Kemi passed on. Apart from the phoenix flames, the other ingredients are relatively common:

*The base—a mix of standard lotus water with purified spring water from the Hallah mountain range.*

*Galium root and honeydew secretion—sticky to keep the phoenix flame embedded within the potion.*

*Pixie dust—to help even distribution of the potion around the body and aid the body in recovering from the influx of magic.* (I'm hoping if I increase the amount of pixie dust, it may help the affected Talenteds recover from the lack of magic, too.)

*Emerald and ruby powder—for easier absorption into the blood.*

The Waidan is already working on mixing the lotus-water base that Tao Kemi described. I'm glad I'm not doing this on my own. While the final mix will be down to me—especially as I have a sneaking suspicion Tao Kemi didn't reveal *everything* about the recipe for the cure—I'm grateful I have experienced alchemists around me to consult.

"So you think you can save Molly?" Mum asks, after I explain what I saw at the palace. The relief on their faces when they heard she looked stable was palpable, but so was the alarm when they heard she had been put into a magical sleep.

"Yes," I say. "I have to believe it. And Mum, whatever you do—don't leave home. I don't want you getting sick too. It seems like all it takes is a single touch from an affected person for it to spread."

Mum shakes her head. "If they let me in to see Molly, no threat of a virus is going to stop me!"

"But Mum—" The look on her face stops me. It's a battle I won't win. I set my mouth into a firm line. "We know now exactly what's wrong and we have a recipe for a cure. The cure is supposed to be for the source of the magic drain—but I can adapt it to help the Talenteds who are affected. Help them take their magic back. Then Zain can get our cure into the palace." The thought of Zain makes my heart pang, but I have to grudgingly accept that maybe he was right. It's good to have him back in Nova—as long as he can stay safe.

"But first, you need to find that phoenix flame," says Trina.

"Yes," I say, cringing as reality sinks in. Phoenixes are extremely rare creatures, elusive and also protected. Most phoenix ingredients are dried, not fresh, and we need the freshest—it will make the potion more powerful. We have the benefit of being near a volcano, their preferred habitat. But what I need is an experienced Finder to help. "Did you manage to track down Kirsty?" I ask.

Mum shakes her head. "She's gone completely underground after the announcement about the ORA."

I'd feared as much. Thankfully, I have others I can ask who would rock this task. "What about Anita and Arjun?" My elite team. Arjun is a Finder-in-training, but thanks to his help on the Wilde Hunt and the royal Tour, he's got more experience than most qualified professionals. If there was any justice in the world, he'd be a Master Finder just like I'm a Master Alchemist. And Anita could be an alchemist just like me and her dad, if she wanted to be. But she would prefer to be a doctor, administering the cures, than an alchemist, mixing them. Her diagnostic skills are invaluable to me—and so is her ability to keep me sane.

"As soon as we knew Kirsty wasn't available, we put them on a plane—especially once the travel restrictions were announced. They caught one of the last flights out."

Relief floods my body. "Things are escalating quickly in Nova, huh?" I say, chewing my lip. "Be careful, please. Stefan didn't see me at the palace, but he knows someone was watching him through the Queen Mother. He might come to the store to find me."

"We will be careful," says Dad. "And you promise us the same. We know you have to do this and that you're the best person for the job. But that doesn't make us worry any less."

"I know." A lump appears in my throat and I can't talk any more. Thankfully, Dad clicks off the screen.

Mei and the Waidan walk into the room from the lab and I look up, hoping for good news. The Waidan smiles. "We have almost everything we need to help you make this recipe. It is just the phoenix flame left."

"You said that a phoenix lived in Yanhuo?" I ask Mei.

"I said there were rumors that a phoenix lived in Yanhuo—once upon a time."

"But with the volcano getting more active—that's a sign that there might be one there again, isn't it?" I say, wincing inwardly at how desperate I sound.

"It's at least a place to start," Mei says, trying to boost my spirits.

I stare down at my diary. For once, making the potion is going to be the *relatively* easy part. I have the recipe, and the expertise and resources of the Jing labs at my fingertips. Soon Anita and Arjun will be here, and I have a lot to prepare before they arrive.

Dai comes running in, muttering something in fast Zhonguoan. The Waidan raises an eyebrow and reaches for the television remote. Mei translates for our benefit. "We need to turn on the cast again. Apparently there is news from the Novaen Palace."

Once more, Prince Stefan's face appears on the screen. I hate how it looks as if he is staring directly at me. I wrap my arms around my stomach, daring myself to watch.

"We have tragic news from inside the palace tonight. The ORA continued their assault, this time with a brutal attack on the Queen Mother. She is in critical condition now, and we ask the nation to pray for her recovery. I hope that the next time I address you, I will have news of the successful capture of her attacker. Good night, Nova."

A broadcast journalist with an expression of pure shock takes the screen next. "Well, there you have it, folks, breaking news from inside the palace. Wait, hang on a second." The journalist puts her hand to her ear. "Ladies and gentlemen, here at *Nova National News*, we have been given an exclusive photograph of the Queen Mother from inside the palace. I am warning you now, this photo may be disturbing to our viewers and we advise if you have young children to ask them to leave the room now."

A few moments later, we gasp as a picture of the

Queen Mother flashes up, her body lying crumpled on the floor.

"Stefan is the only one who could have leaked that photo!" I say. "I can't believe he's blaming the ORA for her attack, when *he's* the one responsible." I feel my hackles raise and my determination grow. He needs to be stopped before it gets even more out of control.

"I can't listen to any more of this," says Trina. "He's trying to divide Nova between ordinaries and Talenteds. But Sam—you not only have the cure, but you can do something else to stop him." Trina's fingers fly over her keyboard. "His photo is spreading like wildfire across the internet. But you can fight fire with fire."

I frown. "What do you mean?"

"You can tell Nova that Stefan is wrong. That it's not the ORA behind the release of the 'virus.' Even that little snippet from the FollowMe is convincing."

I blink. "Not convincing enough for Daphne Golden . . ."

"Then you should film an introduction to go alongside it. We can upload the footage and with a bit of help from me, you can make sure it goes viral."

"What? But . . . I can't." I shake my head.

"Your sister is one of the affected. People will listen to you. Sympathize with you."

I hesitate, my shoulders slumping.

Trina sighs. "Right now, the Novaen people are only

hearing from Stefan. You can offer them something else—a face that people recognise and trust—on both sides. You're trying to save everyone, remember? They'll listen to you."

Everything that she says makes sense, but I have other cues that I can't ignore. My shaking hands for one thing. The dryness in my mouth. I'm not made to be a spokesperson.

Before I do anything, I have to get in touch with Kirsty. Something has been eating away at me since seeing Prince Stefan's face in the palace. He didn't tell me who the source was—but maybe that's because he genuinely doesn't know?

And now I can't help but wonder . . . maybe the ORA do know more than they are letting on.

# CHAPTER TWENTY-SIX

# SAMANTHA

I DISAPPEAR INTO THE WAIDAN'S OFFICE, sliding the door shut and sitting down at his desk. I open up Connect on my laptop and search for Kirsty on the chat function. It's a long shot, especially as my parents couldn't reach her, but I need to try everything. I open up several browser windows, logging into message boards I know that she frequents. Hopefully word will get out there that I'm trying to reach her. Almost instantly, she gets in touch with me on Connect chat.

> Kirsty: SAM!!!!! I don't even know what to say right now but many many exclamation points. Where are you?

> Sam: Hey Kirsty! I'm in Zhonguo.

Can you video chat?

Kirsty: No—that program is too easy for the prince to trace at the moment. It's better that we use Connect instead—it's based out of New Nova, so it's not easy for him to access. He has no control over this platform.

Sam: I'm glad you're okay. I was worried when my parents said you'd gone underground. Look, I have a question.

Kirsty: Shoot.

Sam: I have to know: did the ORA have anything to do with the virus at the palace?

There's a long pause while I bite my nails in anticipation. I can see the annoying words *Kirsty is typing . . .* but she must be writing me a *really* long message or she's unsure how to put what she has to say to me.

Kirsty: No, we didn't.

Her reply comes finally. I let out a loud puff of breath.

Sam: Thank god.

Kirsty: We're in the dark as much as you are.

Wow, Sam. I thought you would be the last person to believe the prince's lies. Do you really think I would put your sister in danger? I'm leaving. Good-bye.

Sam: No, wait!

I wait a few moments, and when Kirsty doesn't log off, I assume she's giving me a chance.

Sam: I just had to ask to be 100% sure. But I do know who's behind the "virus."

Kirsty: Then spill.

Sam: It's not really a virus at all. It's a person. Someone with the ability to drain Talenteds of their power. The only problem is—I don't know who.

I hesitate for a moment. I want to write more, I even start typing the sentence ("There is an ordinary out there who *took a potion* to become Talented"), but I don't know if that's the kind of information I want spreading.

Kirsty: ......

I wish I could see Kirsty's face right now. I have no idea what she's thinking.

> Kirsty: Sam ... you mean to tell me that every Talented who is affected is losing their power? Including the princess?

> Sam: Yes. But I'm about to find the cure ...

> Kirsty: What?! There's a cure? But this could be the perfect opportunity for us. If every Talented lost their power, things would be instantly more equal.

Now it's my turn to be silent. I can't believe what I'm reading. Luckily for me, I don't have to reply, because Kirsty is typing responses so fast, I can barely keep up.

> Kirsty: Who else have you told about this?

> Kirsty: Can I keep you from making any moves until I've figured this out?

> Kirsty: I know your sister is one of the affected. So I know you have to do this. But this is exactly what we've been waiting for.

Kirsty: A moment to show to the Talenteds, to
*prove* to them, that they need us. That they're not
as strong as they think they are. Was this what had
been happening in Gergon too? No wonder they
hid themselves away.

Kirsty: Sam? You there? There's something you
should know.

I tap my fingers along the edge of the keyboard. This
whole conversation has made me so uncomfortable. I
don't know whether to rise to Kirsty's bait and ask her
what that "something" is. But eventually, I give in.

Sam: What's that?

Kirsty: The palace is trying to keep it quiet, putting
blocks on all the media, but you should know. The
invisible floating palace was seen about an hour
ago from the ground. The royal magic is waning.
You know what might happen if it goes altogether.
If you were hoping to find the cure and contain it
before it's too late ... it already is. If the palace
falls, no one will ever trust a royal family of Nova
again.

I log out of the chat before I can say anything that will make it worse. I got my answer: the ORA is not involved. But that doesn't mean they won't take advantage of the situation when it looks like things are turning in their favor.

Events are spinning out of my control. The thought of the floating palace falling ...

The ORA will blame the royals.

The royals will blame the ORA.

It will be ordinary versus Talented at the highest level.

I can't let such an imbalance take place. Maybe Trina is right after all. Maybe I do have to put my voice out there. I can tell the people that there's someone else behind this. A third party. A real enemy.

It might unite us.

Whatever trust I might have built up with the Novaen people in the wake of the Wilde Hunt and the Royal Tour could be so important now. Hopefully my reputation hasn't been damaged too much.

It's worth a try.

I step back out into the living room. "Okay, Trina. I'm ready."

She leaps up from the chair, her bright red hair flying like flames.

We set it up a bit like the private interviews I was going to be doing on the reality TV show. She chooses a dark wall, and creates a makeshift light for my face out of the lamp from one of the labs and a piece of cardboard she folds around the naked bulb to direct the light. Now that there is no one Talented around to make it hover, we prop the FollowMe up on a pile of books, so that the lens is at eye-level.

All of a sudden, this feels so different to the kind of filming I was going to be doing. I thought that I could give an insight into my past, but this is all about bringing the viewers into the present.

This video, if it's to have any impact at all, has to go up before Kirsty and the ORA make any announcements of their own about the palace.

I take a deep breath and look myself dead in the eye. *You can do this.* I stare straight into the camera and start talking.

# CHAPTER TWENTY-SEVEN

# SAMANTHA

LONG-SHI IS BUSTLING. DESPITE THE increased activity from the volcano, life continues as normal in the town—the people here are used to living in the shadow of danger. Until the sirens go off, they won't evacuate. Mei tells me that news of what's going on in Nova has hit mainstream Zhonguoan media, but it's so far away—and there's so much confusion—that it's hard for people to grasp the severity of the situation. "Until it arrives on our doorstep, it will be hard to make anyone care—or understand."

I nod, even as my heart constricts at the thought. If the drain really gets out of hand it could be dangerous for the whole world. "It's the same in Nova. When events take place in other parts of the world, it's hard to get people to care."

The Waidan has gone to pick up Anita and Arjun, as well as to try and find us a local guide to take us up the volcano, but everyone is reluctant to go up when Yanhuo is clearly so active. My eyes drift to the cone of the volcano that looms over the town. Plumes of white smoke rise from the opening. It fills me with dread, but also reminds me that I still have time. The volcano hasn't erupted. There's still an opportunity to see if a phoenix has nested there, basking in the fiery heat. Even if we find the phoenix, collecting its flames will be challenging. My memory flickers back to the time I watched Kirsty as she collected dragon flame. She came close to being seared alive. Collecting from the phoenix will be just as difficult.

*Phoenix flames—even more volatile than phoenix feathers, an ingredient that is known to restore balance to the natural order.* I add a mental note: *Can be used in potions to stem the drain of magical power.*

It's strange to think that this time I know exactly the potion I need to make. It's going to be getting the cure to the affected people quickly enough that's going to be difficult. My throat closes as I think of the falling palace, of my sister locked in sleep and of the Queen Mother, who risked her life to help me. There are people counting on me. I can't let them down.

Thankfully, Zain is going to be on the inside. All I need to do is find that ingredient.

Mei and I are on a quest in Long-shi to gather all the equipment I might need. I've been up all night doing research, reading the book on the Wild creatures of Zhonguo that I'd brought with me—and trying to ignore the fact that my video is up on the internet, gathering views. Trina posted it in the early hours of the morning, which would have been peak viewing time in Nova. I know I should have tried harder to get some proper sleep, but it was impossible. My mind wouldn't settle, no matter how much deep breathing I tried. It was a whirlwind of activity, my heart racing inside my chest, and only a bit of reading so I could trick my body into thinking I was being productive would allow me any respite.

I didn't really need to do much research when it came to the phoenix, though. It's always been my most favorite of magical creatures, and—with its status as one of the rarest—something I never thought I'd get to see in real life. I know almost everything there is to know about them, from how best to approach one, where they live, what they eat—even the average wingspan (it's over four meters, for the record). I know they're one of the few creatures to respond to human speech. That they are noble, solitary creatures that hate imbalance (and that's just one of the reasons why they're symbols of alchemy). We have a stash of dried feathers at the store for potions. Kirsty didn't even Find those, we had to buy them from an alchemist who was shutting down in New Nova. They're not often used in potions.

*If you were a real Finder, you'd be figuring out a way to*

*bring feathers home as well as flames. And maybe ash too, if it exists on the ground.*

I'm snapped back to the present when Mei comes out of a grocery store with two bags of trail mix. "I know you're not planning on being on the volcano long, but it's a hard climb. You're going to need all the energy you can get."

"That's great, thank you."

"So is that everything?"

I nod. "I think so."

"Then let's head back to the compound. Your friends should be arriving soon."

We walk the short distance back to laboratory, and my heart leaps as I spot the Waidan's car parked in the drive.

"Sam?" I hear Anita before I see her.

"You're here!" I shout, and drop the shopping bags I'm carrying. I practically tackle-hug Anita and Arjun to the ground as they appear in the courtyard. The two of them are my rocks.

My world.

I burst into tears.

"Hey!" says Anita. "None of that. We're here now."

"What do we need to do to save the world this time?" Arjun asks, rubbing his hands together.

I wipe my eyes and grin. "You ready to climb a volcano?"

"I thought you'd never ask," he grins back.

Despite the fact that we are all keen to leave as soon as possible, preparations can't be rushed if we're going to be safe. Without an official guide, we're going to be reliant on my research and Arjun's intuition. We spend the next few hours inside the compound, putting together our volcano-climbing kit.

"Do you think this will fit you?" Arjun holds up what looks like a crash test dummy but is in fact a full-length jumpsuit.

"Uh, maybe?" I hold it up under my neck. It skims the ground, so I nod. "I think it will work."

"Good. Apparently we're also going to need crampons for further up the volcano. It might get icy."

"Oh yeah—Mei and I picked up some of those from a hiking store in town. But are they really necessary? Isn't it boiling hot on a volcano?"

"Yeah, but there's a glacier up there. I've been reading up on other Finders' trip notes climbing Yanhuo, but they're ancient; there's not much to go on. Without a guide ... it's going to be tough figuring out a safe route. Our aim is to get up and back as fast as possible. And that's going to be interesting considering it's almost two thousand feet straight up."

I gulp. I'm not exactly a fitness queen and even throughout the Wilde Hunt I never needed to do anything truly physically tough. Once again, Anita is going to be our point person on the ground, with Trina continuing to scour the internet for clues as to who the source could be—any rumor of an ordinary person suddenly gaining magical power is worth investigating, not that there are many of them.

"Holy dragons, your video has just passed the 100k mark in views," says Trina.

My jaw drops. "What? You're kidding me."

"Nope. It seems like people are sharing it on their feeds after they've viewed it. Come look."

We crowd into the small office room, where Trina has set up a battery of electrical equipment that boggles my mind. She thinks *alchemy* equipment is complicated, but to me it feels like nothing compared to the maze of wires and monitors and various beeping, flashing devices that populate the area around her.

Trina herself is deep in the zone, her bottom lip sucked in between her teeth, headphones covering her mess of red hair. We crowd around behind her, staring at the large monitor. She plays my video, and I see she's cut in some of the fake newsflashes that have been going around so that people everywhere know what I'm talking about. I cringe as my face appears on the screen, and I subconsciously raise my hand to my hair, wondering why I couldn't have taken a moment to brush it before filming.

"It's so good, Sammy," says Anita, squeezing my shoulder. "You sound so awesome and natural. Like it's coming from the heart."

"I'd believe you," says Arjun, nodding in agreement.

"Thanks, guys. I think I just look ... untidy. I don't know if I would trust me."

"I would. I think: Now, there's someone who cares more about getting the truth out rather than whether their hair is done properly," says Anita.

I grimace. "If you say so."

I hear my voice, tinny through the speakers. *We are Novaens—all of us, Talented or ordinary. This is not a conspiracy by ordinaries to control the Talenteds. This is not a conspiracy by the Talenteds to oppress the ordinaries.*

I cringe. "And what's the reaction like?"

Trina shrugs. "Mixed at the moment—a lot of scepticism, but that's to be expected. Still, you're so convincing that people are sharing widely. At least they know you're working on the cure. Wow—it's going up by almost a thousand views a minute! This video is really going viral."

I close my eyes for a second and wait for the fear to pass. I can't think about it. I don't have time to worry about people believing me. It's time for me to make sure I can turn the promise of a cure into an actual working potion.

Arjun's voice brings me back. "Okay, you have your own boots, right? I've packed pick-axes, headlamps, gloves, hats, several coils of rope, the heatproof and specially sealed pots to collect the fire, the ribbon for the fire-traps, icy-powder in case of lava lizards, goggles, gas masks—"

"Gas masks?" I interrupt.

"Well, we are going into the heart of a volcano. Who knows what we're going to find down there. What else am I missing?"

"Snacks?" I ask.

"Got them," says Anita, dumping out a series of enhanced nutrition bars on the table. I wrinkle my nose at the crinkled packets—they tend to taste like sludge rather than actual food. "Hey, don't turn your nose up at these! They'll keep you from going hungry and they could basically survive any kind of disaster—natural or magical."

"Mei's trail mix looked much nicer."

"Don't worry, I've got that too."

"Okay. I'll eat them. In fact, pack a few more than you think we'll need." I remember being stuck up on the mountain with Zain after the avalanche and how much we would have killed for a nutrition bar at that point. I wish he was here to help with this.

"I'll stuff them in your bags wherever I can," Anita says with a smile. "Can't do with you getting *hangry*."

I mock-snarl back at her, and we laugh. It feels good to break the tension. The muscles in my shoulders are so tightly knotted together I feel like they have more in common with stones than flesh. The laughter eases the pain.

"Do you miss him?" Anita asks, reading my thoughts in the way only a best friend can.

I give her a small smile, but she's not convinced. She grabs my hand and gives it a squeeze. That breaks my resolve to put on a brave face. "I know it's so much better having him working with ZA—but I wish he was here. I'm worried for him. I'm worried for Mum. For everyone."

"I know what you mean. This is big, huh?"

"Really big. Maybe the biggest thing we've ever faced."

She nods, her mouth set in a firm line.

Trina speaks up next. "Okay, I'm scrambling all the electronic signals leaving here so that our location can't be tracked. And I hacked the FollowMe to place you in a different part of the world every time you upload. That should throw everyone off for now."

Anita has fashioned a hands-free mount for my FollowMe out of elastic hairbands and a watch strap. It fits around the strap of my backpack, so it should capture everything that I see on the journey. I want to have irrefutable proof that I've been working to help Nova.

"I've also swapped out the memory card for the biggest one I have—it should be enough."

"We're planning on being up and down within twelve hours," says Arjun. "The plan is *not* to camp on the volcano or stay a moment longer than we have to."

"Take these too," says Trina. She hands us both small

black objects that look like buttons. "They will work as tracking devices, but only switch them on in an emergency—the signal might get picked up outside of our channels."

"Got it," I say. I guess we're ready, then.

The next morning, I'm up early to dress in my jumpsuit and boots.

Already the first of the sun's rays are starting to creep across the dark sky, purple and blue rising like a bruise. We need to start our hike soon. There won't be any shortcuts for what we're about to do.

Arjun checks his Finding device for the hundredth time, even though we know we're the only Finders on the volcano in ages. No one else is going to have seen a phoenix around here. We're going in basically blind. It makes sense that the phoenix would nest near the place where the Talent potion was first created, though. Nature has a way of providing a cure nearby. Just as dock leaves grow near stinging nettles or jewelweed blooms by poison ivy, often a poison and its antidote live side by side. It's just a matter of knowing where to look.

My first step is to pull on long underwear. Even though we're headed into the depths of a volcano, the likelihood is that it will be cold—not warm. And my skin needs to be protected as much as possible. Who knows what kind of toxins will be in the air.

The jumpsuit is trickier to put on than I imagined, partially because it is so stiff and thick around the knees and elbows. I can't imagine hiking in this is going to be easy. I manage to get it most of the way on, when there's a knock on the door. "Can I come in?" asks Anita from the other side of the bedroom door.

"Sure thing," I say.

"Oh, let me help you with that," she says. She rushes over to my side and helps me pull the suit up and over my shoulders, then zips it up in the back. When it's done up, it feels lighter, the weight redistributing around my body. "You doing okay?" she asks, when I turn around.

"Scared. Nervous. Anxious. I want to get the ingredient and get back here ASAP."

"Us too," Anita says with a laugh. "But you've got this, Sam. Think of everything you've come through this year. What's a little volcano?"

I chuckle even as I shudder.

"You might get to see a *phoenix*," she says, the wonder evident in her voice. Her eyes widen as they connect with mine, and I let the awe of it settle in my bones. She understands. She's the one who drew me my first picture of a phoenix. I suck at anything artistic, but she captured it perfectly: the flicker of bright orange feather into red and yellow flame, the marble-black eyes. I still have that drawing framed above my bed.

"You'll have everything ready for when I get back,

right? This can be a potion that we make together."

"I'll be the apprentice to your Grand Master," says Anita with a wink.

"Don't say that."

"But I mean it. You're amazing, Sam. And you're the only one on this planet who can help. Now, how about those boots?"

I nod, then perch on the end of the bed to put my boots on. As I do so, I let Anita's words sink in and form a casing around my heart; protection against the self-doubt that threatens to gnaw its way to my soul at every moment. This is what best friends do. They not only lift you up but they give you the tools to keep going even in the darkest moment. Her friendship, her love, becomes the armor that I wear against every kind of battle: external and internal.

Her belief in me means more than I can ever say.

Boots fully laced up, I stand with renewed energy. "I'm ready," I say.

"And we'll be ready for you when you get back."

# CHAPTER TWENTY-EIGHT

# SAMANTHA

"I'VE JUST BEEN UP TO MY EYEBALLS MAKING more sleeping draughts," says Zain, his voice crackling down the line. I've managed to get him on the phone before we leave for the volcano trek, but the connection is weak. It's late in the evening his time— and very early in the morning for me.

"Any news?"

"The prince is still trying to keep it quiet that the virus—sorry, the drain—is affecting the floating palace. How long until you can get a cure ready? I'll prepare some kind of excuse to go see her so I can wake up the princess to give her the cure."

"We're just about to set off to see if we can find the phoenix now."

"And if you can't?" Zain asks the question I have been blocking out of my mind.

"Then we search for another volcano. Research

other sightings. Anita is on it," I say, with more confidence than I feel. "Are you being careful?"

"Trying to be. They're making us wear these full coverage suits when we go in to see the affected, so we don't touch their skin. Still, some people are scared of being put to sleep and are trying to leave the palace. The prince caught a couple of Talented servants attempting to sneak out."

"Oh my god." Just because some servants were caught, doesn't mean that others didn't slip through the net. "Keep on being vigilant. I'd better go. We're almost at the monastery."

"Good luck," he says. "I love you."

"I love you too." We hang up the phone.

I can tell Arjun is getting antsy. His leg jiggles up and down next to mine in the back of the car, his fingers playing some imaginary piece of music on the keys of his knees. I want to grip his hand and tell him to stop, but he needs to let this nervous energy out. If he had his way, we'd have at least another week to properly prepare for this hike. There was an earthquake as we left—just a small one, enough to rattle the teacups on our saucers but not to knock the books of the shelves. It's a reminder not to take this trek to the volcano lightly. By contrast, I feel as still as a millpond, my breathing calm and even. I might have slipped a tiny bit of a calming potion into my morning tea. Anything to stay sane.

The Waidan drops us off at the monastery, but from there we have to go on foot. There are no roads up to the summit and no way for cars to cross the craggy ground. "Do not anger the gods," he says ominously as we leave.

"Um, I'm pretty sure we have no control over what happens to this volcano ... nature is going to get angry whether I have anything to do with it or not." Now is probably not the time to be flippant with the person who has been helping me so much, but I can't stop myself: his warnings are fraying my already frayed nerves.

I get out of the car before I can say anything else and stare up at the volcano. It's like a child's drawing: a triangle straight up into the sky, topped with white fluff. *No, Sam, not white fluff. Glaciers and ice. Dangerous stuff.*

Arjun is already getting his bearings with the compass. "In the past, Finders took a slightly western direction—we'll follow that as we're not going to be able to walk straight up, obviously, so we'll have to take a kind of zigzag pattern."

"Let's start walking or else I might chicken out."

Arjun turns back to me and laughs, his face barely visible under his beanie hat and with his jumpsuit zipped up under his chin. "Come on, then."

The first hour of the walk is not too bad: although

we're traveling upward all the time, the ground is solid beneath my heavy boots: mud and topsoil and even a few low-growing shrubs. To pass the time, Arjun and I sing songs that we learned at summer camps when we were little. Even though Anita is my best friend, Arjun has always been there—a big brother to me when I've always felt like I had to take on the responsible "older sibling" role at home. I've always been the one to look out for Molly, the one to pick up the slack when my parents are busy, the one who runs the store and who has taken on more responsibility than I needed.

But Arjun was always the one to take responsibility for me—for Anita and me both. I appreciate having a friend like that.

We take a break after that first hour, pausing to sip some water. "Wow," says Arjun as he stares over my shoulder.

I turn around—and I have to agree. We're quite high up now—almost halfway up the side of the volcano, and all around us the sky is lightening, the previous streaks of purple and blue now turned vibrant shades of violet and crimson that are plastered across the sky as if by a kid with a paintbrush. The volcanic ash that's been thrown up into the sky seems to have intensified the colors of a normal sunrise.

"Come on," Arjun says. "I want to get higher so we

can use the light to look for the clearest path up."

I nod, taking a final swig of water.

The next hour is much, *much* harder. The ground beneath our feet has changed from hard-packed mud to thousands of shards of tumbling, slippery scree. Suddenly I'm being forced to use muscles on the insides of my thighs that I haven't used maybe ever in my life, just to stay upright. Arjun has shortened our zigzags, so the way up is steeper, and occasionally he has to stop to help pull me up when I lose my footing. I realize now why the gear is so necessary: the weirdly padded jumpsuit and the gloves. I end up falling onto my knees more often than is dignified and if I wasn't wearing protection, I would be ripping my skin into shreds.

"There's got to be an end to this," I shout up to Arjun, who's gone on ahead of me to help clear a path. My pride's not too dented, because I can see that he is out of breath as well, leaning on his thighs when he thinks I'm not looking. I'm using the pick-axe now like a walking stick, keeping it constantly on the upward side of the mountain, changing sides every time we zig or zag.

"There is, but I don't think you're going to like it," he says.

He's stopped a few meters higher than me, and with a burst of energy that comes from a place deep down inside of me—I don't know where—I run up the scree mountainside to meet him. Then I see what he means. Ahead of us the gravel merges with ice covered in a layer of ash. It's dirty and grimy, and even though it crunches underfoot, it's also much more slippery.

"I think we're going to have to put on those crampons," Arjun says.

I nod, reluctantly, and we slip on the sharp spikes over our boots to give us extra grip. There are even spikes that stick out horizontally, to help us when we're walking at an angle. "Just take extra wide steps," he reminds me the second time I catch myself on the spikes, the metallic claws grinding against each other and almost making me stumble.

Easier said than done.

It hardly looked like it from the bottom, but every step on the glacier is twice as hard as the scree. It's not just the icy surface: the path has become a lot steeper, until sometimes I feel like I'm walking at an angle, leaning in toward the summit. To try and take my mind off the hard labour, I go over everything I know about the phoenix with Arjun.

"It's a creature that doesn't have a normal life and death cycle, that's what makes it so interesting."

"What, more interesting than the abominable?" he replies. "Abominables *never* die. Isn't immortality better than rebirth?"

"How can it be? Phoenixes live entire lives, start young, grow old, and die—one phoenix might live a thousand lives and each time it's evolving. And no one has any idea how they come into existence. All that's known is that they're linked with volcanoes."

"So they're sort of like merpearls then."

"What do you mean?"

"Well, every pearl is grown in a mermaid shell, but not every mermaid shell contains a pearl. That's why so many Finders don't bother with phoenixes. Imagine having to search every volcano in the world to see if there was one around . . . impossible. Now, Garuda on the other hand . . ."

"Come on. Their rarity makes them even more exciting. Garuda, hmmph. They're practically like sparrows."

"Hey now, Garuda are pretty cool."

"Okay, I'll give you that. But phoenixes are still number one."

"You might change your tune after today," he says, and even though I screw my nose up at him, I have to agree. With every continued step that we take, talking gets even harder. It becomes an effort just to remember how to use my muscles, let alone think of a witty comeback or join in some banter.

I look down at my watch: Already three hours have passed. The sun is now high in the sky, beating down on us with such ferocity that I have to admire the glacier for its tenacity. How is it sticking around? In all the layers, with all the exertion and the heat, I'm sweating like a pig. "Almost ... there ..." says Arjun ahead of me, and I can't help but be glad to hear the strain in his voice. It makes me feel less terrible about being so out of shape.

I knew I should've tried harder in gym class. But what can I say? I was always more of a chemistry lab rat—and no one bought me one of those cute wheels to run around in.

There's a big boulder in our path that looks like it's been shot out from the center of the earth. Arjun gives me a boost up, so I'm the first one over it.

And the first breath I take on the other side fills my lungs with searing fire. Without even thinking, I push back off the boulder and scramble down to the previous level, almost squashing Arjun in the process. "Sam? What is it? What's going on?"

I cough and splutter until I feel like my lungs are going to explode. My hands grip my throat, trying to massage the pain away. My eyes are watering and I can barely speak. "Rotten eggs," I say eventually. "And vinegar. Or acid."

"Oh, dragons ... we need our gas masks. There must be a vent over that way. But hey, think of it like this ... it means we're *so close* to the summit now, Sam!"

I gulp down air, but I can't seem to get a proper breath. Arjun looks down at me, his eyebrows drawn together in a frown. "Are you okay? We're up pretty high up here … you're not getting altitude sick are you?"

I take a big swig of water and—now that the pain has subsided—try a few deep breaths. "I'm okay."

Arjun kneels in front of me and stares into my eyes. "No headaches? Dizziness? Any of those symptoms and we turn round straightaway."

I shake my head. I hadn't even thought about the altitude—stupid, considering my last experience on a mountain. Zain would not be happy with me. But it's all been too much of a whirlwind. "Wait," I say. "Do you have any more of that tea the Waidan prepared for us? I'm sure that I smelled coca leaves in there—it might help with the height."

Arjun reaches around to the flask in his backpack's side pocket. "I might have a drop or two left."

"We should drink up before the gas masks go on."

"You got it." He unscrews the lid and passes it over for me to drink. Instantly I can think more clearly, and I silently thank the Waidan for whatever magic he mixed in for us. Even my throat feels better. I have a feeling we're going to need gallons of the tea once we get back to Long-shi.

"Once we get to the summit, what's the plan again?"

I ask. I think I know, but I need the extra few moments to sit and breathe.

"We find a safe place to anchor the rope and begin what looks like a clear descent into the crater at the top of the volcano. Then we look for signs of a phoenix nest on the crater walls: fallen feathers, boulders of sparkling quartz that look out of place, that sort of thing. I'll be setting my watch timer for seven minutes. Even with these gas masks and all the heat protection we have on, we shouldn't spend any longer than that inside the crater. You got it? Not a minute more—if we don't find the phoenix by then, we come back another time with better equipment and more people."

"You got it," I say. I pull the gas mask over my face and clench the rubber bit between my teeth. It takes me a second to regulate my breathing: it's almost like when we went scuba diving together—that same stale air and slight sense of claustrophobia, knowing that I can't properly breathe without it. But within a few seconds, the feeling passes.

Arjun signals to me that he's going to go first over the boulder this time. I curl my fingers together into a step and help him up. Once he's there, he reaches back down and pulls me up. I brace myself for the searing breath, but thanks to the gas mask, the air entering my lungs is neutralized. It doesn't completely take away the gross eggy smell though. I'm not even sure I'll be able to survive one whole minute, let alone seven.

I don't have any time to think about it. Because Arjun takes a step toward the crater and a hole opens up beneath his feet.

And in that instant, he is gone.

# CHAPTER TWENTY-NINE

# SAMANTHA

"ARJUN!" I SCREAM, BUT ALL I SUCCEED IN doing is making a noise that sounds like a cat being strangled, and fogging up my eye mask. I scramble to where I last saw Arjun, and see the hole created in the ground where it gave way underneath his weight. The edge starts to shake under my feet too, and I throw myself back against the boulder. "Arjun!" I shout, but the wind on this side buffets my face, stealing away any sounds he might be making in return.

*Think, Sam, think!*

I unravel the coil of rope from around my waist. So far this boulder has been the most secure object I've seen, so it will have to do. Hugging the boulder tight, I slowly edge my way around it, bringing the rope with me. Once it's hugging the boulder's circumference, I tie one of the knots I was taught at summer camp. My fingers shake, but I order them to behave. Every second I spend faffing around with the rope is a second that Arjun is alone—injured, or possibly worse (although I don't let my mind dwell on that thought for even a second. It skips it like a stone skimming the water—if it drops in, I might never resurface).

Once I'm satisfied the rope is *somewhat* secure, I give it a few sharp tugs. It doesn't budge. It's good enough for me. I wrap the other end around my waist, securing it through one of the carabiners.

Then I get down onto my belly and tentatively shuffle back to the edge of the hole.

It's pitch black down there. I reach up and turn on my headlamp, frantically scanning the dark. I think I spot Arjun through the dust and smoke sent up by the collapsed earth, curled up in fetal position a few feet below. I want to shout down to him that I'm coming, but I can't risk the burning gas in my throat again. Instead, I flash the headlamp a couple of times, hoping he gets the message.

I throw the rest of the rope into the gaping hole, glad that for now, I can't see exactly how far down it is. It's cumbersome work with the heavy gloves, and I rip one off my hands with my teeth to move faster. It drops down into the darkness. Once I'm fairly certain I've done the right knot to be able to rappel down into the cavern, I shuffle to the edge of the hole and throw my legs over the side. With one last sharp tug of the rope for reassurance, my determination to help Arjun overtakes any fear or doubt I might have. I drop my bodyweight onto the rope, and into the hole.

The rope slides through my gloved hand, as slowly and steadily as I can manage it. I keep my focus on a fixed point on the rocky wall in front of me, trying not to spin to the ground and lose my orientation. What I think is a groan from Arjun spurs me on to go even faster, even though I know I don't have endless lengths of rope.

Thankfully, I have enough. My feet hit the ground with a thud, and I scramble upright, undoing the knot as quickly as I can. I rush over to Arjun and turn him over gently onto his back. His gas mask has been knocked askew, but I can see that he is still breathing. I put the mask back on his face, and he takes a deeper breath. Slowly, his eyes flutter open, and my heart lifts in relief.

I gradually help him up to a sitting position, supporting him with my arms around his back. When he's upright, he removes his mask, and my eyes widen in alarm. "It's okay," he says in a low whisper. "It doesn't seem like it's as bad in here as it is up there. The wind must've carried some noxious gas from somewhere else." He lets out a spluttering cough and gives himself a shake. "I'm okay," he says. "Just a bit winded."

I remove my arms from around him, and he remains upright. I loosen my own mask, pulling it off my mouth so that it sits beneath my chin. I take my first tentative breath, and although the reek of eggs is still there, it's much more subtle. There's no fire in my throat, so I take another, deeper breath. We're alive.

Now we have to figure out where on earth we are.

Arjun turns his headlamp on too, and between us we have a look around the cavern we've fallen into. The ground around us gently steams, wisps of smoke curling up from the mud, and when I put my ungloved hand on it, it feels warm. I search around for the missing glove, and am grateful when I see it lying not too far away. There are still plenty of sharp fragments of rock around that I don't fancy cutting myself on.

"Holy cow," Arjun says. I have to agree with him. The walls are splattered with great swathes of green and yellow rock, some of it luminescent as an oil slick. The walls themselves look as if they're made of shards of black glass, reflecting back the light from our lamps. Of all the places I've been this year, this one is the most ominous. Even the cavern in Gergon can't compare.

"Look, over there." I point in the direction behind Arjun. "There's some kind of tunnel."

"A lava tube," Arjun says, craning his neck to confirm. "It's a place where lava once flowed and has carved out its own unique pathway. You can see there's dried lava on the floor. We might be in luck. If we follow the tube, it might lead us to the crater—just a little bit lower down than we intended."

Sure enough, when we shine our lamps on the floor of the tunnel, it looks different to the muddy texture here. It looks almost rippled, like black waves that have been frozen in time.

"I'm guessing you didn't use a kamikaze knot for this," says Arjun, tugging at the rope that I've left dangling through the hole.

I bite my lip and shake my head. "No . . . I don't know that one."

"That's okay. It's dangerous . . . hence the name. It just means we only have my rope left."

He's right. The way that I tied my knot means there's no way to recover the rope. If I'd been smart and thought for even an extra couple of seconds, I maybe could have tied it in a way that we could have rescued the rope afterwards. But that would have involved halving the length of the rope *before* climbing down, and I wasn't sure I had enough to begin with. When I think of Arjun lying on the floor, I know I wouldn't have had the strength—or the courage—to do that.

"Well, hopefully we won't need any more rope than this," Arjun says, plastering an encouraging smile on his face, even though I know he's worried. I appreciate his effort all the same.

"To the tunnel?" I say.

"Let's go."

It's much warmer down here than outside, and eerily

silent without the wind. But up ahead, I spot something that makes me squeal. My torchlight shines on a long feather, lying on the ground. Well, the spine and tiny spindles of a feather, the actual thing itself is burnt to a crisp. But then, phoenix feathers *are* highly combustible when exposed to the air—except when they're attached to the phoenix itself. It's another reason why they're so difficult to work with, and why we have to have special jars to seal them in.

"We must be getting close," I say, picking up the spine between my fingers. I place it into one of the jars we've brought with us—anything that comes from a phoenix might be useful for the potion. "That might mean there's a nest around here." Excitement makes the tips of my fingertips tingle.

"Look for rocks that don't belong, that seem out of place," says Arjun. "A phoenix will bring rocks from other parts of the world with it to form its nest."

I nod, and we keep on walking, until we come to the end of the tunnel. It opens up onto what we've been waiting for: the enormous crater at the very top of the volcano. I can hardly believe that this is the same place I've been staring at ever since we arrived in Long-shi. The very peak of the mighty Yanhuo. I crane my neck up and see how tall the sides of the crater are, like someone has lifted the top of the volcano off with an ice-cream scoop. The bright sunshine stings my eyes, so glaring after our time in the dark tunnel. Smoke plumes from the caldera—a gaping hole in the crater that signals the most active part of a volcano.

The lava tube has opened up about halfway up the side of the crater walls, so we still have a little way to descend before we reach the crater floor itself.

The ground rumbles and I grip Arjun's sleeve. From the smoking hole, we get our first glimpse of the true power of this volcano: spurts of lava thrown high up in the air, a shower of red and gold sparks. If I wasn't so afraid, I'd call it a Midwinter celebration.

Arjun whistles low. "Hopefully we don't have to go anywhere near that."

"Is it safe from back here?" I ask.

He shrugs, which is far from the most reassuring gesture. "Who knows? Let's look for this phoenix and then get out of here."

"Plan."

We've got several terrifying feet down from the entrance of our tunnel to the floor of the caldera. Rather than look down, I scan the perimeter, trying to see any sign of the magical bird's nest. "Over there," I say, pointing along the caldera wall. There's a sparkling patch of rose-pink rock clinging to the wall—it's too far away to see clearly—but it looks out of place. It might be a nest. Arjun squints in that direction, then pulls out a pair of binoculars.

He's always so prepared.

He nods. "I think you might be right. If we can get over there, then we can set up the fire-traps."

"So we need to climb down, then?" I say with a gulp.

"We need to climb down." Arjun unhooks the length of rope from his belt, then gets to work tying it around a broken column of hardened lava. It doesn't fill me with confidence—especially when he cuts part of the rope inside the knot clean through. He looks me dead in the eye. "Remember, maintain the tension the *whole* way down—if you let it go slack for even an instant, it will tumble to the ground. We want that eventually, just not while we're on it."

"You got it," I say.

"I'll go first, that way I can spot you as you come down."

"Okay, thanks," I say, relieved that I don't have to go first and worry about leaving Arjun stranded up here. Maintaining the rope's tension with one hand, he threads the rope through the carabiner at his waist, then without any further hesitation, starts lowering himself down toward the caldera floor.

He makes it down with ease, though, giving me no more time to think it through. I mentally run through all the steps I need to do, then launch off as well. Within a few short pushes, my feet touch the ground. Arjun steps in front of me and grabs the rope. He lets the tension go and then sharply tugs. The knot at the top unravels, and because he sliced the rope in two at the very top, the majority of it drops down to our feet, meaning we still have most of the length if we need it in the future. Genius.

A rumble deep inside the volcano sends lava spurting from the caldera, and we sprint toward what looked to be a phoenix nest. As we approach it, I can see that we were right: There's a bunch of quartz crystals melted onto the side of the crater wall that couldn't have gotten there by accident, mixed with a tangle of wood and ash, perched between a jutting boulder and the caldera wall. Somewhere behind there will be a cave big enough to hide the phoenix. The wall is almost as smooth as glass, probably melted and cooled repeatedly by the heat of the flames from the phoenix's tail feathers. There's no way for us to get up there.

Arjun tries to use his crampons like miniature picks, but the hardened lava is so solid, he can't even chip into it. "It's no use," I say, as he bashes his foot against the wall a third time. He's only going to break a toe that way. "The phoenix might not even be there. They can be gone for days at a time."

"I know that," says Arjun. "We'll have to call it back."

Another rumble from inside the volcano brings us to our knees. The smoking hole that seemed so far away from us suddenly seems close as it shoots out a new burst of fiery hot lava. The furthest thrown dollops land only a few feet from us, so close we can hear the lava sizzling as it makes contact with the relatively cooler ground. The hole also lets loose more noxious gas, and Arjun and I cough until we pull our masks back on.

Our eyes are enough to communicate. Arjun's are filled with undisguised, unfiltered panic—and I bet mine are the same. I put both my hands down on the ground, which is almost too hot to touch, and in my mind I scream the words: "HELP US," and I picture what is happening in Nova.

I think back to the old legends I know. Isn't that what being an alchemist is all about? Studying from those who have walked the alchemical path before us, learning from their mistakes but also never forgetting their successes.

*The phoenix is a creature with a grand sense of justice.*

*It hates the abuse of power.*

*It will not tolerate lies.*

*It is sentient and older than us. It must make its own decisions.*

"I will use the flame to stop the drain! To stop whoever is trying to take magic that doesn't belong to them."

I have no idea if the phoenix can hear me or not, but a roar fills my ears that seems to emanate from the center of the earth itself.

A bright flare almost blinds me, and I throw my arms up over my face just in time. I stay curled up in a ball on the ground, until I feel Arjun tugging on my elbow.

"Sam! Sam! We need the fire-traps, quick!"

I look up with a jolt. All around us flickers a bright, unnaturally green fire. *Phoenix flame.* I scramble to my feet, at the same time detaching one of the jars from my hip. I place it gently on the ground, while Arjun unravels the spool of ribbon we're using as a kind of fuse.

Once we're set up, Arjun throws the end of the ribbon into the flame. It catches, and the flame rushes down the trap and into the jar. Arjun jumps on the end and seals it with the lid. "Got it!" he cries out. "Let's move!"

But I don't want to have come all this way, come so close to a phoenix without actually seeing one.

Even though part of me knows it's madness, I stay where I am. "Please!" I shout into the air. My eyes sting with the intensity of the smoke that's billowing out of the caldera.

Arjun is looking around desperately for an escape route, for the place where we can climb out of the crater. He risks taking his mask off and shouting at me: "Sam, we gotta go! It's going to blow!"

I fall to my knees. "Please," I beg one final time.

There's no answer but another roar.

*Oh, dragons*, I think. *I've pushed my luck.*

The hole explodes again, and this time it's not emerald flame that shoots out but red hot lava. It starts pouring out of the caldera, bubbling over the side like molten gold, spreading all over the crater floor. I'm paralysed at watching how fast it's moving, how quickly it's heading toward me. Smoke pours out of the hole like a steam train. *Move, Sam, move.* Some kind of self-protection instinct finally kicks in and I barrel toward Arjun, my arms pumping as hard as my legs.

He's already running up a narrow line of hardened lava that only leads about halfway up the crater wall, a natural pathway to nowhere. From there, he starts to climb. I follow him, running as quickly as I can.

I breathe a sigh of relief as I see him scramble over the top of the wall, before turning back around to help me. He lets down a length of rope, which I grab hold of. But he's not going to be able to pull me up on his own. I'm going to have to climb.

I'm no good at this. I have the upper body strength of a T-rex. Still, I know I have to try. I take off my gloves, jamming them into my pocket, and dig my fingers into the small holes made by the rough, jagged lava, so different to the pillowy smooth kind that was on the crater floor—it's painful to climb, but at least possible.

The problem is, it's burning hot. The whole crater is steaming up, and the black lava absorbs the heat faster than anything I've ever known.

"I can't!" I scream up at Arjun. "It's too hot!"

"You can do it," he shouts back down to me. "Only a few big pushes."

I grimace and start to climb—my thighs are trembling, every muscle groaning. My hands are slick with sweat, and I swear I can feel the flames that dance across the lava pooling at my heels. I close my eyes, wishing for one second that I could be anywhere but here: clinging to the side of an active volcano's crater, with the key to saving my sister's life in my pocket, choosing between pushing my body beyond its physical limits or dying in a molten lava flow.

That one second is all I give myself.

I grit my teeth and scream again, but this time as I scream I push with every inch of power and strength I have left in my shaking limbs. My fingers slip on the rocky wall but I push them further in, begging them to cooperate. Two great heaves from my legs bring me close enough to the edge that I can grip Arjun's wrist. He grips mine too, and with a huge pull from him and another final push off from me, he is able to haul me over the edge and onto the icy surface of the glacier.

From his backpack, he pulls out two round plastic discs.

"What are those for?" I ask, my eyes widening in alarm.

"We have to get out of here before this entire thing blows," he says. "And the fastest way to do that?" He hands me one of the discs, before sitting on his. "Is to slide our way outta here." Without a second thought he pushes off from the snow and hurtles down the side of the glacier on the plastic slide.

"You've got to be kidding me," I say, before sitting down and sliding after him.

# CHAPTER THIRTY

# SAMANTHA

ANITA IS WAITING FOR US IN A BIG PICK-UP truck at the monastery. As soon as she sees us, now half-running, half-sliding down the scree hill, she starts up the car. We fling ourselves into the back seat, collapsing on the bench, our bodies wrung out with adrenaline and exhaustion.

"The warning sirens were going off in the village and I was freaking out! I had to come up here to make sure you were both okay." She sneaks a look over her shoulder. "Did you manage to get the ingredient?"

I nod, unhooking the jar from my belt and placing it down in the footwell in front of me, protecting it between my heavy boots. "We got it," I say.

"Oh, thank the dragons!" Anita says. There's an explosion from behind us and a column of fire shoots into the sky from the caldera. We don't need any more encouragement. Anita puts her foot down on the accelerator, and we zoom down the mountainside. Thick black smoke turns the formerly bright day dark and dingy, as if it's twilight at noon.

I spin around in the seat and watch the column of fire as we speed away. Even though the brightness of it hurts my eyes and leaves halos of white when I blink, I keep watching. Waiting. Until ... maybe, I see it: the shape of a bird against the fire—wings flapping, trailing tail feathers and a long curved neck. It could just be my imagination, or wishful thinking, but I believe that the phoenix is there, reveling in the explosion.

With the phoenix's blessing, its fire on our side, how could we fail?

*Unless what we're up against is stronger,* my annoying brain says. *We've been working on this cure for five minutes. The drain has been raging for months.*

*That someone would do this ... it speaks of desperation. A desperate evil.*

*Well ... good can be desperate too.*

*I will go to any extreme.*

*I will go to any length.*

*I will do anything to save my sister. My friends. My country.*

*So, come at me, evil. We'll see who's more determined in the end.*

"Hey, are you okay?" Arjun puts his hands over mine, which are clenched into hard fists.

"We're going to do this, aren't we?" I ask, staring straight into his dark eyes.

He squeezes my hands. "Easy, right? This is the part where you get to shine. We'll all pitch in."

"Right, we'll both be your apprentices," says Anita. "When the three of us are together, there's nothing we can't do."

"I just wish we knew who we were up against." Now we're far enough away that I can't see the phoenix, I settle back down into my seat.

"You and me both," says Anita.

"Well, let's puzzle this out," says Arjun. "What do you know? That this clearly affected Gergon before everywhere else, and it started within the past year, so it's got to have started in Gergon."

"Yes. And someone stole the page with the recipe on it. Then somehow, it spread everywhere in Gergon—including to the royal family. But they had Emilia Thoth, and she was able to create some kind of pill that stopped her and Stefan from being contagious—while they were taking it."

Just saying her name makes me shudder, but I remind myself that she's dead: She can't hurt us any more.

"Why?" Anita wrinkles her nose.

"Stefan said he had recruited her. She probably owed him."

"Okay, so they must be looking for a cure too," Arjun muses.

"Yes. At the time of the Royal Tour—when I was hunting down the aqua vitae—Emilia was working against the Gergon royals, that was clear. She was rebelling against them because she saw that they were weak. It was her one shot. She blew it, yes, but she didn't count on having us working against her."

"The ordinaries there are so downtrodden—I can see why they might be desperate to be Talented," says Anita.

She's right. Ordinaries are notoriously suppressed and shunned in Gergon. The alchemists are the only ordinaries who have some respect, and that's because synthetic potions aren't trusted. They haven't joined the modern world like the rest of us. I see the scepticism in Arjun's eyes too. "Or maybe someone was trying to find a way to make themselves more powerful. You know . . . a way to drain other Talents of power and transfer it to someone else, a bit like what happens with the princess when she gets married?" muses Arjun.

"That seems more likely . . ." says Anita.

"That must be it," I say. "Any way this truck can go any faster? We need this cure ASAP."

"I'm on it," says Anita, and she puts her foot down a little harder on the accelerator.

There's a niggle in the back of my mind that I can't ignore, though. A hint of something *else* I saw in Stefan's tiger eyes, back before I was his captive, and when I thought he might be my rescuer. When I think about everything he's put me through, my heart turns to stone against him again.

"Maybe when we've cured the princess, and Stefan is arrested for his crimes against ordinaries, he can be sent back to Gergon and we can be done with them forever," says Arjun.

That thought sends my stomach reeling too. The people of Gergon didn't deserve this any more than the people of Nova.

We pull into the town, where the siren is still wailing. Some people are loading up their vehicles and evacuating—I would be one of them, if I lived in the shadow of that volcano. But when we enter the Jing laboratory compound, everything is quiet.

"Should we be evacuating?" I ask Mei, who comes running out to meet us. I really hope not. Their laboratory is the best chance we have of making the cure in time.

She shakes her head. "Our monitoring system says that although there's activity, it's still below our evacuation thresholds. So—was it a success?"

I nod, holding up the filled fire-trap. Her eyes go wide with relief. I follow her into the main mixing room of the lab, and when the smell of ingredients rendering and potions bubbling away hits my nostrils, I instantly relax.

The Waidan looks up from the cauldron he's leaning over and raises an eyebrow.

"We got it," I say with a smile.

"You did?" Trina rushes in from the other room. In her hand is her tablet. "Awesome. Look, our plan worked."

"What do you mean?" I place the jar containing the phoenix flames on the table, then crane my neck to see what's on the tablet. There, on YouCast, is the video I shot before we left for the volcano. It's already had over a million views and rising. "Wow, seriously?"

"Yeah, apparently it got picked up by a major news outlet for a while, but then they stopped showing it. Must've been pressure from the palace. Stefan keeps trying to block every website that shares the video—but every time he does, I find a way around it. He might have people that are good, but trust me, I'm better. Connect is going crazy—you have so many shares."

"So people aren't freaking out about the ORA anymore?"

Trina shakes her head slowly and switches off the tablet. "I wish that was the case. If anything, the situation might be heating up."

"What? But they've heard the truth now—they know it's not the ordinaries behind this after all!"

"You have to remember, while you have a lot of credibility, you're up against the *palace* here. The royal family have ruled for centuries and once Stefan married the princess, he became one of them."

I bite my lip. I hadn't thought about it from that perspective. Trina continues: "Plus, there are more and more restrictions being added all the time. There's no more travel into or out of Nova anymore. Reports of the 'virus' are spreading around the world, and other countries don't want it in their borders—understandably. All the Transport streams are blocked. Look at this." She switches on the tablet again and swipes to a news page. The headline reads: ORDINARY UNION BUILDING VANDALIZED. It shows a picture of a building with broken windows and GIVE US OUR TALENT BACK, SCUM written in bright red spraypaint.

Fear grips the bottom of my spine and makes me choke. "Oh my god." We haven't seen that kind of hate speech for a century or more. I don't have a moment to waste. "Come on," I say. "I've got a potion to make."

# CHAPTER THIRTY-ONE

# SAMANTHA

ANITA AND ARJUN ARE STANDING BY. ARJUN and I have changed out of our heavy jumpsuits, into more casual clothing ready for hours of work in the lab. "We're ready when you are," Anita says with a smile.

I nod. "Let's go."

I set them to work immediately: chopping and slicing and boiling the different ingredients. "Arjun, there's a bit of tough work to do pounding the emerald powder."

He flexes his bicep. "Tough manly job, coming up."

Anita throws a cloth at him, then turns to me. "Hey, are you trying to say I couldn't pound emerald powder? I'm just as strong as my stupid brother."

"I know that," I say, my eyes twinkling. "That's why I need you to crush the ruby powder. Just as hard, I'm afraid."

"Oh, I was kind of worried you would say that."

Arjun throws the cloth back at Anita, and it lands on

top of her head like a flat cap. "Serves you right."

"Are you sure you don't have some galium root I can cut up or some pixie dust I can sieve?"

"What, and let the man do all the hard work? I don't think so," I say with a wink. "Besides, sieving the pixie dust has to be done straight into the cauldron, so I'd better do that." This is my potion, and I need to make sure all the ingredients are mixed in properly.

"Okay," she finally concedes.

I've brought my potion diary and placed it on my workstation, so I can consult it as needed. But I've read the recipe so many times now, I think I know it off by heart. Still, it doesn't hurt to read it again.

*Sieve pixie dust into lotus-water base.*

See? I knew I had it right. *Trust yourself, Sam. Trust your talent.*

I stir the lotus-water base, admiring the consistency as the wooden spoon ripples across the surface. It's slightly more viscous than water, so it moves more like a gel than a liquid. It looks like you could bounce off it, if you were small enough to fit.

I take the jar of pixie dust and balance the sieve over the gently simmering base. With a few taps, the dust falls like snow into the liquid. I hold my head back to keep from inhaling any dust particles launched into the air, but when I'm confident everything is settled, I tilt forward to watch the reactions as they take place.

Watching a potion come together is the ultimate balm for my mind: I find that I can't panic when I'm fully engaged with mixing. The logical part of my brain takes over, pushing out almost everything else: emotions like fear, anxiety, or even dreams. I'm totally focused.

It blows my mind that the cure for this raging virus can be relatively so simple. This isn't half as complicated as making the love potion cure—even with the fact that I have the recipe—and it's far easier than it was to cure my grandad. This is like making a sleeping draught—all I have to do is make sure I put everything in the right order. The pressure I have now is time—before the drain spreads in Nova and before the volcano erupts and we need to evacuate.

Of course, *that's* where the difficulty level comes in. It's a challenge to Find all the ingredients: the phoenix flames being a case in point. The rubies and emeralds to make the powders: they're far from cheap, and not something we would normally store in our stockroom.

But now that it's all here ... I could be back in Nova tonight, even.

"Finished," says Arjun, almost at the same time as Anita. I hadn't realized they'd been racing until I hear Anita's groan of disappointment at coming second. I grin. I'm so glad I have my friends with me.

"Okay, pour it in there," I say. He tips the crushed-up contents of the mortar into the cauldron, and the precious jewel powder makes a satisfying sizzling sound as it settles in.

"Me next," Anita says. "See, I wasn't *that* far behind," she continues, sticking her tongue out at her brother. She tips the ruby powder in after his emerald, and I stir it with my wooden spoon. It's weirdly sludgy and surprisingly not expanding too much inside the large cauldron. I hope we're going to have enough cure for everyone in Nova. They should all hopefully only need a drop, but we're going to have to get into the palace before the virus spreads too far.

There certainly isn't going to be another trip to get any more phoenix flames any time soon. The phoenix has likely left by now, since we disturbed it. I feel a pang of sadness that I didn't get to see it properly—but I have to be content for now.

"I think we need to leave it for a bit, guys. Just to let the ingredients simmer together before we add the final ingredient."

"Is that what it says in the recipe?" Anita looks over at my diary.

"No ..." I say. But then, I'm a Kemi—and I know something about Tao that I don't think the others know. The secrets he hides close to his chest. The shorthand he uses to disguise the proper sequence of events—except to people who know the code. I imagine that there are steps he left out deliberately in dictating the recipe—and filling in the gaps is left up to me. Kemis don't believe in following recipes to the letter—nor leaving recipes so easy to follow that they could be mixed by anyone. We all stand on the shoulders of our ancestors, becoming giants in the process. But ancestors like Tao wanted to make sure we could stand on our own two feet, too.

No one said that alchemists were perfect, after all.

I'm sure that this potion just needs a little more time. A bit of breathing room, before the final ingredient is added.

Anita studies my face, then shrugs. "You are the master," she says with a small smile.

I puff out my cheeks. "Let's go see what Trina is up to. If we sit around here, we'll just drive ourselves crazy. And I'll just second-guess myself."

We find her in the next room, hunched over her laptop. "How's the potion going?" Trina asks as we walk in.

"Surprisingly well," I say. "Suspiciously well. I just hope it's right. We don't have a second chance at this."

"No second-guessing, master."

We collapse down onto the sofas, and I close my eyes to take some deep breaths. We don't turn on the TV—it's too distressing to watch as the media struggles to fill in the gaps in their knowledge with speculation and misinformation. Instead, after I've calmed my heartbeat, I read over the notes in my diary again and again, making sure there's nothing that I've missed.

After an hour or so, I look down at my watch. "Okay, let's go back and check on the potion."

Anita and Arjun jump up as soon as I speak, and together we hurry back into the lab. I peer over the lip of the cauldron. The potion is an unappealing gray-brown color which ... it's not supposed to be. But that's okay. Maybe. There's still one ingredient left, and sometimes the final ingredient can change everything.

Anita, Arjun, and I hold our breaths as I open the jar of phoenix flame. I direct it down into the liquid and it slithers out like a snake. Our hands squeeze together beneath the table. A puff of smoke as delicate as a cloud rises into the air as the fire reacts with the liquid, and the cloud settles above the cauldron like a cloth. We hold our breath, counting down inside our minds. *Five ... four ... three ...*

The smoke disappears and instantly the potion changes color from the murky gray to bright red.

Exactly as was described by Tao Kemi.

We've done it.

We've made the cure. The one that could save my sister and the princess and the whole of Nova.

I take a vial and dip it into the liquid, stoppering it with a cork. Then I turn to Anita. "How are we going to get into the palace?"

"Simple. I will take you there."

The deep voice makes my heart stop. I spin around

269

and Trina takes a step forward so that she's in front of me, her bodyguard instincts coming out in full force. But even her solid form can't hide me from the fear I feel at the sight of that silhouette darkening our doorway.

He steps forward, emerging from the shadow. The light hits his sharp, angular face, his tiger eyes lit from within by the flames of madness. He takes another menacing step, then another.

"Stay back from her!" says Arjun, using his most commanding voice.

"Samantha, I came because I need your help."

In a burst of speed that is almost superhuman, he leaps forward, closing the gap between us. Trina draws a weapon I didn't even know she'd been carrying, and aims to fire. With barely a flicker of his hand, he flings her to one side. Even though I know she is wearing clothing that is designed to help her withstand a magical attack, she's no match for Prince Stefan. Not when he's married to the heir to the Novaen throne.

Now there's only the heavy wooden table between the prince and me. I don't know what to do. I can't throw the potion at him—it's the only cure we have for my sister and the princess. I have no weapon.

There's no one here who can save me. And I can't even save myself.

Trina jumps at Stefan, but it's a split second too late. Stefan launches himself over the table, crawling like a bear on all fours, and he reaches me before I can scream again. He grabs my arm, wrenches it behind my back, then claps his other hand over my mouth. He stares at Trina. "We'll be back," he says.

Then before I can stop him, he throws something over my head and I feel a wrenching darkness pull me down, down and away from everything that I've ever known.

# CHAPTER THIRTY-TWO

# SAMANTHA

WHEN MY FEET HIT THE GROUND AGAIN, I pause. I've been Stefan's prisoner once before, and I have no desire to be it again. I need to be alert, focused. The problem is, I'm surrounded on all sides by dark, cold stone and I'm a prisoner to his magic.

"Where have you brought me?" I ask. My eyes dart around the room, trying to take in any clues. There are none. It's a perfect square, the same rectangular gray stones forming the walls, ceiling and floor.

"Home," he says. I spin around and take in the sight of the prince. He's down on one knee, dressed in a black suit and matching black shirt, the cloak he used to transport us settling over his shoulders. His tiger eyes face the ground; he doesn't look up at me. "You'll need to wear this before we can leave," he says. He throws me a similar cloak, this one in a rich sky-blue velvet. The traditional color of alchemists—the same color that ribboned along the edge of the Waidan's white robes. "Your modern clothes have to be covered up as much as possible. Not that there will be anyone around to witness you, but *she* might get agitated."

I stare down at my white-soled trainers, my scuff-kneed jeans and button-down shirt. Then at the velvet cloak in my hands. It has a clasp to attach around my neck, a bright gold pin. I run my fingers along the rich fabric, fighting the urge to dig my nails in and attempt to rip it to shreds. "Who is *she?*" I ask, through gritted teeth.

"You will see soon enough. Put the cloak on."

"And if I refuse?"

Stefan stands up and now stares me straight in the eyes. "You want to save your sister, don't you?" His eyes are wild and desperate, but it is a different kind of desperation that I expect. He doesn't look as if he wants to stop me. He looks as if he wants my help.

What's a stupid cloak in exchange for saving Molly?

I throw it over my shoulders.

"Fine, let's go," I say.

"Good." He flings an arm out wide, and at the same time a gap appears in the stone wall in front of me. "This way," he says.

He strolls out of the gap and down a hallway. The hallway is made of the same cold stone but—unlike the tiny room—it is more opulently decorated. Or maybe opulent isn't the right word. There's a layer of decay visible alongside the veneer of wealth. At first glance the carpets that line the floor look rich, but as I walk across them I can see they're moth-eaten and threadbare in places, dust filling the gaps where the wall meets the floor. No one has swept these halls in months, at least. Large windows bring some light into the hallway, the glass frosted with dirt, and as we pass them I sneak glances outside. I see a sprawling town, a mix of old and new—concrete towers like ugly blemishes on an otherwise perfectly historic thatched-roof town.

Another modern element helps me to figure out exactly where we are. It's a billboard. The words on it are in a language I recognise, even if I can't translate it. *Gergonian.* "Are we in your capital city?" I ask as it dawns on me.

"The main castle," he confirms, without turning around.

Alarm bells sound in my head. We're deep in the heart of Gergon. No Novaen citizen has been here in years, even though I know of a few brave adventurers who wanted to try. There had been maybe one public visit that I'd heard about, but it had been conducted under the strictest regulations, with the visitors being accompanied by government officials and only shown the very best parts of the city.

"You know the virus has affected all the Talented in

Gergon," Stefan says as we continue to walk down laby-
rinthine hallways.

"The drain, you mean."

He visibly flinches as if I've slapped him. "When I
heard what you said through the Queen Mother ... it's
obvious to me now."

I nod but clench my fingers into a fist, my anger spik-
ing at the mention of Queen Tabitha.

"She ... she's going to be okay," continues Stefan.
"The spells were meant to paralyse temporarily, but her
magic and her body were too weakened by the drain. I
don't want anyone to be hurt. You have to believe me
on that."

*No, Sam*, I tell myself firmly, as I feel my heart begin
to soften by his honeyed tongue. He has to do more than
just say the right things to make me believe he's different. I need to change the subject.

"Where are the ordinary people in Gergon?"

"They are sleeping too. It was my final act before I
married the princess."

We come to a stop outside a pair of heavy-set iron
doors. We've passed a series of rooms and doors on the
way here, but my first thought is that these doors look
modern. Reinforced steel. Big stainless-steel bolts. A
fancy modern keypad on the front. I can even feel the
hum of magical security. There's something dangerous
hiding behind that door, that's for sure.

Stefan places his palm on the high-tech-looking security pad, and it flashes blue before flashing twice in green. Then a light comes out and scans us both from head to toe. It seems to find whatever it was looking for acceptable, as the bolts begin to clink and turn.

The doors open.

And what's on the other side is not what I would expect. It's a child's playroom, dominated by an elaborate doll's house along one wall, almost as tall as me; its chateau-style frontage wouldn't have looked out of place in Pays. The walls are covered in heavy velvet damask wallpaper, and everything is draped in layers of white lace and chiffon. There's even a rocking horse in the corner—or actually, on close inspection, it's a rocking kelpie, the rocker itself a wave from which the kelpie is emerging. It's stunning.

In one corner, there's sign of a struggle—or some kind of disturbance that hasn't been tidied away yet. There's a broken doll in a frilly nightie, her face marred by a huge crack, one glass eye rolled back in her head. Books are open on the floor, their pages ripped. And on the wallpaper there are scratches like fingernail marks—and burns, as if it's been scorched by something fiery. I frown, wondering why no one has cleaned up the mess.

It's a time warp. A child's room from centuries ago.

Stefan's face looks drawn and pale as he stares around the room. "No one knows about this room except the royal family and a few servants. Mute servants, I might add."

"Who . . . whose is it?"

"This is my sister's." He waves his hand, and using a burst of magic, shuts the door behind us and opens another to one side.

In the next room, I spy a four-poster bed, draped in chiffon. And a young woman lying under the yellowed sheets, the gentle rise and fall of her chest the only sign that she's fast asleep—not dead. Her curly brown hair lies strewn across the pillow, her hands clasped serenely over her heart.

"Your sister?" I say, my frown deepening. I know I've never been top of my World History class, but I certainly don't remember there being any mention of a female descendant to the Gergon line.

"My *twin* sister," he clarifies. "My dear Raluca."

"But—"

"She was born ordinary," he says, his voice barely a whisper. He walks up to the doll's house and runs his finger along the dusty roof. He gazes over at his sister with a mixture of love and something else. Something I can't quite define.

My brain struggles to process what I've heard. Royal blood is *never* ordinary. The streams of magic running through their veins are just too strong, too powerful, too *present* not to be passed down. There are royal families

277

all over the world and as far as I know, it has never happened.

A voice inside my head asks a key question: *But would any royal family tell the public if it happened?*

He gestures for me to come closer. I don't want to, but my feet obey his command without my brain's say-so. I could pretend it's his magic making me do it, but I know what it really is. It's curiosity.

"She was a surprise to my mother. To all of us. I was born first, but she followed not long after. My shadow. Her deficiency was immediate. We used the old way."

I shudder. In Nova, we check whether babies are Talented using a sophisticated, totally noninvasive technology that tests their reaction to magical energy. If they absorb it, they're Talented. If they block it, ordinary. It's done at the same time as the first weighing, so there are no surprises.

But the old way ... To test whether a baby was Talented, parents used to submerge infants in a deep bowl of water. If it protected itself, it was Talented. If it didn't ...

A lot of ordinary babies died that way. Or if they didn't, when they emerged from the water, their minds were damaged by the experience. It contributed to the stereotype that ordinaries were somehow "lesser" than Talenteds. I thought the practice had been outlawed all over the world, but apparently not in Gergon. "My parents wanted to get rid of her," continues Stefan. "But even when I was a baby, I protected her. They tried to separate her from me and I screamed until I was blue in the face—I almost died myself. If they wanted me, they had to keep her."

"And they did?"

"In secret. I was presented to the public, and Raluca was not. They hoped maybe her powers were latent. That they might somehow develop over time. But of course, that's not the case."

"How ... how did they keep her hidden this whole time?"

"It wasn't easy. They tried to send her away—to the mountains, to the forest. They didn't succeed. I wouldn't let them. Whenever I thought they might try to take her away from me, I would throw legendary tantrums—just like when I was a baby. They built this wing of the castle for her and hid it from everyone with their magic."

Something about that rings a bell. About a young prince in Gergon who wreaked havoc. A wild prince. It was always written off as just the antics of another young brat—and when I first met him, Stefan was imbued with this arrogance that made me instantly dislike him. *Mingled with a hint of intrigue*, I remind myself, and I find myself staring at his strong jaw and furrowed brow. Then I check myself and swiftly push that idea from my mind. I look to see if the prince has noticed anything different about my demeanor, but he's still talking. It's as if I'm not there—he's so wrapped up in his own world.

"Then someone came to us who changed everything. An alchemist—but someone who dared push the limits that no *true* alchemist would bend—let alone break. Someone who was willing to twist her soul for a potion. And someone who was *Talented*, so my parents were willing to trust her."

"Emilia," I say, my voice low.

His eyes snap up to meet mine, as if suddenly remembering that I'm here. Then he nods. "Yes. Now you know why she came to Gergon."

My theory had been so close to the mark—and yet so far. Emilia really had intended to turn an ordinary person Talented. A *royal* ordinary person, but still.

Stefan continues his story. "For a while, my sister lived at the Visir School with Emilia. It was the only time I allowed her to be separated from me. She seemed to like it there. It was more in the countryside, she could see the rolling green fields from her window. And she could play in the caves. For once, she didn't care about having magic power. She just enjoyed being free."

I shudder; I still couldn't think of anything worse than being locked up in a castle with only Emilia Thoth for company.

"In the Visir library there were old books from all over the world—one of which contained a legend about an alchemist in Zhonguo who might have done the impossible in the name of love. Emilia always said that alchemists look to the past. If something has been done once, it could be done again. Emilia made no progress for a long time—until the news broke of the discovery of the buried monastery near Long-shi, an archaeological dig that was turning up ancient alchemy secrets. We gave her our full permission to do whatever it took to get her hands on those secrets."

"And that's when she came to Long-shi and stole the page out of Tao Kemi's diary," I say, filling in the blanks from the story I know already. "That woman had no respect," I can't help but snap. Somehow to me, after all she's done, desecrating an ancient book is up there with the worst.

To his credit, Stefan chuckles. But it's a dry sound that seems more like a choke. "Yes, well. She did what we asked. Emilia brought Raluca back to us, with the potion in hand, so that we could all bear witness.

"Raluca was brought to this secret wing of the castle, kept under lock and key. Her rooms had been left in the exact manner they had been when she was a child. All the toys to occupy a child's mind, but no real freedom. The whole family was there to watch—my mother and father, my older brother, and me. We even had the story prepared for how we would welcome her back into the royal fold—as a full member. The long-lost child, stolen from the castle when she was born and raised in a remote region. And it might well have been true. She had different mannerisms to us—wilder, more feral. She had eyes that were more cat than human."

"That goes for both of you," I say.

"Well, we are twins," he says with a shrug.

"So what happened when she took the potion?"

"She was sitting almost right where you are standing. In front of this doll's house. She had the potion in her hand—I remember it, because it was the most fantastic emerald-green color. She looked us all in the eye and then, without a second's hesitation, she drank it.

"We all felt the change in energy immediately. I had for her a present that I'd prepared especially for this occasion. A royal wand. I didn't know if that would be her preferred object once she was Talented, but it matched mine. We were so alike, she and I. I thought she would be pleased." He casts his eyes down—for the first time in this speech taking his eyes off Raluca.

"And would you know it? It worked. She took hold of the wand, pointed it at the closest object—her doll—and made her fly. The doll flew straight into that wall over there and fell, cracking its face. My sister was saved.

"Then Raluca looked at us, and the drain started almost straightaway. My mother was first. She had a coughing fit right then and there. But we were so proud of Raluca. We barely noticed anything was wrong; we were so pleased by the result. We thought if we could train her a little, give her a bit of time to master her magic, we could present her to the world. All was going according to plan. Even as the coughing, the weakening, spread from my mother to my father to my brother and any Talented servants in between.

"We didn't know what was happening. The 'virus' spread faster than we could have anticipated. All our magic was weakening. Then my father got trapped in his bedroom. It's a doorless room, and suddenly he didn't have the power to exit. We had to blast through the wall to get to him.

"I was the least affected. Now, looking back on it, I think it's because I am her twin. Regardless, it looked as if I was the only one less affected by the virus. Well, Raluca too. In fact, she got stronger every day—but I didn't connect it to everyone else's drain at that time. I thought she was simply getting better at controlling her new magic.

"No, it was Emilia I wanted answers from. She created this potion. I tracked her back to the Visir School and demanded answers.

"I found her, coughing up clouds of powder, and ter-rified as to what she had unleashed. When she saw that I was more-or-less immune, we struck a deal. I said I would give her my blood to manufacture a small amount of serum that would keep the drain at bay—and keep me from being contagious, so I could continue to inter-act with the outside world. It wasn't a cure. But it was something.

"But Emilia told me she believed it was Raluca who was doing this. That the only way to stop her would be . . . to kill her. I refused to believe that. I had already saved my sister once from being killed. All those years of confinement, after everything that we did to her . . . I wasn't going to give up so easily.

"The enchanted sleep was my idea. I wanted to give it to Raluca to keep her safe. I didn't want her leaving the castle. If people found out that she was behind the drain, she would be a target." His face darkens. "I had to keep the fact that it was Raluca's doing from my parents and brother too. They would have had no hesitations in ending her life, I'm sure.

"She trusted me. I came to her . . . I sat with her. She delighted so much in her new power. She made the toys in here come alive. They danced all around this room. Her power was not so great yet that she could leave her room, but it was getting there. I convinced her to show me her favorite thing—that doll over there, in the corner. She brought it to life, had her perform for us. And that's when I did it. I slid the sleeping draught into her neck." Almost as if he conjures it, a sleeping draught appears in his hand, in a syringe with a long, sharp needle.

"It put her to sleep. But it didn't stop the drain. If

anything it must have angered her ... The drain continued, faster than ever. It spread throughout the palace, passing through our staff—and then, as they went home, it began to spread throughout the country."

"You needed to put the people affected to sleep," I say, my alchemist brain working to connect the dots.

"Exactly. That way around, it *slowed* the drain— stopped an affected person from losing their magic completely. It was necessary. To protect our royal family. To protect our bloodline. To stop the total annihilation of our country's Talent!

"I stayed awake. With the pill from Emilia stopping me from being contagious, it was possible. I commissioned Emilia to find a solution. She claimed no cure had been written in the place she found the recipe, and I had no choice but to believe her."

At least Emilia hadn't deceived Stefan on that front. Only I was able to find the cure.

"Her first idea was that if I was to have any hope of overcoming the drain, I would have to become more powerful. I needed to marry Evelyn and have her transfer half of her enormous power to me. We got waylaid by the hunt for the aqua vitae, which we thought would work as a cure—and we wouldn't have even known about if it wasn't for your television broadcast a few months back."

"Oh yes, that."

"But once Emilia betrayed me once and for all and took the aqua vitae for herself ... I had to go back to the first plan. And this time I succeeded. I convinced Evelyn to marry me."

"But it didn't work."

"No. On our wedding day, I stopped taking the pill that Emilia had created. I touched Evelyn's hand, and—"

"You let Raluca drain a Novaen Princess, opening the door for her to drain all of Nova. You put everyone in the world in danger."

Stefan doesn't even wince. "Marrying Evelyn was my last resort. I shared the remainder of Emilia's pills with the princess until I could get a sleeping draught made."

"And so you could decide who to blame. The ORA? How could you?"

"I couldn't tell people the truth. They would hunt Raluca down. They would kill her! But all that doesn't matter now. Because you're here. You can change her back."

I swallow hard and grab the vial of cure from underneath my cloak. It feels warm in my hands, as if the phoenix flame is responding to Raluca's proximity.

I hesitate. "We have to wake her up for the cure to work. What if she's too strong? She has so much power . . ."

"You're right." His tiger eyes lock onto mine and refuse to let go. "Samantha, she won't understand why I'm doing this. All she's ever wanted is to be Talented like me. Now she is, and I'm taking it away. Will you talk to her? You are ordinary. She might listen to you."

"I can ... try." I move toward the bedroom, but Stefan stops me again.

"No, you should do it now."

"But how? She's asleep."

"I know that. All I need to do is send you to sleep too." He lashes out like a snake and grabs my upper arm, pulling me close. Before I have a chance to raise an arm to defend myself, to kick or scream, he jams the needle into my neck and sends me into oblivion.

# CHAPTER THIRTY-THREE

# SAMANTHA

I OPEN MY EYES TO THE SIGHT OF A GIRL IN front of me.

She cocks her head. Her dark hair is a mess of curls, her eyes round and glassy. She's thin—so thin her collarbones jut out of her skin and her hollow cheeks look like caves. She's wearing a long white nightgown that hangs off her frame and doesn't quite reach her ankles—once, maybe, it fit her, but no one seems to have bothered to give her a longer one. Eighteen years living alone or in exile. She looks as mad as anyone might, in that situation.

Glowing shapes seem to fade in and out of existence as they orbit around her, ghostly shapes with long trailing gowns. I recognise them at once.

*Oneiros. Creatures that inhabit dream space, often blamed for creating realistic nightmares. Rarely are they known to pass into the physical world, but when they do,*

*the hallucinations they cause can have devastating conse-*
*quences. They have few uses in potions as they rarely leave*
*behind physical matter when they die, but strands of their*
*hair can be used in potions to help sleepwalkers.*

When I manage to tear my eyes away from the girl
and the oneiros, I realize that I'm in a circular stone
room—not dissimilar to the room I've just come from
in Gergon. It saddens me that even in a dream world,
the girl lives in such a cold, hard place.

"Raluca?" I ask tentatively.

I blink and suddenly she's right in front of my face,
moving at lightning speed. She reaches up a hand as if
to stroke my face, but I recoil.

"You are not one of them," she says, in a voice no
louder than a whisper.

"One of who?" I ask, taking another step back. She
doesn't seem to care, and I would like to put as much
space between us as possible, so I keep retreating.

"A Talented."

"No."

She's in front of me again, this time lifting my wrist.
Her touch is feather-light, her skin papery and dry.
"Then why are you here? What do you want with me?"
Now she is the one to recoil, snapping her hand back
as if she's been bitten by a snake. "You don't want to
give me another foul potion, do you? I won't take it!
It's a potion that's keeping me here! Where's Stefan?

He promised he would keep me safe!"

Her arms flail in the air; I'm worried she's going to attack me. I hold up my hands. "Please, it was Stefan who sent me here. He put me to sleep. He wanted me to explain why I'm here."

"He thinks so little of me that he sends a child here to talk to me? Why has he not come himself?"

My hackles rise and my eyes narrow at being called a child. If she's Stefan's twin, then she's only a couple of years older than me.

"What then?" She floats away from me. That's the only way I can describe it. It doesn't seem like her feet touch the ground.

"Do you know what's happening to the Talented people in the ... real world?"

"Oh yes, they tell me all the time."

"They *tell* you?" I dart my head around, looking from side to side, all thoughts of talking to the hidden princess gone from my mind. I spot a window so I run toward it. I see a built-up town far beneath me, protected by a wall. "Evie?" I shout out of the window. "Molly? Are you there?"

"*Don't* ask for them!" Raluca's eyes are wide with fury. "Don't you know that they're Talented?" She says the word like it's poison in her mouth.

"My sister is Talented!"

"So? My parents are Talented. Both my brothers. And

they would not accept me. They had to 'fix' me. Well, I am fixed now. More than fixed. I am powerful, more powerful than them. I have seen them in this dream world and they are weak, so when I wake up, I will take all of the magic in the whole world."

I shake my head, but my entire body is trembling. "No, you don't want that. If you take away all of someone's Talent, they die. Do you realize that? This dream world is the only thing preventing you from killing everyone here!"

Raluca's eyes flash. "So? You think a world divided between Talenteds and ordinaries is fair? No. If all people can't use magic, no one should."

Her fierce resolve hits me like a slap, and tears spring up in my eyes at the thought of all the Talented people I know and love ... gone. I wipe them away furiously. "You think ordinary people don't have magic? It's not true. We can experience all the same kinds of things that Talenteds can—we just use our brains, our intelligence, our ingenuity to make it happen. Talenteds can fly? We build airplanes. Talenteds can communicate across vast distances? Heck, they still prefer to use their *ordinary*-created smartphones!"

Raluca is frowning at me, and I wonder whether I'm making any sense to her—whether she knows what smartphones and airplanes are, given her sheltered existence. I take a different tack. "I know you have been treated so, so badly. It's unfair what they've done to you. But it's not the same everywhere else in the world. You can find a place where you can be happy. Even as an ordinary."

She seems to consider it for a moment, but then she reaches out and grabs both my hands, forcing me so close I can count the flashes of magic in her eyes. "I know a place where I can be happy. A place where I can access every stream of magic." The oneiros descend on me, and I feel the cold touch of their fingers in my hair. They start to spin a web of images in front of my eyes, building a world of fire and brimstone. I recognise it all too well. It's Yanhuo. "Emilia told me about it. From here," Raluca whispers in my ear, "I can take all the Talent in the world."

It's her dream.

It's my nightmare.

"Stay away from her!"

The stone walls around me melt into the blank white space—and all of a sudden I see Princess Evelyn striding toward me. The vision of the volcano disappears—the oneiros flee. Evelyn has an army of teenagers around her too, although she looks the most formidable, an expression of fire on her face.

The oneiros aren't the only ones that run. Raluca disappears too.

Before I know it, Evelyn's arms are around me, pulling

me into a tight hug. I feel other arms grip my waist, pinning my arms to my sides, and I lean into them as much as possible.

"Sam!" Molly's voice is muffled by the tight hug, and reluctantly we step away from each other. I can't help it though; I reach out and give her another hug and a hundred kisses on her forehead.

"Mols, I was so worried about you!" I say, when I finally break away.

Her cheeks are flushed, her normally neat hair in disarray. "I'm okay. The princess has been keeping us away from the oneiros and we've been building our own walls for protection from that woman."

"That woman is Prince Stefan's twin sister," I tell them. "She was born ordinary and her parents hid her away. Stefan was the only one who cared about her. He commissioned Emilia Thoth to create a potion to give her magic power. But what Emilia and Stefan didn't realize is that magic doesn't come from just anywhere. Raluca takes it from any Talented person she can."

There's a choked sob from Evelyn, and my attention snaps over to her. "It's all my fault," she says, through gasps.

Molly touches Evelyn's back. "Princess, no one blames you. You couldn't have known."

"Couldn't I?" She drags her hands away from her face, her cheeks tracked with tears. "I could've done a *bit* more research before I married the guy. I mean, dragons, I could've listened to Sam when she came running! There's so much I could have done. I could have waited and maybe one day married the person I loved. Sam had the solution right there—a way to store my excess power so I didn't have to marry anyone. If only I'd had a little patience . . ."

"Your city—your country—was in danger. You did what you had to do," I remind her. Evelyn stares at me, but I keep my face impassive and my voice firm. I've seen the stakes now. I know she made the decision she had to.

"And now look what I've done to our country." She throws her hands up in despair.

I can't help but show the unease on my face. "Evie, can I speak to you on your own?" I stare at Molly's classmates and at the crowd of Kingstown citizens who are gathering around. I search the crowd, but thankfully I can't see Mum or Zain there yet. I breathe a sigh of relief.

"And me, right?" says Molly, her voice with a dangerous edge. I know better than to ever leave her out.

"Of course, and you too."

"Anything for you, Sam." Evelyn turns to the crowd and raises up her hands. "I'm afraid I have official royal business to attend to. Remember how we practiced keeping the oneiros at bay? You can do this, I know you can."

I'm always amazed at how Evelyn manages to get

people to do her bidding: her gentle but firm persuasiveness. I know it comes from being born with power, from never assuming that people *won't* follow her orders. Whenever I ask someone to do something, I do it couched in apology, wrapped up in ribbons of pre-made excuses so they can choose one to pull out if they want. Evelyn offers none of that. It is either her will or nothing at all.

Molly and I walk with Evelyn until we are apart from the crowd, then Evelyn throws up some dream walls around us. I'm impressed that she's learned how to control her power here so smoothly, but again—I shouldn't be. This is a woman who's never known what it's like to not have power. My mind instantly compares her life to Raluca's—Princess Evelyn's equivalent who has never known magic until now. "So? What are you doing here?" Evelyn asks me. "Have you come to save us? Is there a cure?"

I smile. "I have—Prince Stefan brought me here."

"You're talking to the prince!" Molly's jaw drops.

"Are you being held against your will?" Evelyn asks immediately.

"Yes and no," I say, honestly. "I think Stefan has finally had the wake-up call he needed to stop Raluca. And he's sent me here to cure her. But I wanted to ask you something first. When this is all over—and you're safe—don't punish Raluca. Her accumulating power was just a side effect of the potion—she probably couldn't have stopped it anyway. Even if she wanted to."

"The Gergonian Princess," says Evelyn, her lips pursing together tightly. For a moment, I think she's not going to relent. Then her shoulders drop. "It's despicable what they've done to her. Disgusting. And I don't mean the attempt to give her power. But to keep her hidden all this time?"

"I know."

Evelyn grips my arms. "Tell me what's happening in Nova?" she asks.

I hesitate, but I know I can't keep the truth from her. "Because all the Novaen Royal family members are affected . . . it's hurting the palace."

"Well, of course it is. I mean, there's no one there to run anything . . . I've seen both my parents but not my grandmother. I hope the Prime Minister has been quarantined and that actions are being taken—"

The reminder of the Queen Mother makes my heart lurch, but I know I can't drop that news on Evelyn now—not with everything else that's going on. Plus, I can't let her get distracted from the main issue at hand. "No, you don't understand. The actual palace itself is in danger. People have been seeing it from the ground."

"What? Imposs . . ." The words die in the princess's mouth before she can continue, and realization dawns.

"The magic keeping the palace invisible is failing," she says.

Molly gets to the next step even faster than the princess does. "Does that mean that it might fall?" she asks, her voice squeaking with alarm.

"Oh god," the princess moans. She stumbles and I catch her with my arm. "What can we do, what can we do?"

Molly looks up at me, her eyes wide and her lips trembling with barely disguised fear. "If the palace falls ..."

I shudder, despite myself. "I know," I say. Then I shout, "Stefan! Wake me up!"

Evelyn's face distorts as my vision tilts on its axis. My knees buckle and Evelyn grabs my arm to keep me upright. But I barely feel her touch.

"Sam? Sam, what is it?" she asks, her voice filled with concern.

"I think ... I think I'm waking up."

"Good luck!" Molly shouts.

"We're counting on you!" says Evelyn.

The world shifts again, this time I can see Stefan's face. I'm thrown back one more time into the dream, enough to see Evelyn wrap her arms around my sister's shoulders. My consciousness is leaving.

"I'll be back," I say. "Just ... be ready."

"We will," I think I hear Evelyn say, before I finally resurface in the real world.

# CHAPTER THIRTY-FOUR

# PRINCESS EVELYN

"BE READY? HOW CAN WE BE READY? THE palace is falling, our magic is fading," Molly said, and she didn't have any answers.

Evelyn took a deep breath. *You are the princess. There is nothing you cannot handle—not when your citizens are the ones who are suffering.*

The palace was her responsibility. Hers—and her parents'. She thought about them in that walled city, their minds trapped by the oneiros, their power slowly draining from them. But their lives weren't the only ones affected. Now, there were millions of lives at stake.

She turned to Molly. "Come on, we need to stop Raluca. Do you think you and your friends can handle it?"

Molly straightened, her fingers flexing inside her gloves. "We can do it."

Evelyn nodded. "Who's your best general?"

"Bethany?" Molly called out to her friend. The other thirteen-year-old came running over, the beads at the ends of her braided hair clattering together as she sprinted.

"Okay," said Evelyn, "I need you to spread out again, but this time we're going to all direct our power to destroying the walls of the town. Understand?"

"We can do this, Princess," said Molly.

Evelyn smiled. "I know we can."

Evelyn took up her position at the iron gate. Then there were ten students to her left and ten on her right. Maybe, with enough effort, they could bring the wall down.

"Ready?" She looked left and right, and both her young generals nodded.

Evelyn set her mouth in a grim line.

But before she could say "fire," Raluca appeared in front of her.

"Oneiros are nice, aren't they? Keeping all these Talented people calm while their power drained toward me. I've promised them lots of dreams when I am the only Talented Queen in a world of ordinary people." She lifted up her hands, and all around, oneiros gathered. Then she lowered them, pointing toward the two groups of teenagers.

The oneiros swarmed. Molly screamed.

And then Raluca laughed. It was the most chilling

sound. She laughed and laughed and as she did, her face turned shimmery, her body losing its solidity. It was an exact repeat of what Evelyn had seen happen to Samantha.

That could only mean one thing.

Raluca was waking up.

Evelyn didn't think it was because she'd been given a potion. She'd *forced* herself awake.

And if Raluca could do it, Evelyn was sure she could, too. She wasn't going to let some power-mad princess drain her people and take over her country.

Maybe Samantha would succeed; maybe she wouldn't.

She wasn't going to take that risk. Nova was hers.

"Wake up!" she screamed at herself. And suddenly the world began to shift.

# CHAPTER THIRTY-FIVE

# SAMANTHA

"QUICK!" STEFAN SCREAMS AT ME. "SHE'S gone!"

I struggle to orient myself after waking up from the dream, my head filled with a dense fog. "I'm sorry, what?"

"Look!" The bed in front of us is empty, and Stefan is nursing an ugly-looking bruise on his forehead. "She broke out of the potion-sleep spell *by herself*. I thought that wasn't supposed to be possible?"

The fog, I realize, isn't just in my head. It's filling the room. It's smoke. That's when I gasp. "The cure!" My precious vial of cure is smashed on the stone floor, bright red liquid pooling everywhere. The phoenix flame was still burning inside it, and it's caught on the fringe of threadbare carpet, spreading to the wooden toys and up the sides of the curtains.

The whole cursed bedroom is on fire.

But at least I know where Raluca has gone.

"Stefan, we have to go back."

"Go back where?"

"To the Yanhuo volcano. That's where your sister is going to be."

"But why?" he asks, in disbelief. "Why would she not just go to Nova and continue to drain Talenteds?"

"The Yanhuo volcano is where all the streams of magic in the world come to meet. If she goes there, then that means she can drain Talenteds all over the world. She wants all of it. So she can rule a world made up only of ordinary people, as the only Talented Queen."

Stefan shakes his head in slow disbelief. "No, she wouldn't do that."

"I've seen it in her dreams, Stefan. She will do it. She truly believes it's the only way."

Something seems to snap together in his brain and he nods. "Let's go, then."

He removes his cloak again, swinging it off his shoulders. "It's a Transport panel. Old-fashioned style."

I think of the rumors of Gergons being able to fling their cloaks and disappear. I guess this is how they integrate new technology into old fashions. I almost let myself be impressed. Until I remember that Gergons also got the nickname vampires.

It is convenient, though. If I could get my hands on one of those . . .

"Don't get any ideas," he says. "You have to be a high-level Talent in order to use it."

*Great*, I think. *There goes one potential escape plan.*

I'm also a bit disturbed that I'm that easy for Stefan to read.

He throws his cloak over us and, this time, I hear him mumble the name of the volcano under his breath.

We arrive to fire and brimstone and lava, just like the nightmare. But this time there's added heat. Extreme, choking heat—compounded by the gases—that makes me want to faint. I throw my arm over my mouth, but it's not good enough. The smoke stings my throat and every inch of exposed skin. We're perched right on the side of the crater, and looking down on the chaos below. The caldera has opened to fill almost the entire crater floor. Only islands of solid rock remain, surrounded by rivers of molten red lava.

"Are we in the Wilds here?" Stefan asks, his wand out and ready.

I nod—there's no way Stefan can use his magic predictably here. Thankfully, he understands that—and instead he pulls my cloak off my shoulders. He rips it in half and throws one section to me. I wrap it around my mouth and nose, and immediately I can breathe a bit easier.

Raluca is standing on one of the larger islands of rock down on the crater floor. It's as if she's living and breathing the fumes; they are energizing her, conducting her magic. Unfortunately, she spots us almost immediately and her black eyes narrow. "Don't try to stop me, brother," she says, her voice amplified to reach us. "I need to do this. It's for the good of everyone."

Bubbles of lava rise up to the surface, sizzling and acquiring a gray crust as they come in contact with the cool air. There's a path of rock leading to where Raluca is standing, but it's narrow; it could crack at any moment, and then we would be stranded.

"Come on," Stefan says to me. "We have to get down there and stop her."

"But how?" This volcano is at the center of everything—if the streams of magic are like veins, then Yanhuo is magic's beating heart. If Raluca manages to use the veins to spread the drain around the world . . . there will be no stopping her.

"I don't know. But we're not going to figure it out up here."

"There." I point to the path that Arjun and I climbed up. The rope from our ascent is still there. Stefan nods and rushes over to it.

There's a flash of light, and the rope disintegrates in front of us. Raluca's hands are spread in our direction.

"How can she do that? I thought magic didn't work here. Not that accurately."

"It shouldn't." My eyes open wide. "It must be because she was born ordinary. It's a potion that's changed her. Ordinaries have a different relationship with the Wilds."

"I don't want to hurt you, Stefan," she says, her magically amplified voice rising up above the noise of the cracks and shakes of the volcano. "Nor a spectacular ordinary soul like you, Samantha. I am close now. Then there will never be a divide between people again."

"You can't do this, Raluca!" Stefan turns to me, and I see tears shining in his eyes. "There's only one way out of this. I know what I have to do. So please, take this." He slides off a ring from his forefinger—a heavy gold signet ring with the new Novaen crest on it—and places it in my palm. Then he stares down at Raluca, takes two steps, and follows them with a flying leap to the crater floor.

"Stefan!" I scream. He's going to kill himself.

But his magic works enough to keep him steady.

"I told you not to try to stop me, brother. I don't want to have to hurt you." Raluca emphasises her point by flinging her arm out in his direction and pulling, her hand closing into a fist. Stefan reacts like a ragdoll in the air, and in the smoke of the crater I can see a stream of gold-flecked magic drain, the Talent she is pulling out of him. Whatever immunity he had—whether by virtue of being her twin or from the serum Emilia made—is now gone.

When he drops to the ground, he is unable to cushion the blow. By the grace of the dragons, he lands on a patch of rock, missing the rivers of lava. But I don't know how he could survive an impact like that. Especially with his restricted magic.

With coldness that turns my own blood to ice, Raluca turns her back on him, focusing back on the lava lake.

"Sam!"

I spin around as I hear my name being called from behind me. Three figures I recognise are powering up the side of the volcano. Trina, Ani, and Arjun.

"We saw the commotion from the crater and then your FollowMe location signal started buzzing that you were there too. We had to make sure it was real and not some kind of joke," says Anita.

I've never been happier to see familiar faces in my entire life.

Trina's face is red with sweat and exertion. They look like they've sprinted up the side of the volcano, crampons and all. "Sam, you have to hurry. The palace is not only visible now, it's falling."

"What?" I cry out.

"Something must have happened over the past few hours. Every Talented in the city is lined up, pointing their wands at it, trying to stop it from happening. Your grandad and parents are handing out potions to keep people strong. But everyone is weakening."

"Oh my god. Since Raluca is awake, she must be draining Talent faster than ever."

Trina nods. "Kirsty and the ORA are organising the evacuation. They're so grateful for the Talented help that they're working together to stop it. And you know who's leading the charge on the Talented side?"

"Who?"

"Zain."

"Oh." My mouth sets in a firm line. Everyone I know is doing their part to save the world. Now I have to do mine. Because my home—my city—is about to be demolished.

"We've bottled up the cure," says Anita. "We all have vials in our backpacks."

My heart leaps, and Anita turns around so I can grab a vial for myself. But when it's in my hand, it looks so small. A tiny bottle against now the most Talented person in the whole world. "I don't know if I can get close enough to Raluca to use it. She has to drink it," I say.

"There's another option," says Arjun.

The realization dawns on me. "You're right. We need to summon the phoenix again. This time it's urgent. PHOENIX!" I shout, but my voice cracks.

"It won't work from here. We have to get down there," says Arjun, loosening the rope from around his waist.

"Raluca's too powerful. She's already destroyed one of our ropes. She drained her own brother!"

As evidence to my statement, Raluca sends a ball of fire in our direction, sending us flying backward. Her voice is all around us. "Oh, you. The girl who claims to have a 'cure.' The girl who has been sharing videos around the world. Well, are your cameras rolling now? Come down, and I'll let you show the world who they are facing."

I exchange fearful glances with Arjun and Trina, but Trina nods. I turn on the FollowMe. I walk to the edge of the cliff, and Raluca's power picks me up, flying me across the crater floor to her feet at the lava lake.

The ground cracks and sizzles beneath my trainers, but I try to hold on to my composure. The vial is my hand, unstoppered, and I need to be able to use it at a moment's notice.

"Look at me," she says. A second later, Raluca is on fire with power, magic pouring out of her, surrounding her, a beam of glittering light extending out into the sky as high as the volcano's column of smoke. This is no simple stream of magic—she is an ocean, the owner now of all the Talent in Gergon and almost all of it in Nova. My sister's power. The princess's. The King's and the Queen's.

"I feel it," she says, her eyes ablaze. "All around me there is power, there is Talent, there is *magic* and it is flowing through the cracks in this ground. Here beneath our feet are the currents of magma that lead all around the world. Can't you feel it? Samantha. You are ordinary. Soon you will have the respect you deserve. There will be no one to laud their Talent over you and make you feel lesser."

I shake my head, squeezing my eyes tightly shut. "I don't feel lesser," I say. "I am ordinary, and I have power too. I don't want to be Talented."

But she grabs my chin, forcing my mouth open.

"You don't? Why not try? My brother . . . his Talent is there for the taking. I resisted draining him because he was the only one who ever cared for me. And now look. He's opened the whole world of magic to me. So why don't you try it?"

She forces a liquid down my throat just as I open my eyes, raising my hand up so I can get my cure between her lips. But she is faster than me. The vial of cure tumbles from my hand and smashes on the ground as I stretch, arch my back, and recoil, trying desperately not to swallow the liquid.

But swallow it I do. When she sees it, she lets go of me, stands back and waits, a huge grin on her face.

At first, nothing happens. Then, slowly, warmth begins to creep through my veins, starting at my fingertips and spreading through my body. It almost ... hums, the cells of my body vibrating. Singing.

Connecting. Molecules of magic in the air connecting with the cells of my body. Is this what it's like? Is this what Talented people feel every day?

I almost weep at the unfairness. That I will never get to experience it. To live like this.

But then I realize that I *do* experience it. Whenever I'm mixing a potion, the buzz that I get. It's not just magic. It's creativity. It's passion.

I stare at my hands, thinking they should be glowing by the way they are feeling.

Opposite me, Raluca smiles. "Take the rest of his power," she says. "Do something with it."

I feel the power settle in my palm. One dose of it. My first thought is to use it against Raluca. But I know she would be able to throw up shields before I'd made a move. And besides, it was such a small amount.

So instead, I use it to float the FollowMe. My eyes go wide as I make it lift and spin. I hope it's capturing everything.

A shot rings out, echoing around the caldera. There's a flash in front of me, and Raluca shrieks in anger. I whip around to see Arjun and Trina have made it to the floor. Trina's arm is extended, her stance wide, her aim absolutely perfect for the gun in her hand. The bullet thuds into the ground at Raluca's feet. A warning shot.

"You messed with the wrong princess, Princess," Trina says.

"You are almost too late," Raluca replies. "I feel the power accumulating from all parts of the world. Soon there will be no Talent left except what I have, and there will be no one else to fight."

Trina fires again, and Raluca blocks it with a sweep of her magic. "Suit yourselves," she says. Raluca turns her back to Trina and raises her hands toward the lava lake. Out of it—and all along the rivers of magma that spew through the cracks in the caldera floor—crawl monsters made of fire and brimstone, lava demons with amorphous bodies that ooze into existence. Arjun is prepped with some of the icy-powder from the Waidan, throwing handfuls that freeze the demons in their place, but there are so many of them. They converge on Trina, who races and ducks their attacks like a pro, keeping Raluca distracted.

Distracting me as well. I shake myself into action. I sprint toward the phoenix nest, hopping from island to island across the rivers of lava as fast as I can while watching my feet. "Phoenix!" I cry out. "Please come! We need you!" I stop beneath its nest, my legs shaking with fear. I try to get enough breath to call it properly. But every breath I take is choked by the adrenaline and the smoke.

"What are you doing?" In an instant, Raluca is next to me. She grabs my collar and drags me at superhuman speed back to the center of the crater. "I'm bored with this," she says. "If you won't join me, it's no loss."

Then she shoves me backwards into the lava lake.

# CHAPTER THIRTY-SIX

# SAMANTHA

THE HEAT IS SO INTENSE, IT FEELS LIKE it's going to sear the clothes off my back. I close my eyes and think of my family.

But my life doesn't end there. There's a screech as loud as a thunderclap in my ear. I fall onto a bed of flames. Except it's not flames. It's feathers.

A phoenix. Red and gold and orange and yellow and bright as the lava itself. It's huge—far larger than I ever could have imagined. It's bigger than the dragons I've seen.

My hands instinctively claw for purchase. They find it, amidst the barbs and vanes of the phoenix feathers. My heart soars as we fly up, away from the boiling lava. I'm on the back of the phoenix. It came to save me.

It lets a burst of emerald fire seep from its pores, which washes over me—painless and cleansing, like bathing in ice-cold water. Whatever vestiges of Talent I might have left from the potion leave my system thanks to the phoenix's flames, and I couldn't be happier. It didn't feel natural to me. Whatever envy I might have had for my sister, for Zain, for the princess ... it's gone. I'm happy being me. And it assures me it's exactly what we need for Raluca.

Clinging on for dear life with one hand, I dare to adjust my position, rotating around so that I'm lying on my stomach, looking over the phoenix's wing at the ground below. It's chaos down there, with Anita, Arjun, and Trina back-to-back, battling Raluca and the lava demons. I know that none of them will have much ammunition left—bullets or potions. We only prepared for a hike—not for a battle.

They need to get out of there. "Phoenix, over there," I say, pointing over its wing at Raluca. "She's the source. You have to help me stop her."

I don't know whether the phoenix understands, but there's another ear-splitting screech that I can only hope means it does. It takes a swooping dive in her direction, and I brace myself against its body for the burst of fire. But it doesn't come. Instead, the phoenix flies over the Patels and Trina, and I feel the phoenix sag under their sudden weight. It's picked them up in its talons. We soar up and over the caldera, where with a heave and shiver of its feathers, it throws me from its back and onto the hard ground.

"We have to go back!" I say, scrambling to my feet. But the phoenix looks at me with sad eyes, before exploding into a fiery inferno. Its body disintegrates before my eyes—along with our chances of stopping Raluca. All that's left in the end is a tiny chick, naked and pink against the black lava floor. But I can't bring myself to be anything but grateful. It saved my life—and the lives of our friends. The last effort proved too much.

There's a cackle from inside the crater that raises the hackles on my back. Raluca has won. But determination solidifies in my body and turns my passion into marble. I'm not going to stop. Even if we have to spend every day trying. Track down another phoenix in another volcano in another part of the world. Capture as much fire as we can in bottles. We will take her down. I won't let her take my sister. Not for good.

I step to the edge and force myself to watch.

Raluca is hovering above the lava lake, her power suspending her. She feeds her energy down into the magma. I can't reach her from here with any weapon. I can only wait, helpless, letting the FollowMe capture it all as the plan we constructed unravels in front of our eyes.

There's movement from nearby—and it's not one of the lava demons, which are all just pools of magma now that her energy is not feeding them. Instead, it's Stefan. He's moving slowly, trying not to draw attention to himself. He's edging closer and closer to her.

At any moment she's going to spot him. "Trina," I say. "I need to distract Raluca. Quick. What can we use?"

"I'm out of ammo," she says, tossing her useless gun to one side.

I have to use the only weapon I have left. A bluff. I grab an empty jar from Arjun's belt and hold it high in the air. "We have the phoenix flame!" I shout. "I will use it on you."

Raluca's attention jumps to me, and the snarl on her face sends shivers down my spine. "You're mine," she says. I brace for her to use her immense power to smite me.

But behind her, Stefan gets to his feet, and even from this far away, I see his tiger eyes settle on mine. Then, in a burst of speed and energy, he runs at the lake, jumps, and tackles his sister.

She throws out her hands, rope exploding from the air in front of her palms, trying to save herself as she falls. But the momentum is too unexpected, too forceful, too sudden.

They both fall. There's a flash of green light, and the ground beneath our feet begins to shake.

Trina grabs me by the arms. "Come on!" she says. I turn to make sure Arjun and Anita are following—they have tears streaming down their faces and so do I; the gases are too much.

"How are we going to get back to the palace?" I ask.

"What's that? On your hand?" asks Trina, pointing at my finger.

"It's Stefan's ring. He gave it to me just a few moments ago."

Trina's eyes light up. "It's a royal ring. I've seen it before on Princess Evelyn. It can get us back to the palace. Ani and Arjun, hold Sam."

They grab my hand, fortifying it. Then I take the ring. I see that it has a catch on the side, right underneath the giant ruby. I flick it open, and that's where I see a tiny notch. I turn back to the crater one more time—in case there's a chance . . .

"They're gone!" whispers Anita.

I know that. I don't waste any more time. I put my finger over the notch.

And in an instant everything—including the volcano—disappears.

# CHAPTER THIRTY-SEVEN

# SAMANTHA

THE RING FLINGS US INTO THE FLOATING Palace of Nova, and I land skidding on my knees on the polished ballroom floor. I take the briefest moment to compose myself, but before I can get my bearings the floor tilts again and I'm sliding the other way. I collide into Anita and Arjun, who are in crumpled heaps on the floor.

"We need to wake everyone up!" I shout to them. "I'll call Zain."

Trina tosses me her phone and I dial Zain's number as quickly as I can. "We need to wake everyone up!" I say into the phone as soon as he answers, not even giving him time to say hello.

"I'm on it," he says, without questioning me. "I'll meet you in the ballroom in one minute."

We hang up the phone. "Did you hear that?" I ask the others. "We need to get to the ballroom."

Trina looks up and down the hallway, then gestures to the right. "This way."

"We don't have long before the palace is going to fall!" I scream, as the floor beneath us lurches ominously to one side.

"Then come on, we'll need every ounce of Talent if we're going to stop it."

We race down the hallways—or as fast as we can with the force of the tilt pushing against us. The ballroom doors loom before me, and Trina slams her way through, bursting the lock with her shoulder.

The ballroom is oddly the calmest place in the palace. It's eerie the way everyone is asleep, blissfully unaware of what's going on outside. I sprint toward where the princess is. But that's when I get another shock. "Dragons!" I shout.

"What is it?" Trina asks, but the words die in a choke. "What on earth?"

The princess's bed is empty.

"I'm here!"

Silhouetted in the light streaming in from the balcony at the far end of the ballroom, her hair streaming out behind her in wild blond tangles, is Princess Evelyn. Her ice-blue eyes are crazed with power. Her hands are splayed as far as her fingers can stretch. "I'm keeping the palace up—but I can't do it on my own for much longer."

Trina rushes to her. "Be strong, Princess!" she says.

Evelyn nods. "I will. For you."

"Sam!"

I spin around to the familiar sound of Zain's voice and I almost collapse with relief. Instead, I fling myself into his arms, sparing the briefest second for a hug. Then it's back to business. "I've got the antidotes to the sleeping draughts. They should work straightaway."

"Good, we need to wake and cure everyone as quickly as possible if we have any chance of saving the palace," I say. "Guys?"

Anita, Arjun, and Trina each throw down their backpacks. Inside are enough vials to cure everyone in the palace. We each take a handful and I turn to Anita. "You wake the Queen. Zain, you take the King. Arjun and I will make a start on the others." *Starting with Molly.* I don't even need to say the words out loud.

"You got it," Zain says.

None of us waste another moment after that. I clutch my cure in one hand and the sleeping draught antidotes tightly in the other. I have to trust in Zain's synths this time. I know he won't let me down.

I run to Molly's bedside, throw back the blanket, and pour the sleeping draught antidote between her lips. To my relief, her eyes flutter open. "Hi, Molly," I say. "Drink this."

She drinks it without protesting. "What can I do?"

she says, bolting upright in the bed. Her gloved hands crackle as her magic returns.

The palace judders so violently, the chandelier shakes and glass begins to rain down from the ceiling. Molly screams and I throw the blanket back over her. When there's a momentary break in the shaking, I say: "Let's move. You need to help the princess."

"I got it," she replies. "You wake up more people." We hug quickly and run in opposite directions: she, toward the window and I, toward the next sleeping teenager.

The king is climbing out of bed too. Arjun is frantically trying to explain what's happening, and when it dawns on the King, he storms forcefully to one of the balconies next to the princess. The Queen, when she awakens, rushes out to join him.

With the three members of the Royal family out on the balcony, their powers returned to maximum capacity, the palace slowly begins to right itself. It's only when I step out onto the balcony that I realize just how close things got.

The foundations of the floating palace are touching the Z of the ZA headquarters, the Z leaning—but not quite broken yet. I'm staring at the distressed-turning-into-relieved face of Zol Aster—Zain's dad and maybe, one day, my future boss.

Then, the next step is that we begin to rise. As we wake up more and more of the palace guards and workers, they lend their Talent to the effort. Slowly the palace returns to its original position above Castle Great.

"The last step," the king says, raising his arms, "is restoring the invisibility."

"I don't think we should, Father," says the princess. "The people of Nova have just experienced one of the darkest periods of our times. They need to see that everything is okay—see that their leaders care—not just disappear into oblivion."

"But that's how it's always been!" the king protests.

"And it's not how it needs to be." Evelyn's voice is firm, and the king relents.

"I heard you in the dream world, daughter," the king says. "You kept your wits when we all allowed ourselves to succumb to the oneiros."

"I couldn't have done it without my citizens," she replies. "Speaking of whom, I must check to make sure they are all okay." She turns around and sees me standing in the balcony doorway. "Sam! You saved us again."

"It was a team effort *again*," I say with a blush.

"I know it was more than that." She embraces me, kissing me on both cheeks. "Come on. I want to help wake everyone up."

It takes a couple of hours before everyone in the palace is awake and accounted for—even the Queen Mother—all their powers tested and seemingly back to normal. Finally, the princess gestures for me, Molly,

Zain, Anita, Arjun, and Trina to step into her private quarters.

As soon as the door closes, Evelyn turns to me. "So . . . what happened?"

It doesn't take long to relate to her the goings-on from the time I saw her in the dream world until now. When I get to the part about how Stefan threw himself into the depths of the volcano—with Raluca as well—Evelyn gasps.

"So . . . my husband is gone?"

I nod.

"Are you sure? I thought . . ." Evelyn looks down at her hands. I frown. What is she wondering about? And then I remember: her power. It hasn't come back to its *full* force. It's full, uncontrollable force.

Evelyn flings her arms around Trina, and it feels as if she's been waiting for this moment for a long time. The shackles that she placed around her heart have been lifted, and they share a passionate kiss. I squeeze Molly's hand and we grin. Finally, it's a story that might have a happy ending. Then, my heart does something that surprises me: It sends a pang of sadness up to my brain. The fact that Prince Stefan and Princess Raluca both had to die for this to happen. In the end, through everything, all he was doing was trying to save his sister. Can I blame him for that?

I pull Molly toward me and give her a hug.

"Oh, am I interrupting?" Stefan asks in a small voice. He's just appeared in the center of the room, using a piece of his tattered cloak.

Molly shrieks and the princess and Trina step apart straightaway. Trina stands in front of the princess, her hands on her hips, while Arjun, Anita, and I all stand ready to intervene at any moment.

It's not even an exaggeration to say he appears in a puff of smoke. He's a mess. His clothes are burned and smouldering, his face covered in soot. I think he's even burned one of his eyebrows off. It makes his face look comically lopsided.

"You . . . you're alive," I stutter. "You made it back."

"It wasn't without its struggles."

"And Raluca?" I have to ask, even though the sheer fact that everyone is well again is answer enough.

"She's alive too," he says, in a voice that's barely a whisper. "The lava lake behind us was filled with phoenix flame. When we fell, it reset everything—and it gave me back my magic. I was able, just, to carry us to safety before we hit the inferno below us." He turns away from me, to face Princess Evelyn. I see Evie's shoulders stiffen as she steps out from behind Trina. She puts a finger on Trina's arm as she passes, and Trina blinks. Then, with a wooden expression that must hide a universe of disappointment and regret, Trina steps to one side to let the princess go to her husband.

"Prince Stefan," Evelyn says, stiffly.

"Princess." He drops down onto one knee. "I want to apologize for what has happened here. I've taken Raluca back to Visir. It's the last place she was properly happy—amongst the green fields and the fresh air. She will have freedom again, I promise you. I won't let my parents hide her any longer."

The princess draws herself up as tall as she can. "I've met your parents—and your older brother—in the dream world. They might not be as lenient on your sister as you."

"I can help with that," I speak up.

Both Stefan and Evelyn turn to look at me. I hold up the FollowMe in my hands. "I've got everything—and I mean everything—on video. You have to promise me you'll treat Raluca properly from now on. Otherwise all of it—the fact that *your family* were behind this Talented drain—will come to light. And I don't think the Gergon people are going to like that very much. Let alone every other Talented person in the world."

Stefan nods. "Trust me, that is not something we want to be common knowledge. My parents will understand that too. And besides, I have to return to Gergon to help my people rebuild. To help them heal. And it would seem that since I violated the contract of our marriage by—" He chokes up, the words catching in his throat.

325

"By willfully endangering me, allowing an unknown drain to spread throughout my kingdom and possibly threatening the life of every Talented in the world?" Evelyn says gently.

"By doing that, I'm asking you to draw up the papers for our annulment. I will sign them at the earliest moment. I . . ." He fiddles with his empty finger, where there once had been a ring. He lifts his eyes to me.

"Oh!" I exclaim, before rushing forward and handing Stefan the ring. Stefan takes Evelyn's hand, then gently places the ring inside her palm, closing her fingers over it.

"I'm sorry if this places the burden on you to find someone else to marry, but I think it's for the best."

At that, Evelyn's eyes lift to mine, and I smile. There might be a need for that magic storing system I devised at the end of the Royal Tour, after all.

"I think Sam's got it covered," Evelyn says.

# CHAPTER THIRTY-EIGHT

# SAMANTHA

I LIE BACK ON MY OWN BED, IN MY OWN room, my laptop warming my knees as I stare at the constellation of glow-in-the-dark stars on my ceiling. I could almost reach up and touch them. Everything about my room feels small since I've come back. It's nice to be home. But there's a big, wide world out there, and I know I need to see more of it.

This adventure stuff is addictive.

When I arrived back from the palace with Molly, and we escaped from the shower of parental hugs, I had a moment alone with Grandad in the store. Our first order of business was to call the Jing monastery and let the Waidan and his team know that it worked. The natural balance was restored.

They, in turn, reassured us that the volcano's eruption hadn't threatened the town of Long-shi, and—in fact—the volcano seemed to have quieted down once again. There could never be words to express my gratitude to the Waidan. Without his help, and the help of his team . . . I never would have known how to make the cure.

Even my short visit in Long-shi showed me that there was so much more to know that I would never get a chance to experience if I stayed here. At Kemi's Potion Shop. In Kingstown. In Nova.

*You've ridden a phoenix. You've walked in the ancient footsteps of your ancestors. You've climbed a volcano.*

It's the first time I've truly felt that call for adventure. And I want to answer it.

"The store will always be here for you," Grandad had said.

The words both terrified and excited me. It changed everything I thought about what I wanted for my future: even the ZA job just doesn't seem *enough*. There's too much to explore. When I leave high school . . . who knows where I might go? Who knows what I'll accomplish?

My laptop beeps. I frown at the screen, which is currently loaded with about a million different tabs, all offering different versions of what's happened over the past few weeks. I'm trying to see if one of them has come close to getting the facts right.

So far, I haven't found one that's got the whole story yet. But that's okay. This time I'm not going to correct the media—and at least they're no longer blaming the ORA.

Mostly, I've been trying to avoid my emails, and I'm frowning because I've got notifications that another *five* messages have come through. All of them with similar headings: FOR ATTENTION OF SAMANTHA KEMI: ADVANCED CURE NEEDED. People from all over the world with unusual problems, things that can't be solved by their local alchemist, all coming to me for help.

One email address in particular catches my eye. FROM: YOLANDA GRANDINE. It's gotta be a fake. Yolanda is one of the top actresses in New Nova, star of a dozen films, winner of all the top acting awards. She's megafamous. World famous.

Hoax, I decide. I file it under "Spam."

There's a knock on my bedroom door. "Come in," I say, without thinking about it.

"Samantha?"

The voice makes my heart stop, and I have to close my eyes and take a breath before I close my laptop and look up. "Zain?"

Seeing him standing in my doorway makes me smile—it's like a reflex that I can't control. "Can I come in?" He looks sheepish, his head hanging low. I almost tell him to stand up straight. I want my confident Zain back. This isn't the person that I recognise.

But then, maybe as I'm changing, he's changing too.

"Sure," I say. I gesture to the bed, and we sit down together on the edge of it.

"So, you saved the day again?"

"Something like that," I reply. My shoulders stiffen. My first fight with Zain was over my being in the spotlight, and I don't want to feel that guilt again.

He notices, and puts his hand over mine. "Sorry, that was the wrong thing to say. It was pretty inconsiderate."

"Yeah, it was."

He sighs, then unleashes that irresistible smile on me. "I'm proud of you, Sam. I knew you could do it."

I bite my bottom lip, trying to consider my words carefully before speaking. "I don't want you to be proud of me. I want you to be there with me. But ... that's not going to be possible, is it?" I catch his blue eyes and I can see the reality that's written there.

"I need to find out who I am, if I'm ever going to be worthy of you."

"I don't need someone worthy!" I protest, but he stops me.

"I know you don't. But this is something I need to do for me. I need to figure out who I am. All I know is that I'm not meant to take over ZA Corp. Synths and Potions ... it's not my field."

"So what next?"

"Well, I loved visiting Long-shi and the thought of

exploring that ancient monastery. I thought maybe history would be something I was interested in. Archaeology."

I smile. "You did get really into the research."

"Yeah! So I applied for a new degree program. In New Nova. It starts next semester, so I thought I'd take the rest of the semester off. Travel for a bit. I know this isn't what you wanted to hear."

"It's okay. It really is." As I say the words I can feel the truth of them in my heart. I love Zain, but I also know he has to figure out who he is. If, one day, when we both know ourselves, we realize that we were better together ... then I know my heart will always be open to him.

"You're the most amazing person I've ever met, Samantha Kemi. You make me want to be the best version of me that I can. I'm sure this is not the end. We're just ... a potion that needs to be left alone for a while before all the ingredients come together."

His attempt at a potion metaphor makes me smile. "We always were an odd mix, you and I."

"Oil and water."

"I hope one day the conditions will be right and we will form the perfect potion." I can't help it. I stand up and throw my arms around him. We kiss, my hands running through the unruly strands of his dark hair, until we run out of air and finally have to break apart. It's impossible to deny the chemistry that we have. Maybe one day things will work out for us.

But for now, that one day will have to wait for us *both* to be ready.

# CHAPTER THIRTY-NINE

# SAMANTHA

*Three months later*

RED CARPET—CHECK.

*Popcorn—check.*

*All my friends and family*—I look around, catching sight of my favorite faces: Mum, Dad, Molly, and Grandad on the plush red-velvet pull-down seats in the front row; Anita, Arjun, and their parents behind; Kirsty with her Finding friends. Princess Evelyn waves down at me from the royal box, Trina sitting at her side—*check. Check. Check.*

I guess this isn't a dream, then. I really am backstage at my own documentary premiere.

Comforted by the familiar faces in the crowd, I step back into the darkness behind the screen, allowing the curtain to fall back into place. When I turn around,

Daphne is standing there, smiling at me. "Ready to play?" she asks.

I run my hands over the front of my simple, silvery dress—one that Evie helped me choose, that flatters my height and my skin tone. "I guess so," I say with a nervous smile.

"Everyone will love it," she says. "Don't worry—I'm always nervous at these things too. But introducing your documentary is going to be a breeze. Your story speaks for itself. For a director, you're dream subject matter."

"You did a great job putting it together," I say, honestly. I should know. I've seen it almost ten times already, nervous I'm going to spot something that I'm going to hate, or hear my words twisted beyond recognition. But Daphne has been amazing ever since she got back in touch and apologized for leaving me in Zhonguo, for not believing in me. I accepted her apology, because I could understand why she doubted me, what with all the lies Stefan was spreading. It's part of why I wanted to tell my story.

And now, she's created something truly special. A warts-and-all look into my life as a Master Alchemist, from the late nights researching ingredients, mixes gone bad, to the triumphs of creating the exact perfect potion.

True to my word, though, I didn't choose the story of Prince Stefan and Princess Raluca to feature as the main subject. Evie gets messages from him every now and then, assuring her that Raluca is recovering from her ordeal and learning to be happy again, that Gergon is rebuilding, that Stefan himself is stepping up and demanding better from his parents and brother. Evie and Trina have gone to Gergon too, to oversee that what he's saying is true. I trust their judgement.

Instead, I chose to record the creation of the potion that is enabling Princess Evelyn to store her excess power *without* being forced into a marriage she doesn't want—a potion that enables her to fall in love, in her own time, with the right person. When the documentary airs, it will help explain her and Prince Stefan's annulment to the public, reassure Talented and ordinary citizens alike that the balance—and safety—in Nova is the top priority. It's a good story, too.

The first few bars of the intro music fill the theater, and Daphne gives me a nudge with her hand. "You'd better go to your seat," she says.

I nod, take a deep breath, and slip into the auditorium while everyone's eyes are glued to the large screen in front of them. The introductory sequence is playing, ending with the title: *Samantha Kemi: Alchemist Extraordinaire.*

That breath feels like the only one I take through the hour-long showing (even though I know it can't be true). It's the standing ovation the documentary gets at the end that finally releases all the tension in my shoulders and the air from my lungs. Ani throws her arms around me from behind, and Mum has tears in her eyes. Even Grandad's eyes are a little glossy as he makes a grumbling comment about how they filmed me leaving the lab really messy after mixing my potion. I can tell he enjoyed it, really.

"Oh my god, Sam—that was amazing!" says Anita, clambering over the seats to give me a proper hug.

"Really?"

"I wouldn't lie. Is it too late to retrain to be an alchemist too?" she laughs.

"I'd have you on my team anytime, you know that," I say, her smile infectious.

A crowd of people builds around me, jostling Anita and me as we talk. She presses something into my hand: It's her phone. I left mine at home, not wanting to read any reactions or receive any messages from anyone except the people who are right here in front of me.

Well, with the exception of *one* person, of course.

"Take the call," she whispers in my ear. "Somewhere private. I'll run interference on the crowd."

I nod and slip through the swarm of people as Anita guides me through—it's not easy ghosting through a crowd when you're as tall as me, but somehow we manage it, and I hide behind the curtain of the screen again.

A familiar face fills the screen of Anita's phone.

"Zain?"

His face lights up as he sees me, and that smile speeds up the beating of my already-hammering heart. "Sam! I couldn't let this night go by without saying congratulations to the most kick-ass alchemist I know."

"Thanks," I say, a blush rising in my cheeks. "How's life in New Nova?" Zain's started on his new degree and he's been studying nonstop for weeks to catch up from starting a whole semester behind.

"It's amazing. You have to come out to the campus here for a visit—you'd love it. I went and checked out their labs for you—they have even more tech here than in Long-shi."

"Seriously? Well, sign me up, then," I say with a grin.

"So—have fun tonight. I can't wait to see the show."

"Thanks—and happy studying."

Although neither of us speak, we don't end the call either. Our eyes lock on the phone, and my throat chokes with all the words I want to say—but can't. Then I close my eyes and press the button to end the call, and I'm left in momentary darkness.

That is, until a moment later, when a bright light flashes nearby. I walk over, filled with curiosity. There's a package sitting on the floor, wrapped in plain brown paper and tied in a red bow. My name is written on the tag, but there's no sender name.

I pull on the ribbon and unwrap the paper. What's inside makes me gasp.

It's a potion diary. A stunning leatherbound diary filled with fresh sheets of creamy, textured paper, blank and ready to be written on. On the cover, debossed into the buttery soft, dark brown leather, is an intricate line drawing of a phoenix rising out of flames. I run my fingers over the phoenix, unable to get over how beautiful it is.

I know it's lame, but I want to smell the pages: that perfect, musty scent that only seems to be noticeable the first time a book is opened. I peel back the leather cover and prepare to take a sniff. But something stops me. Written on the first page is an inscription in handwriting I recognise:

*Just remember, Sam. You have always been extraordinary to me—Z*

I clutch the diary to my chest as the curtain opens.

"Sam?" It's Daphne, with Anita following close behind—a look on my best friend's face that says *sorry I couldn't stop her!*

"Ah, there you are," Daphne continues. She charges over to me, a spring in her step that seems powered by the audience's ovation of her—and my—film. "I'm off to the after-party now, but I wanted to give you this in case I don't see you again tonight." She winks as she hands me a sleek business card with the name YOLANDA printed on it in neat capital letters. It's glamoured to play trailers from her movies on the back. "Yolanda tells me you've been ignoring her emails. You should get in touch, she's dying to meet you to talk to you about a mix."

"Seriously?" My jaw drops.

"Seriously," Daphne says. She gives me two quick kisses on the cheek. "The documentary is a triumph, Samantha. I hope you're really proud."

She leaves in a swirl of her long skirts, leaving Anita and me alone behind the screen.

Anita grins at me. "So, Samantha Kemi, documentary queen, Master Alchemist and soon to be potion-maker to the stars … what do you want to do now? There's drinks going on in the lobby, or I heard talk of an after-party."

I bite my bottom lip. "Well, an after-party does sound fun … but you know what I really fancy?"

"What's that?"

"An extra-hot vanilla bean latte with whipped cream."

*Caffeine—it might not be an aqua vitae, but it's as close to a cure-all potion as I'm ever going to find.*

She laughs and links arms with me. "Coffee Magic?"

"Where else?" I pull away toward the back exit, where

we can slip out of the theater without anyone being the wiser.

"What's that?" Anita asks when we step outside, pointing at the diary I'm still clutching tightly in my hands.

"This?" I look down at the potion diary, at the phoenix rising from the ashes, and I smile. "This is where the magic happens."